The Gifts of Poseidon

The Gifts of Poseidon

Anne Zouroudi

First published in Great Britain 2016

www.annezouroudi.com

ISBN 978-1-910990-14-8

DRAMATIS PERSONAE

Hermes Diaktoros, the fat man	– An investigator
Alexis Hardouvelis (Papa Alex)	– A priest
Tassos Hardouvelis	– Papa Alex's brother, part-owner of a fish-farm
Lambros Hardouvelis	– Their father
Agni	– Their mother
Vaios Tsinamis	– The Chief of Police
Tomas & Panos	– Police constables
Stathis Rigopoulos	– A retired fisherman
Maritsa	– Vaios's wife & Stathis's daughter
Circe	– Stathis's dog
Apostolos Androutsos	– Captain of the Coastguard
Sevi and Andreas	– Junior officers of the Coastguard
Orestes Stangos	– Tassos's partner in the fish-farm
Vassilis	– Orestes's cousin, a fisherman
Pericles Kassimis	– Proprietor of the Poseidon Hotel

Tina	– Pericles's wife, a chef
Costas Iordanidis	– A young man who discovers a corpse
Elias Zoulas	– Proprietor of the Neraida café
Noula	– Owner of a tobacco kiosk (periptero)
Sammy	– Noula's brother
Dr Nikos Vatopoulos	– The local doctor
Popi Dritsaki	– A pathologist from the Examining Magistrate's Office
Prof Pantelis Maglinis	– A professor of Pathology at Athens University

GLOSSARY OF GREEK LANGUAGE

Baklava – Syrup-soaked pastry
Chairo poli – A pleasure to meet you (formal)
Despinis – Miss
Frappé – Iced coffee
Glyko – Sweet
Gomina – Girlfriend (slang)
Gyros – Kebab
Hasta – Leave it, forget it
Kafebriko – Long-handled coffee pot
Kafenion – Café
Kali mera – Good morning, good day
Kali spera – Good evening
Kali orexi – Bon appétit (lit: Good digestion)
Kali epistrofi – Safe passage
Kali nichta – Good night
Kalo taxidi – Good journey
Kalos tou – Welcome
Kataifa – Sweet pastry with walnuts
Koukla – Doll, beautiful woman
Koproskilo – Strong term of abuse
Koulouri – A kind of pretzel
Kyria – Mrs, madam
Kyrie – Mr, sir
Malaka – Very common term of abuse

Mezedes	–	Small plates of food
Metrio	–	Medium sweet (coffee)
Oriste	–	Here you are, may I help?
Panayia mou!	–	By the Virgin!
Pasticcio	–	Greek version of lasagne
Pedia	–	My friends (lit. Children)
Poulaki	–	Slang for penis (lit. Little bird)
Poustis	–	Slang for homosexual
Stifado	–	Beef stew with onions
Sto kalo	–	Farewell (lit. Go to the good)
Tavli	–	Backgammon
Tsipouro	–	Strong alcoholic spirit
Tzatziki	–	Yogurt & garlic dip
Yammas!	–	Cheers!
Yamyotes	–	Strong term of abuse
Yassou	–	Hello/goodbye (sing.)
Yassas	–	Hello/goodbye (pl/polite)
Yia moto	–	To hell with it

Honour your father and your mother, so that you may live long in the land the Lord your God is giving you.

From the Ten Commandments, Exodus 20:12 (NIV)

Too late! For already, mortar and trowel
And great stones were waiting, the girl to embowel
'Alas!' she cried out, 'our blood must be cursed!
What hope when the Fates are intent on their worst?'

From The Bridge at Arta,
A Greek folk tale translated by Menelaos Stephanides
& Fotini Stephanidi

Prologue: Scales of Gold

Mikey always said mermaids sang in these waters, eerie, melancholy songs with words men couldn't understand. *Don't ever be out there by yourself, cousin*, Mikey used to say. *Bad things will come and get you.*

But now Mikey was gone, and Stathis had no other choice than to be out here alone, drifting between the islets of Paximadi and Kromithi where the sea was at its deepest, running dark as ripe fig's skin in an underwater fissure the old folks claimed reached to the centre of the earth.

Stathis thought Mikey had been brought up too superstitious, with his bulbs of garlic dangling from the wheelhouse roof and a blue glass eye at every porthole, and no women, not even his own mother, allowed aboard. Stathis had no belief in the supernatural and he didn't subscribe to superstition. He found enough to worry about in the real world.

If only Mikey could have been here now! This fish was bigger than any the two of them had ever landed together, bigger, Stathis reckoned, than any catch ever made in this district. And it was angry, switching backwards and forwards trying to break loose, diving fast and deep and rocking the boat, spinning her slowly through all points of the compass as though *Panayiotissa* were no more than a stick of driftwood.

Stathis had been afraid at first he'd hooked a shark. When the fish was still at the line's full length, he'd thought its flanks were black, and he'd had his knife ready to cut it free. Yet he had held back.

He turned the winch handle. When Mikey was captain, the winch always ran smoothly, but Stathis never seemed to find the time to grease the cogs and cables, and the mechanism squealed as he wound in a few more metres of line. Forced closer to the surface, the fish twisted and flailed, not black but midnight blue. When it inverted itself to dive again, the rays of its tail flashed gold.

The line was taut and the drag on it so heavy, Stathis dared not wind in more. Better to wait it out. Either the line would snap and the fish would be gone, or it would tire and he'd have a fighting chance of landing it.

He sat down on the engine housing and lit a cigarette, shielding the flame of his lighter from the mild September breeze. The fish plunged again under the hull. Despite *Panayiotissa*'s breadth of beam, she rocked alarmingly to port, but Stathis wasn't troubled; he was holding the aces of brains and patience, and while the fish might beat him on strength, it had swallowed the mackerel bait whole, and the steel hook was embedded through the roof of its mouth. Its fate seemed in his hands.

As the fish passed close to the surface, the scales on its back glinted.

Jumping off the engine housing, Stathis crossed to the deck-rail and flicked his cigarette over the side. Catching oxygen from the breeze, the cigarette's tip glowed red until the butt hit the water, where it floated until its paper was sodden grey. The line had gone suddenly slack, and the sea was settling back to silky swell. He waited, and the calm prevailed, and the part of him which doubted himself was relieved the fish had got away.

'Eh, Mikey,' he said. 'It was a good one.'

But as he spoke, there was a glimmer in the water like the torpedo-fast propulsion of squid or the flicker of snapper, and the fish leapt, rising in a balletic arc, the water streaming off its back rendering marvellous the iridescence of its skin. Plunging back into the sea, it raised a monumental splash which soaked Stathis from his shirt down to his sandals.

The shock of the cold water was galvanising. Stathis ran to the wheelhouse, where Mikey's trident was hanging from a pair of hooks screwed into the ceiling. *You've got your gaffs and you've got your harpoons,* Mikey was fond of saying, *but with swordfish, you'd always do better to trust a trident.* Stathis snatched down the weapon and tested the weight in his hand. Spearing had always been Mikey's job; he'd had the confidence, the power, the aim. Stathis was the winch-man, and the expert at the wheel. Without Mikey, Stathis hadn't seriously expected ever to land another big fish. Now here was the catch of a lifetime, and he was on his own.

But he'd watched Mikey make the kill a thousand times, and he knew the technique and the timing. All it needed was one straight throw.

Above the dashboard, a photograph in a cheap frame showed him and Mikey together, the young men they had been thirty years ago captured in black-and-white, blood-stained and windswept and grinning with a huge swordfish hanging between them. Stathis kissed the pads of his fingers, and touched them to the glass covering Mikey's face. Tucked behind the oil-pressure gauge was a small brass coffer embossed with a cross, and Stathis signed three crosses over his heart before lifting the coffer's lid. The box was lined with burgundy silk, and had a place set in it for a cylinder the size of a baby's finger, though the cylinder was missing. Stathis laughed at tales of the supernatural and gave no credence to superstition, but his faith in St Nicholas, patron saint of sailors, had never wavered. He kissed his fingers again, touched the burgundy silk and said the prayer they had always said over the relic, even though the relic was no longer there.

'Keep us in your care, St Nicholas, for God's ocean is so wide, and our boat so small. Amen.'

He closed the coffer. Outside, he leaned the trident on the deck-rail and wound the winch a few more turns. The fish was held close to the surface now, its thrashing diminished but still creating a whirlpool in the water, as if Poseidon himself were rising from the depths.

Stathis gripped the trident and stood, heart pounding, at the rail, watching the creature circling, beautiful in its shimmer of gold and blue. When it turned to charge the boat he knew the moment, but with the weapon aloft he was struck by doubt. Did he have the right to take its life?

Doubt, or lack of guts? Knowing Mikey would have damned his hesitation, he hurled the trident with all his strength behind it, driving its spikes through the fish's skull.

The kill was clean. Amazed that he had made the shot, Stathis at first did nothing but watch the floating carcass. The fish's eyes were bright and staring; its lower jaw sagged in what seemed an expression of dismay, and its tail was sinking as if it might slip away, back down to the depths from where it had come. For the first time he could recall, he felt remorse, as if this death were an act of vandalism he had no business committing. From the holes in the skull where the trident was lodged blood was seeping, turning the water purple, billowing and diffusing like smoke.

He hurried to the wheelhouse and switched off the engine. Behind the lapping of the sea lay a deep silence. Mikey would have been whooping and laughing, clapping Stathis on the back and lighting a celebratory cigarette, but Stathis stood at the deck-rails looking down at his prize, and felt his eyes inexplicably fill with tears.

If Mikey had seen that, he'd have told him he was going soft, that he was acting like a woman, a *malaka*, a *poustis,* and the thought of Mikey's gibes brought a smile which, as he began to wind the winch, became a grin. He wound until the fish was hoisted high above the deck, its burnished scales gleaming as it dribbled saltwater and blood onto the boards. By any measure, the sea had brought him a great gift, and he was grateful. The fish would fetch big money, and Stathis was looking forward to becoming – for a while, at least – a wealthier man than he had ever been before.

Summer's Beginning

One
Fifteen Years Later

There were small green crabs everywhere, carried in on the waves washing the beach, low-scuttling and sidling over the shingle.

The young man was realising his mistake. Calf-deep in the water at the cave-mouth, the crabs were tickling his feet. The girl peered down, pouting, and gripped tighter onto his hand.

'I don't like this!' she said. 'Costas! They're eating my toes!'

'It's nothing,' said Costas, but the sensation was peculiar and unpleasant. He felt nibbling on the heel of one foot, soft nipping at the arch of the other.

Mid-afternoon, mid-siesta, the sea was sleepy. Anchored behind them, their little boat rocked on a light swell. Costas had chosen this cove for its shelter both from the breeze and prying eyes: no pathways in, no danger of discovery. Above the cavern the precipitous rocks were barren, except for odd blooms of green plants even the goats couldn't reach.

'Ow!' complained the girl. 'It bit me!'

He was going to lead her from the water, but the beach was alive with a swarm of shiny-backed crabs. The girl let go of his hand to push her sun-bleached hair off her face and peered more closely into the ripples. Her toenails were painted coral and a silver bracelet dangled charms around her ankle – a conch-shell, a starfish, a curve-tailed sea-horse. She wore nothing but a white bikini, a halter-neck whose knot he was keen to untie.

She was a beautiful opportunity. Even so.

'I think we should go,' he said. 'Maybe come back tomorrow.'

'But I want to see the cave. I want to see if the smugglers have left anything.'

He was regretting the tale he'd spun her of law-breakers and tax-dodgers, of night-voyages and Turkish contraband. He'd known there'd be nothing here; there'd been no smuggling, no need for it, since he was a child. A weekly boat ran from the island to the Turkish town visible, on clear days, from this eastern coast. Now everyone on Liteos did their own smuggling, buying their contraband in a weekly souk.

He took a step forward and felt the crack of shell under his foot, the ooze of innards.

'I know somewhere else,' he said.

'Let's look before we go. We might find something valuable.'

He batted away a fly; the drone of flies was as loud as the lapping waves. She took back his hand to lead him forward, looking down in wonder and repulsion at the multitude of crabs.

'Why are there so many of these things? Where have they come from?'

'I don't know. I've never seen it like this before.'

Stepping carefully to avoid the creatures as best they could, they made their way onto the hot shingle. The air smelled odd, of the mossy fishiness of the crabs, and of something like the underside of beached seaweed.

She pulled him towards the black arch of the cave-mouth, but he resisted.

'We should go,' he said. 'It's not healthy, with all these flies. Maybe there's a dead goat in there. They're so stupid, always falling off the rocks.'

'You're right,' she said. 'Look.'

She went forward, the crabs scurrying away from her feet, blinking their robotic eyes, threatening with their pincers. Enough light seeped into the cave to show a low mass lying under an overhang of rock, crawled over by feeding crabs and flies.

'What is it?' Coming from sunlight into gloom, it was hard to see. 'It doesn't look like a goat to me.'

'I'm not sure,' said Costas. 'Maybe a dolphin. But it's not good for us to stay here. We have to go.'

'I've never seen a dolphin up close.'

'There's nothing to see. Whatever it is, is dead.'

There was a piece of driftwood near her foot, a plank from a packing-case, and kicking several crabs off it with her big toe, she picked it up. Using the wood like a scraper, she knocked as many crabs as she could from their feast, wafting away the scores of disturbed blow flies.

She uncovered an object broad to narrow, no dolphin but a man, who, mercifully face-down, had one arm by his side and the other pointing forward, as if trying to swim from land to water. He wore nothing but a pair of shorts, and if his condition were judged by his legs, which were intact, he might have been taken for someone sleeping. But on his upper body, what skin remained was grey and waterlogged; in the places where it was missing, his flesh was red and wet as a newly flayed lamb.

'Oh my God.' The girl dropped the driftwood and covered her mouth. 'Oh my God.' Stepping back, she crushed a crab under her heel, and squealed.

Costas felt his stomach lurch and his vision grow hazy. He wanted to be far away from her, but with nowhere else to go, he made it as far as the water's edge before vomiting on the rocks.

The afternoon was going badly, and he knew his luck with the girl was out.

∞∞∞

She gave him no argument now that they should leave. He took her arm to help her into the boat, silent in his embarrassment until he noticed that she, too, looked unwell under her tan and was covering her mouth with her free hand. The levity and anticipation of their outbound journey was all gone. She sat quietly on one of the benches, wrapped in her French designer beach-towel, as if even in the heat of the sun she was feeling cold.

He hauled up the lightweight anchor. As he stepped easily from bench to stern, he didn't touch her shoulder for unneeded support as he had on the way out, but just took his place by the engine and pulled the outboard cord, and when the engine started adjusted the throttle and moved the tiller to take them back the way they'd come.

Her eyes were fixed ahead, watching the curving patterns the prow carved in the water, the popping white foam and the fabulous, unnameable blue, until her attention was caught by a gull gliding low over the swell. Wheeling and rising, it took up a position ahead of them, and flying lazily in the direction they were steering, seemed to lead the way.

Costas watched the bird for a while, then leaned forward and tapped the girl on the shoulder. When she turned to him, she looked younger than he'd thought, no older than his youngest sister, and he was glad nothing had happened between them. He gave her a smile, and patted the bench beside him. Hesitantly, she made her way to the stern and sat down hard, her thigh against his, as the boat bounced on a seventh wave.

He pulled back the throttle and reduced the engine noise so he could talk to her.

'Listen,' he said, in his imperfect English. 'I have to go to the police, tell them what we found. A body like that, it's a big thing. But you don't need to come with me. In a few days your holiday is over, maybe they won't let you go home. And papers, too many papers. Sign, sign, sign. Greek system. I'll take you to a place near your hotel, you can walk from there.'

Earnestly, she looked into his eyes.

'I don't mind the paperwork,' she said. 'I want to come with you, support you. We both found the body. We should both go to the police.'

He shook his head and squeezed her hand.

'I don't think it's a good idea, you coming with me. Your mother and father may be angry with me.'

At the mention of her parents, a shadow of doubt crossed her face, and he saw the way to disentangle himself.

'If they knew I took you by yourself to that place, what would they think? I think they would ask questions. Leave the police to me, let me come and find you tomorrow, tell you what they said. OK?'

He lifted her face as if to kiss her, then remembered the sourness of vomit in his mouth and instead pressed the back of her hand to his lips.

'*Koukla*.'

She gave him a reluctant smile and nodded her agreement, then rested her hand on his knee. Opening up the throttle, he smiled from a sense of relief. The seagull seemed intent on staying with them, tracking them as they hugged the coast. The girl looked out at the rocky shore and slopes densely wooded with pine. They came to the promontory the people called the Black Castle, and as he steered around its jagged base, he thought of the local legend, that it had once been the haunt of pirates who abducted Liteos's prettiest women and brought them there to be obscenely used, that any troublesome men who came to reclaim wives and daughters were weighted with stones and thrown into the deepest waters of the bay. Costas had never believed those tales, but in the afternoon shadows the clefts in the rocks resembled glassless windows, and it was easy to imagine despairing faces looking down. He was glad to reach the promontory's far side. There, the gull wheeled a full circle over their heads, and flew away.

Beyond the Black Castle was a curve of coastline which he intended to short-cut by motoring straight across to an opposite outcrop, but as soon as the course he intended taking came into view, he saw a small craft like their own directly in their line, not cutting a wake as they were but stationary. He moved the tiller to alter their course; but as their prow turned landwards, the boat's occupant stood up, cupped his hands to his mouth and shouted for help.

Not understanding, the girl asked the boy for a translation.

The shout came again.

'Someone with a problem,' said Costas. 'We should go and see what the trouble is. Probably a rented boat run out of fuel. The tourists who take them out don't know how far they can go on a single tank.'

But as they drew close, Costas saw it was no rented dinghy. The boat was of some age, crafted from pine and painstakingly varnished to a high gloss.

The girl touched Costas's wrist.

'Don't say anything,' she said, keeping her voice low.

He shook his head in the Greek way, signalling lack of comprehension, and cut the engine.

'About the body.' She squeezed his wrist tight. 'Maybe he had something to do with it. We shouldn't tell him anything.'

Costas was about to dismiss her concerns, but then he glanced at the stranger. Between Costas's father's and his grandfather's age, he was more vigorous-looking than either, and for a man at sea very well-dressed, in navy trousers with the cuffs rolled up above his ankles and a sky-blue polo shirt. On his feet were white canvas shoes, spotlessly clean; over greying curls in need of a cut, he wore a straw Panama hat, and he hid his eyes behind sunglasses with tortoiseshell frames. He was a tall man, perhaps even imposing, especially given that he carried enough extra weight for Costas to think of him as fat.

Costas's mind went back to the corpse, and feeling bile rising again, he swallowed it down. All along this coast, there were lonely coves like the one they'd visited, and it was only luck – the dead man's luck, at least – that they had discovered the body before the crabs had done far worse and the man's identity had become an insoluble mystery. Probably his death was innocent, a heart attack or other natural cause, but the islanders heard constant warnings of desperate foreigners, migrants with nothing to lose. Maybe the girl was right, and this man did have something to do with it. And maybe Costas had been stupid to stop and help.

He brought the boat alongside the wooden craft, gripping the rail to hold the two boats together. The fat man did the same, seeming confident in his seamanship and not at all the amateur Costas had expected. His smile made him seem benign, though Costas sensed he was eyeing himself and the girl from behind his dark lenses, assessing them and their situation.

'*Kali mera, kali mera sas.*' The fat man spoke Greek as Costas rarely heard it, each word enunciated without regional slurring or shortening or slang, reminding Costas of the over-groomed men who read the TV evening news. 'Thank you a thousand times for coming to my rescue. Something's wrong with the motor of this old tub and I'm not technically minded enough to get it going. Could you offer me a tow? Wherever you're headed, I'll go along too.'

'Maybe I can get you started,' said Costas. The outboard at the wooden boat's stern was elderly but appeared well-maintained. 'Shall I have a look?'

'You're welcome to, of course,' said the fat man. 'But to be honest, even if you get her running, I'm not confident of keeping her going all the way back to the port. If you wouldn't mind, a tow would be far preferable.'

'We won't desert you,' said Costas. 'If I can get you moving, we'll stay close by.' He turned to the girl. 'Keep your hands here,' he said, showing her where to hold the two boats together. 'Don't let go.'

He hopped into the fat man's boat. On the bench beside the motor was a hunting knife with a carved bone handle and a simple fishing line wound round a spool with the hooks tucked neatly away. A honey jar holding the remains of raw bait, though sealed, was drawing flies, and in a galvanised bucket filled with seawater floated several good-sized bream. Half in, half out of the bucket was a fan-mussel shell as long as a forearm.

'You've been luckier with your fishing than with the motor,' said Costas. 'You're very far out to be catching those bream.'

'I've drifted a good distance since the engine failed. I thought since I was out here I might as well keep dropping my line, and the fish were happy to keep taking my bait. I agree, I've done very well. You're welcome to take the bream as payment for your trouble, since you've been good enough to come to my aid.'

Costas opened the choke and gave a sharp tug on the motor's starter-cable. There was no sign of firing from the motor, only the spinning of the fly-wheel. Costas opened the throttle and tried again, closed the throttle, opened the choke and tried again, and again. Still the motor refused to fire.

'Could be your spark-plugs,' he said, wiping sweat from his forehead. 'Are you sure you have fuel?'

'Unless the tank has a leak. I filled it up myself.' For the first time, the fat man gave his attention to the girl, who was watching them and beginning to look bored. 'I'm sorry, *despinis*, to have interrupted your afternoon.'

'She doesn't speak Greek,' said Costas. 'We'll have to tow you. Do you have a rope? We're going to Liteos harbour, if that's any good to you.'

'Perfect,' said the fat man. 'I'm staying on the waterfront, at the Hotel Poseidon. I've known Pericles, the patron, for many years.'

'I know him,' said Costas. 'And that's where she's staying. I'll take you close, but not to the door.'

'I understand. A small island, and you in a young lady's company. People talk, even when there's no smoke and no fire.'

'Let's get you tied up,' said Costas.

The fat man stepped easily to the prow of the boat where a mooring rope was coiled, and threw its end to Costas.

'Are we secure?' he asked, and receiving a nod from the young man, he took a seat in the stern.

Back in his own boat, Costas opened the throttle gently to take up the rope's slack, then revved the engine and began to motor slowly in the direction of the port.

The girl reached for Costas's hand, and he took it, enjoying the touch of her slender fingers. Maybe he might see her again, after all.

She glanced back, relaxing as she saw the distance between the two boats.

'You didn't say anything?'

'No, I didn't, but I'm sure it's nothing to do with him anyway. Relax, OK? Fifteen minutes, we'll be at the hotel.'

They passed at a distance a group of netted hoops apparently floating on the swell, six of them secured by a metal frame.

'What are those?' asked the girl.

'It's a fish farm.'

In disbelief, she pulled a face.

'A fish farm? There's no such thing! You're joking with me.'

Costas laughed.

'I'm not joking. If you look after what you're growing, you can farm almost anything you like. And here in Liteos, what some people like to farm is fish.'

ooooo

The Hotel Poseidon stood substantial and handsome to the western edge of the port, its balconies overlooking the water and its front door only metres from the sea. Costas steered to a mooring a little distance away from it, and drawing level with the quayside, held the boat steady as the girl climbed out. As he gave his attention to the tow-rope, she watched him uncertainly.

'What will you do now?' she asked, fastening her beach-towel around her waist like a sarong.

‘What we agreed. Don’t worry about me. I’ll come and find you tomorrow.’

She hesitated, reluctant to leave him; but Costas ignored her, and at last she wandered away and up the steps into the hotel. The fat man had lined up his boat alongside the quay, and when Costas threw him the unfastened rope, he tied it with a seaman’s knot around a bollard.

‘My sincere thanks,’ he said.

Costas was about to re-start his engine, but the fat man stopped him.

‘Just a moment. You forgot your fish.’

‘Keep them,’ said Costas. ‘It was nothing.’

‘Nonsense. You’d be a fool to turn them down, and there are far too many for me.’ The fat man swung the bucket onto the harbour-side, and very nimbly for one his apparent age, jumped up beside it. He made a quick count of the bream. ‘There are five. I really was lucky. No doubt I stumbled on a shoal. So, let me keep two and my fan-mussel, and you take the rest and the bucket. You can return it tomorrow, when you come to see your friend. A trio of bream will make your story believable, if you’re intending to say you spent your afternoon with a fishing-line.’

Costas looked at him sharply, but the fat man smiled.

‘Forgive me. I only speak as one man to another. I sense the young lady might be a cause of embarrassment to you, and what other excuse do we men ever use to whomever we offer them – wives, fiancés or mothers – than to say we've been fishing? And if you've brought back a bucket of fish, who could argue?'

He gave a wink, and Costas shrugged, accepting the logic.

'Thanks very much,' he said.

'You are most welcome. Just drop the bucket in the boat, or if it's not here, take it in to Pericles. You know I've been very rude. I didn't ask your name.'

'Costas. Costas Iordanidis.'

'*Chairo poli*,' said the fat man. 'Maybe we shall meet again. My name is Hermes Diaktoros, of Athens.'

Two

Dusk, and the cool of early evening, pewter light at the horizon and reflections shimmying on the water. Along the harbour-front, the lamps at the taverna tables were lit and the first diners had taken their seats; in the bars and *kafenions*, aperitifs were being served.

At the Proteus taverna, the waiter standing out front was doing his best to draw in customers, guiding their eyes with his extended arm to a fridge packed with crushed ice and seafood. He saw the fat man – whose figure was flattered by cleverly tailored Italian linen – walking towards him from a distance, and stepped forward as he grew close, putting on a welcoming smile.

'Good evening, sir, good evening,' said the waiter. '*Guten abend, buena sera, bon soir.*'

'*Kali spera*,' said the fat man.

'Forgive me,' said the waiter. 'I took you for a foreigner. Please, let me show you what we have to eat this evening.'

He led the fat man to the fridge, and the fat man looked down on the dismal display: several bream, a few cloudy-eyed red mullet, grey prawns and flaccid rings of squid defrosting in their own melt-water.

'I caught several of those bream myself this afternoon,' said the fat man, 'so I wouldn't want those. Is the squid fresh?'

The waiter frowned.

'The mullet?'

The waiter shook his head. 'Frozen.'

'And the prawns, from Vietnam?'

'To be honest, *kyrie*, I'm not sure.'

'What I'm hoping for, here in Liteos, is some of your famous golden tuna.'

Again the waiter shook his head.

'It's been a long time since we could have offered you that! The tuna, *kyrie*, is all gone. We're all of us praying for the day when a boat brings us another.'

'And in the meantime, frozen fish? Is there nothing else?'

'The beef *stifado* is good. Please, come and sit down.'

He led the fat man to a table, and held out a leather-backed menu.

'I don't need that,' said the fat man, taking his seat. 'Do you have courgette fritters? I'll have an order of those, and a bowl of olives if they're local. The *stifado* to follow, and some green beans. The house red, where is it from?'

'It's made in Liteos, *kyrie*. It's a young wine, but it's good.'

'A carafe of that, then.'

The waiter left him, and the fat man made himself comfortable in his chair and looked out at the view. The fishing boats were putting to sea; the ragged, smoky rattle of their cold engines drifted above the lapping of the water as they ran out to the harbour mouth and beyond, where their dark shapes grew obscure as the red and green of their navigation lights shone brighter.

As the small flotilla headed out, an inbound launch threaded between them, obscured in the gloom by its grey livery and identified as government property by the white letters and numbers on its hull. Drawing close to the coastguard station, it cut back its speed, and motored slowly towards the quay.

The officers aboard did their best to be unobtrusive. As one manoeuvred the launch into its mooring, three others jumped ashore to tie up, and when the ropes were fast and the engines shut down, the crew stood on the deck discussing strategy, glancing round to assess the likelihood of being observed.

At their feet was a stretcher draped with a sheet, and the mound the sheet was covering was unmistakably a corpse. The coastguard mooring was set apart from the visiting yachts and cruisers. Hopeful they wouldn't be seen and straining as they took the weight, the officers each took a handle of the stretcher and struggled down the gang-plank and ashore.

A breath of breeze lifted the corner of the sheet, and an officer hastily tugged it back into place. Checking again to be sure they weren't being watched, they hurried as best they could with their burden into the coastguard station.

But someone had seen. Noticing their activity, the fat man's eyebrows lifted the merest fraction. Laying down his fork on his plate of *stifado,* he saw the officers hurrying across the quayside and watched their awkward efforts to get the stretcher through the doors.

When finally they disappeared inside, he took up his fork and gave his attention back to his plate, seeming thoughtful as he chewed his beef and dipped bread into the rich tomato sauce of his green beans. When the beef was gone, he picked up the carafe, and as he poured more dark red wine into his glass, lights came on in the coastguards' upstairs offices.

ooooo

Vaios Tsinamis, the Chief of Police, was wearing a pair of shorts and a t-shirt with a grease-mark on the chest. There was a redness to his facial tan from being in wind and sun, and he smelled of wood-smoke and charred fish, and faintly of beer. He had brought with him a constable in uniform, who stood behind his boss clutching his cap.

Apostolos Androutsos, the captain of the coastguard, was a big man, whose thighs challenged the seams of his white trousers and whose belly strained the buttons of his shirt. He kept a picture of his ancestor, Odysseas Androutsos, hero of the War of Independence, on the wall, and modelled his extravagant moustache on the one for which his ancestor was famous. Behind his back, his junior officers joked he took it off at night because his wife complained it tickled, and that he sprayed it every morning with hairspray to keep its shape. He was sitting behind his desk, filling in a form with a silver pen presented to him for twenty five years of service.

As the Chief of Police led his constable into the room, the coastguard captain looked up from his writing, put the cap on his pen and stuck it in the top pocket of his white shirt. He sat back smiling in his chair, his arms spread in welcome.

'Here he is at last!' he said. 'Vaios, *kalos tou, kalos tou*! We are so sorry to have spoiled your day off!'

Vaios was grinning.

'You'd better make it worth my while. I left a beer getting warm.'

The captain became serious.

'Very much worth your while, I'm sorry to say. We have a body.'

The Chief of Police looked surprised.

'A body? Whose body?'

'That's your department, not ours. Male, maybe thirties, average height, a little overweight. Looks like he's been in the water a while and not pretty. I hope you won't lose your dinner.'

'I haven't eaten dinner. Some fool called me over here before I got to it. Don't you know who it is?'

'If you haven't eaten, have a pastry.' He pointed to a box of *kataifa* on a table. 'It's Sevi's name day. No, we've made no identification. Not to put too fine a point on it, there's not much left of the facial features.'

Vaios grimaced.

'If you don't know him, he's most likely a tourist,' he said. 'We'll ask around at the hotels.'

'You want to have a look at him?'

'I don't want to, but I suppose I should. Did you call Dr Nick?'

'I did. Like you, he was enjoying his day off. He asked me if there was any possibility of revival – and take it from me, there absolutely isn't. He said if we don't have a name there's no question of him signing a death certificate and I should pass it straight to the Examining Magistrate's office, so I put a call in to them. They're sending someone ASAP, which I hope means the overnight ferry. The *Marie-Crysanthe* is due just after midnight.'

'Good work. If he can give us a cause of death and sign it off, then all we have to do is find the next of kin, and tell them to come and pick him up. What do you make of it?'

The coastguard captain twirled one end of his moustache to enhance its curve.

'To be honest, it's an odd one. He was too far from the port to be the usual kind of swimmer.

Maybe he was swimming and pushed himself too hard, got out of the water where he could but his heart gave out anyway. More likely he came from one of those holiday apartments down the coast. That's my take on it. You should ask the gentlemen who had the pleasure of retrieving the body. Hey, Sevi! Come and talk to the chief, tell him what you found! Andreas is still in the bathroom washing his hands. He has a hot date tonight, and I assume he doesn't want to be touching the young lady with corpse-stink on his hands. Though happily for us the smell isn't bad, considering how long he looks like he's been in the water.'

'No doubt it will get worse. A few hours in your basement will see to that.'

Sevi came over to join the senior officers, and wished the Chief of Police *kali spera*.

'So how did you find him?' asked Vaios. 'Presumably you weren't just motoring about looking for women and there he was?'

'We had a tip-off,' said Sevi. 'A man out fishing tied up at one of the beaches across from the chapel of the Holy Unmercenaries and found the body there. Costas Iordanidis.'

The Chief of Police nodded.

'I know him. If he was on a fishing expedition, who was with him? High summer and him round that side of the island, I guarantee he wasn't alone.'

'He never said there was anyone with him,' said Sevi.

'Did you ask?'

'I didn't see the need to. He had a bucket of fish.'

'Lucky young man,' said Vaios, 'probably in more ways than one. Show me exactly where the body was.'

Sevi led Vaios and his constable to a vast sea-chart pinned to a wall, and traced Liteos's coastline with his finger, passing over the mapped depths from shallows to hundreds of metres.

'This inlet here,' he said. 'There's a beach – not much to speak of – and an overhang of rock, just about big enough to be a cave. He was in there.'

'Inside the cave?'

'Yes. It wasn't easy getting him out. The place was swarming with crabs, and he was – slippery.' He shuddered at the memory.

'Not just lying on the beach?'

'Not exactly, no.'

The Chief of Police looked at Captain Androutsos.

'But you said he looks like he's been in the water a long time.'

'So he does.'

'So how come he crawled from the water into the cave?'

The men were all silent for a moment, considering the implications of the question.

'I don't know,' said the coastguard captain at last. 'That's a question for you, my friend. We just bring them in. And in truth, I'm keen to move him out again, before he starts to be offensive. I have a steady stream of visiting skippers coming in here with their paperwork, and it would be better for us all if their first experience of Liteos wasn't the stench of the dead. No offence to our corpse, of course. And it's your offices the Examining Magistrate's man will come to, when he arrives.'

The Chief of Police sighed.

'OK,' he said. 'I'll get someone to come and pick him up.' He turned to his constable. 'Tomas, go and find whoever you can, and get him moved. And do it discreetly. Let's not alert the entire island, eh?'

'Vaios?' A woman stood in the doorway, a small child sucking its thumb and clutching the skirt of her cotton dress. 'The children are tired. Aren't you going to drive us home?' She nodded at the coastguard captain. 'How are you, Apostolos?'

'Good,' he said. 'How are you, Maritsa? Your father, how's he doing?'

She shook her head.

'Not so good. He forgets things, and he gets mad at himself for it. And he's spending too much time by himself. I tell him he should go out, find his friends, drink coffee, play *tavli*, but he's lost his spark, you know?'

Captain Androutsos nodded his understanding.

'My mother was the same. They lose a spouse, they lose a big part of themselves. What can you do?'

'Anyway,' she said, 'can I steal my husband back from you? It's his day off.'

'Not any more,' said Vaios, apologetically. 'I'll call you a taxi. You can blame these guys. They've found us a body.'

'Whose body?' asked Maritsa.

'We don't know,' said Captain Androutsos. 'An unidentified male. That's why we need to keep your husband.'

'Poor man,' she said, making crosses. 'No-one to sit with him except the priest.'

Vaios and Captain Androutsos looked at her.

'You have called a priest for him, at least?' asked Maritsa, sternly.

'Sevi,' asked Captain Androutsos, 'have you called our guest a priest?'

'No, sir.'

Captain Androutsos shook his head.

'I can trust them to do nothing!' he said, to the room at large. 'Well, get on the phone and do it, now! Whoever he is, when the family come to claim him, they'll want to know we treated him with proper respect.'

Three

The hand-painted sign welcoming visitors to the Pension Esme – once sunny yellow and decorated with scarlet poppies and purple lupins – used to be fastened to the wrought-iron gate, but the sign had been taken down, and rested now against the inside of the gatepost, its colours fading like the pattern on old china.

The house which had been the Pension Esme stood on a lane above the harbour, set into the hillside and amongst others of its kind – small hotels, apartment buildings, rooms for rent. The tricky plot the house was built on had led to an asymmetrical design, so the house presented a broad face when approached from uphill and much narrower dimensions to the downhill slope of the lane. This narrow gable was the prettiest, with its whitewashed wall and, on the first floor, a French window with a traditional balcony of dark-varnished pine and an overhanging tiled roof. Growing up the wall was a twisted tree of bougainvillea, trained from a division in its trunk into the shape of a tulip which framed the balcony in blossoms of vivid pink.

Lambros Hardouvelis sat on the balcony in a rattan chair. He was elderly enough for age to have provoked growth where none was wanted – in his fleshy ears and bulbous nose, and in the white hair springing from those ears and his nostrils – and to have shrunk him in stature; his baggy shirt and trousers had once been his size. He played with a string of worry-beads carved from walnut shells, and the rhythmic click of the beads melded with sounds that reached into the garden from the harbour below – the roar of a motorbike, the rumble of a truck, a church clock chiming the three-quarter hour. In the chair opposite, his son Alexis sat in his priest's summer robes with his lap full of splinters and shavings and his hat beside him on the floor, whittling a lump of olive-wood with a steel-bladed knife, shaping the wood into the bird's head it resembled, coaxing it from the contours as if the bird were emerging from an egg.

The old man poured himself a restrained measure of Johnny Walker Black Label, and as he sipped his whisky looked out over the garden, whose perimeters were disappearing into the dusk. The aubergines' spiky mauve flowers were setting into purple drupes, and the tomato plants were in their summer vigour, tall and green on their frame of criss-crossed bamboo poles and heavy with red fruit. A tree was laden with green plums, another with unripe quinces, and the first bats of evening were flitting around their branches, lightning-quick as they dived for flying insects.

The priest laid his knife and his carving on the table.

'The light's poor,' he said. 'I can't see. Where's mama?'

'Sleeping,' said Lambros. 'I gave her some camomile tea. I put in one of those powders the doctor left.'

'She'll sleep a long time, then,' said Papa Alex. 'I wanted to say goodnight.'

'Don't wake her,' said his father. 'If you wake her I'll have the devil's job getting her to sleep again.'

Silence fell between them. Beneath an empty wheelbarrow, a black cat crouched, scanning amongst the tomato-stems for prey. In a distant room inside the house, a phone rang. The priest looked at his father. The old man stood up from the table, and went through the French doors into the house. Moments later, the ringing stopped. Papa Alex picked up his carving and studied it in the fading light, stroking the curve of the thrush's crop with his thumb. Somehow the curve of it wasn't right; it was too rounded, more needed to be taken away. He could hear his father talking. Lambros's voice used to be manly and mellifluous – he'd had talent as a singer, and used to burst into comic songs at odd moments, belting out verses which had made the family laugh – but his voice now was weak, his speech tentative, and Papa Alex could almost hear his father summoning his words from the vocabulary banks of his memory, his recall slowed like a failing wind-up gramophone or a run-down clockwork toy.

His father stopped speaking, and Papa Alex listened to Lambros's footfall as he made his way back through the house. When he reached the threshold of the French doors, the old man hesitated a moment, holding onto the doorframe as if unsure of himself.

'Who was it?' asked Papa Alex.

His father looked apologetic.

'I don't know,' he said. 'I forgot to ask. They wanted to speak to you.'

Papa Alex stood, and held out his arm to guide his father to his chair. The wood-shavings from his lap dropped to the ground.

'Come, sit,' he said. 'Drink your whisky. I shan't be a moment.'

The old man sat down heavily. In the house next door, a light came on. The black cat jumped over a wall, and disappeared into shadows.

When Papa Alex returned, he touched his father's shoulder and gave it a squeeze.

'Could you pass my hat, papa?' he asked. 'I have to go.'

He picked up the half-carved thrush and his knife from the table and slipped them into the pocket of his robe.

The old man was fumbling for the hat.

'What time will you be back?' he asked. 'What shall I say to your mother?'

He grasped the hat at last and held it out to his son, who put it on; immediately he looked older, taller, official.

'That was the police,' said Papa Alex. 'They've found a body.'

A look passed between them.

'Whose body?'

Papa Alex shook his head.

'I don't know. They didn't say.'

'Man or woman?'

'I didn't ask, papa. They want me to go and say the Words for the Dead. Look after mama, tell her I've gone to Mass. She won't know whether it's time for services or not. Say goodnight from me, and I'll be back as soon as I can.'

He disappeared inside the darkening house; moments later, he emerged at the garden gate carrying the black case which held his utensils for administering the last rites, and stepping out into the lane, headed downhill towards the port. Lambros watched him go; and when he could see his son no more, he looked out over the almost-dark garden, and made the sign of the cross over his heart.

ooooo

Papa Alex walked briskly. The evening scent of jasmine drifting over a neighbour's wall was tainted by the stink of tom-cats, and the effluent of a washing machine at a house further up the hill trickled down the centre of the lane, the sweetness of fabric-softener rising off the scummy water.

Where the lane joined the harbour, there was pork on the grill at the Tasty souvlaki house and chips sizzling in the fryers. The smell of hot fat and charring meat turned Papa Alex's stomach. He had made fried aubergines for himself and his father, and though he hadn't eaten much – Lambros had eaten less – the food was sitting heavily in his stomach, the oiliness disagreeing with the beer he'd drunk later. Mercifully, his mother had been sleeping. If she'd been awake, she'd have been at his shoulder criticising and interfering, the aubergines sliced too thick or too thin, too much salt added or too little, the oil not hot enough or overheated.

As he made his way along the harbour-side he stayed close to the water, avoiding the inevitable delays of social interactions if he passed close by the *kafenions*, shops and bars. The lights there were bright. Music was beginning to play.

'*Yassas*, Papa!' A young man sat on a bench at the quay where the island ferries docked, though no ferry was due for some hours. In the midst of the evening's liveliness – the buzz of mopeds, the shouts of a hawker selling melons and peaches, the chatter of schoolgirls walking arm-in-arm, nonchalantly trying to catch the eyes of the boys they liked – he was alone, seated at the centre of the bench in heavyhearted confidence that no-one would join him. His face was asymmetrical, the right side handsome, the left drooping like one of Dali's melting clocks. On the back of the bench leaned a woman's bicycle with a pannier attached to the handlebars, in which were several paperback books.

The priest glanced over to see who had called to him, and seeing the young man, raised a hand.

'*Yassou*, Sammy,' he said, and would have walked on without pausing, but the young man called out to him again.

'Where are you going? Shall I walk with you?'

Papa Alex stopped and looked back. Under the streetlamp, he saw desperate hope in the young man's distorted face, and harrowing sadness in his eyes.

'I've been called out in a professional capacity,' he said. 'Are you waiting for the boat?'

Sammy was becoming animated, grateful for this exchange.

'No,' he said. 'I'm just sitting. I could go part of the way with you, if you'd like.'

'I'm not going far,' said the priest, 'and my business is of the worst kind.'

'I don't mind. I shan't ask you about it.'

Papa Alex sighed.

'Come with me a little way, then.'

Sammy got to his feet and collected his bicycle, pushing it with his right hand as he walked. His left arm hung down at his side.

'Where are we going?' he asked, but Papa Alex ignored the question, answering with one of his own.

'What are you reading this week?'

'One of those books you gave me,' said Sammy. 'I love those detective novels. I'm looking for the red herrings, like you told me, but they're difficult to find. When I finished the last one, I went back to the beginning and read it again to pick them all out, or as many as I could find. I don't know if I got them all or not. I'd like to think I did, but how would I know if I did or I didn't? It's not as if they publish a list of them on the last page.'

A couple were walking towards them, a smartly dressed man taking a stroll with his wife. When they drew close, they fixed their eyes on Papa Alex, and wished him *Kali spera* as though Sammy were not there.

Sammy appeared not to notice, and chattered on.

'I got a book from my sister's friend this week. It isn't a detective book. I think it's a woman's book to be honest, but I'm going to read it anyway. Would you like to borrow it when I've read it?'

'I'm afraid I'm rather behind on my reading at the moment,' said Papa Alex. 'My mother isn't well, and caring for her takes up a lot of my time.'

'You should still make time for books. Reading is the best way to better yourself. That's what you told me.'

The priest nodded.

'I remember saying it. And you're right, I should make the time. So, this is where we must part company.'

Sammy looked around them. The closest building was the coastguard offices.

'Here? What are you doing here?'

'Official business,' said Papa Alex distractedly, immediately regretting saying so.

'Shall I wait for you? We could walk back together. Noula would let us have an ice-cream.'

Papa Alex shook his head.

'No, don't wait for me, Sammy. I may be here a long time. Go and find yourself a comfortable spot, and finish that book. I have plenty more you can read when you're done with it.'

Sammy looked downcast.

'OK,' he said. 'Maybe I'll see you tomorrow.'

The priest watched as Sammy wheeled away his bike, head down but covertly glancing into the bars and *kafenions*, where everyone seemed to be enjoying company and laughter.

'Sammy!'

Hopefully, the young man turned.

'*Kali nichta!*'

Disappointed it was no more than that, Sammy's head went down again, and he raised his good arm to say a despondent good night.

Papa Alex climbed the steps to the coastguard offices and pushed open the door. An officer was heating a *kafebriko* on a gas burner, and the room was filled with the aroma of brewing coffee.

Captain Androutsos looked up from his copy of that day's *Ethnos* and grinned.

'*Kali spera*, Papa,' he said. 'Good timing, good timing! If I read any more of this rubbish, I'll burst an artery and then I'll be the one needing your services. I don't know who's the more stupid, the politicians for the ridiculous things they get up to or us for letting them get away with it.' He closed the newspaper, folded it in half and half again and stuffed it into the bin at his feet. 'That's what I think to them. Andreas, bring coffee for Papa Alex. And Sevi is celebrating his name-day. I'm sure he'd want to offer you a pastry.'

But Papa Alex raised his hand.

'Nothing for me, thank you.'

The captain's eyebrows lifted.

'Nothing for you? I never thought I'd live to see the day! You've a sweeter tooth than anyone here in Liteos, and you're turning down the offer of *kataifa*?'

The priest gave a slight smile, and patted his stomach.

'I'm in charge of the cooking at home at the moment, and I don't do a very good job. My poor belly will spend all evening recovering from lunch. Maybe I could take a piece for my mother? She'd enjoy it far more than anything I make.'

'How's she doing?'

'Oh, much the same. We do the best we can for her. Sometimes she's as she always was, and sometimes she doesn't know us at all.'

'You have my sympathy,' said Captain Androutsos. 'That's how it was with my father-in-law. Sometimes he used to get so agitated, no-one dared go near him. Absolute hell for my mother-in-law. You just have to take each day as it comes.'

'Anyway,' said Papa Alex, 'I can't be away too long. Your man tells me you've brought in some unfortunate.'

'I'm afraid so,' said the captain, standing up from his chair. 'A John Doe, possibly a tourist. He was found washed up on one of the small beaches on the coast opposite the Holy Unmercenaries. He's in a bit of a mess, I'm afraid. Not enough left of his face to be identified.'

'Not quite the thing then for my delicate stomach.'

'We've covered his face, don't worry. But we were reminded by Chief Tsinamis's wife that it was only decent he should have your services.'

'Quite so. Assuming he's Orthodox, of course.'

Captain Androutsos shrugged.

'I think we have to make that assumption, don't we? The Examining Magistrate is sending someone on the night boat to have a look at him and we'll be starting the identification process after that. I've managed to persuade Vaios to take delivery of him at the police station, so he'll be on the move shortly. I was wondering whether you know anyone who'd sit with the body? Neither Vaios nor I can spare the man-power for overnight vigils.'

'There are women in the village who'll come,' said Papa Alex. 'In fact with a case as interesting as this one, they'll be falling over themselves to volunteer. How will you identify him?'

'Vaios and I between us will check the national missing persons reports and put the word out to other areas. If no-one claims him in the next twenty-four hours, we'll take him onto Volos and let them take care of him. It's hardly practical to keep him here for long in this heat.'

'Well, I have my box of tricks here and I'm ready to do my part.' The priest patted his black case.

'This way, then.' The captain led him down to the basement, and stopped in front of a closed door. 'I'll leave you to it. Come and say goodbye when you're done.'

The captain made his slow way back upstairs. The remaining pastries were tempting, and choosing a piece of *baklava* he carried it to his desk, but before he could sit down, a dreadful cry of distress rang out from the basement.

The captain looked in alarm at his juniors, and led them at a run to the head of the stairs.

'Papa!' shouted Captain Androutsos. 'Are you all right?'

Papa Alex stepped forward from the shadows in the stairwell, his face ghastly pale.

'Papa?' insisted the captain. 'What's wrong? What is it?'

Papa Alex grasped the stair-rail to steady himself, and sat down heavily on the lowest step.

'The man you have in that room,' he cried, burying his face in his hands. 'I know him! My God, how could I not! God save us! God save us, I would know him anywhere! It's Tassos, my brother, my beloved brother!'

Four

The fat man left only a small tip for what had been slightly neglectful service – a slow response to his request for more bread, a long delay in bringing out his plate of green beans, no-one to be found when he was ready to pay. He was patient for a while, smoking a cigarette, and still no-one came to his table. In the end, he got up and went to the kitchen door to ask what he owed and the bill was brought out with indecent haste, but then, when he discovered he needed change to leave a tip, the waiter was again nowhere to be seen, involved no doubt in the raucous conversation coming from the kitchen. Looking around, he saw other neglected diners looking with displeasure in that direction, so deciding not to wait, he left the waiter nothing but a scattering of copper coins.

As he left the taverna, no-one appeared to thank him for his business or wish him goodnight. Carrying his holdall, he made his way along the harbour-side in the direction of the Hotel Poseidon. He passed a taxi-stand where there were no taxis for hire, and a municipal tourist information office where – though it was well within the advertised evening open hours – the lights were switched off and no-one was inside. The fat man studied the brochures taped to the windows advertising Liteos's attractions, but they were last year's publications and so sun-bleached, the photographs were too faded to be seen.

Alongside the tourist office was a *periptero*, a kiosk whose usual purpose was to sell cigarettes, confectionery and magazines. The *periptero* was of old-fashioned design, reminiscent of the street-kiosks of 1930s Athens, with a base of carved panels which looked to have been lifted from a tour-de-siècle dining room, but for being painted sunflower yellow; and the glazed upper half rose to a tiled, orb-capped roof so the whole might have been taken for a transported French bandstand.

As the fat man approached the kiosk, he saw many of the usual commodities were available – chocolate and postcards, pistachio nuts, chewing gum and cold drinks – yet the merchandise seemed cramped on the shelves, forced into less space than it needed. As he drew closer, he saw why. Where there might usually have been cheap lighters and wafer biscuits, were displays of fishing-lures – metallic minnows striped with ruby and emerald, iridescent plastic squid with feathered tails, lifelike titanium copies of wrasse and parrotfish – all attached to hooks of varying sizes. On the *periptero* roof a sign which used to advertise Ion chocolate was covered by a placard bearing one hand-drawn word: Bait.

The fat man approached the sales window. Behind it was a pretty girl whose face was all but hidden by her hair, which fell, straight and sleek, down to her waist. She was seated on a high stool, and he thought at first she was embroidering, or making lace; but as he reached her, he saw she was making up simple fishing-rigs to sell, threading and tying lead weights and hooks onto lengths of line wound on polystyrene spools.

Seeing the fat man, she pulled tight with her teeth the knot she was tying, and buried the barbed hook in the polystyrene. She smiled at him, and wished him *kali spera*.

'*Kali spera,*' said the fat man. 'I wonder if you can help me. I'm looking for a pack or two of these.'

He brought out his cigarettes. The box was old-fashioned in design, a red background with the manufacturer's name – Konstantinos Brothers – written in gold, and below the name, a slogan: *For the man who knows a real smoke*. At the centre of the lid was the stylised face of a 1940s starlet, a coy platinum blonde with an arch smile.

The fat man placed the pack on the counter, and the girl looked at it.

'We have those,' she said. 'At least, I think we do.'

She slipped down off her stool, and began to search a shelf of cigarettes. Tempted by the illustrations on the ice-cream freezers, the fat man wandered over and peered through the glass lids, but instead of the bright packaging of sundaes and cornets, there were only bags of raw prawns and squid, and plastic food containers labelled mullet, snapper and bream.

Disappointed, he returned to the counter, where an unopened pack of the Konstantinos Brothers' cigarettes lay next to his almost-empty one.

'You found them,' he said. 'That's excellent. But I have to say I'm not impressed with the quality of your ice-cream.'

She laughed, a sunny, convivial laugh.

'I'm sorry,' she said. 'But if you want ice-cream, there are a hundred places in Liteos that'll sell it to you. I use all my freezers for bait. Are you a fisherman?'

'Sometimes. As a matter of fact, I was lucky in my fishing today.'

'Let me guess,' she said. 'You caught bream.'

'As a matter of fact, I did,' said the fat man. 'How did you know?'

She pursed her lips and gave a shake of her head, in the Greek expression which meant, I can't say.

'We'll call it an inspired guess, then,' said the fat man. 'But tell me, how do you come to be selling bait?'

Her eyes flashed with annoyance.

'If I were a man, would you ask me that question?'

'No, I don't suppose I would.'

'You think it strange for a woman to sell bait because women have no business fishing.'

'You misunderstand me. I don't at all think they have no business fishing. I made the remark only because it is rare to find a woman who enjoys it.'

'And it's a rarity because of our insulting superstition, that women are unlucky to fishermen,' said the girl. 'As it happens, I'm an excellent fisherwoman, and if you try my baits, you'll find out why.' She leaned forward in her earnestness. 'I know fish, *kyrie*. I know what they like, and I know what they don't like. I know plenty about the sea, more than most of the men who run these boats. I learned from my grandfather. He used to take me out from being a little girl, and when he passed away, since my brother wasn't able to handle his boat, it came to me. It isn't much of a boat, to be honest. It has no engine, only oars, so I don't go far. But I usually come back with a decent catch, or as good as it can be in these overfished waters. My dream is to captain an ocean-going boat, and to bring back swordfish and tuna.'

'What do you put in your bait that makes it so special?' asked the fat man.

'If I told you that, I'd put myself out of business! My grandfather used to say it came from being half-mermaid. I was swimming when I was three, and I swim kilometres every day. Sometimes when I'm swimming, it's as if the sea-creatures speak to me, and an idea pops into my head, that the snapper would love a little of this, or the pipefish some of that. And I put it in the next mix of my bait, and the fishermen come back, and they tell me, Noula, I don't know what you put in that bait, but those fish couldn't get enough of it. Call it instinct, or call it what you will, I'm not very often wrong.'

'Then next time I go fishing, I shall give it a try,' said the fat man. 'In the meantime, I'll take the cigarettes, and I need a box of matches, if you have one.'

She placed matches alongside the cigarettes, and gave him change from the note he offered.

'Noula, is it?' he asked, as he turned to go. 'My name is Hermes. *Chairo poli.*'

He gave a small bow of his head, and she, amused by this and his formal form if address, bowed her head too.

'*Chairo poli*, *Kyrie* Hermes,' she said. 'I'll hope to see you again, next time you're going fishing.'

∞∞∞

The fat man walked on, staying close to the water, until he came to the empty ferry berth where Sammy had returned to his bench, his bicycle propped up behind him. One of the books from his handlebar basket was unopened on his knee; his eyes were on the dark sea and beyond, looking out to where the black water met the star-speckled sky.

Reaching a nearby litter-bin, the fat man took the matchbox he had bought from Noula, slid off the lid and tipped the unspent matches into the bin, where they fell with a light tinkling into its base. The noise drew Sammy's attention, and he saw the fat man replace the empty matchbox in his pocket.

The fat man sauntered on, feigning great interest in the water as if trying, in spite of the darkness, to spot fish or octopus, until he came to a halt directly in front of Sammy, whom he seemed then to notice for the first time.

'Excuse me!' he said. 'Forgive me! I'm blocking your view!'

Sammy glanced at him and looked away, expecting to have no further interaction with the stranger. But he found nothing in the fat man's expression to suggest revulsion or even curiosity – nothing, in fact, to show his deformity had been noticed at all.

'It doesn't matter,' he said. 'I wasn't really looking at anything.'

The fat man raised his eyebrows.

'Not looking at anything?' Shaking his head, he moved closer to Sammy's bench. 'May I sit with you a moment?'

Pleased at the prospect of company, Sammy shifted to make space for him.

The fat man sat, placing his hold-all between his white-shoed feet.

'Behold!' he said, holding up his arms as if to encompass the heavens. 'Of all the gods' creations, these two surpass all others, the ocean and the heavens, and here we are, with an uninterrupted vista of the two together. And do you see how they complement each other? By night, the sea is blank and mysterious in the darkness, allowing the constellations to shine.' He pointed up at the crescent moon. 'There you see Selene, goddess of the moon, modest this evening with only a sliver of her robe on show, though she is no less beautiful for that. And when day breaks, she and the stars around her will withdraw behind the sunlight, and Poseidon's kingdom will be spread before us, like a mantle adorning the body of the land. Do you know the constellations?' He placed a hand on Sammy's left shoulder, and Sammy felt warmth there, a tingling and trickling as if warm water were running down his useless arm. 'You can see the sea reflected in the sky. There's Cancer there, the sign of the crab, and Pisces the fish.'

Sammy was looking up, following with his eyes the fat man's pointing finger.

'I never thought of it like that,' he said, 'as a reflection of the sea.'

'I was out there fishing today,' said the fat man. 'As a matter of fact, I did rather well. Are you a fisherman?'

Sammy patted his left arm with his good hand.

'My sister fishes, but not me,' he said. 'I can't bait the hooks.'

'I'm sorry to hear that. I see you're a reader, though. What are you reading?'

Sammy held up his book to the light of a nearby streetlamp. Its cover was a line drawing of a man in a trilby, the collar of his overcoat turned up against the cold, a cigarette hanging from his mouth.

'It's *The Fourth Suspect*, an Inspector Bekas mystery. Yannis Maris writes them, and I've seen them on TV. I've borrowed this one from Papa Alex. He has a huge collection of detective stories. I like to try and spot all the red herrings.'

'So you are a fisherman, a fisher of red herrings. Have you found any in that book?'

'I think so. The trouble with red herrings is, you don't know until you get to the end whether they were red herrings or not.'

The fat man nodded.

'That is true,' he said. 'And very true in my line of work. You can never be sure of the truth until you get to the very end. So, next time I see you, you can tell me how many herrings you've caught.'

'I already know how many I think there are. I'm reading it for the second time, to see if I was right.'

'That is very thorough of you. What do they call you?'

'Sammy.'

'*Chairo poli*, Sammy. My name is Hermes.'

'Are you a tourist here?'

'In a manner of speaking. I'm passing through and admiring the views, but I have work to do here, too.'

'What kind of work?'

The fat man considered.

'That remains to be seen. My work takes different forms, but in Liteos I am here, in part, to check on some of my business interests. We are sitting here looking at the sea, from which many people in this country make their livings in many different ways. Let me show you something.'

He unzipped his holdall, and after searching inside for a few moments, pulled out a glossy magazine whose title was in a foreign alphabet Sammy couldn't read. The fat man opened it at its centre pages, which were covered by a photograph of two magnificent globes. The globes were illuminated from within, the pastel-blue oceans and misshapen landforms glowing so that they seemed, in the darkness, to light the pages on which they shone.

'This is a catalogue from the French National Library in Paris,' said the fat man, holding the magazine so Sammy could see it clearly. 'I have visited it on several occasions – it is, of course, the repository of some of the most valuable writings in the history of mankind – and whenever I am there, I always make time to see these wonderful objects. They are the Coronelli globes, glass representations of the earth and the heavens as they were believed to be in the time of Louis the Fourteenth, for whom they were made. Louis was a French monarch known as the Sun King for his ostentation and glamour. Nothing was too expensive or too luxurious for his glittering court, and as a man who had everything he could possibly want or need, his boredom with life led him to seek out new wonders wherever he could. Travel was difficult in those days, so he decided to bring the world to his palace, and had the Italian monk Vincenzo Coronelli fashion the world and the stars, and present them to his courtiers.'

Sammy was gazing at the pictures of the wonderful globes.

'Like a fairytale,' he said. 'A king commanding the world to come to his feet.'

'You're very astute,' said the fat man, 'but King Louis's life was hardly a fairytale. He was Europe's longest-reigning monarch, but he suffered all his life from the misery of ill health. He underwent – and survived – an operation to remove an abscess from his anus which took two months to heal, and in the end he died in agony of horribly painful gangrene. But his taste in art was faultless, and so despite the fact that Louis is long gone, these wonderful globes remain. They look like glass, but they're made of wood and fabric. From these photographs it is hard to appreciate their size, but whilst they were being painted seven men could work together inside each one. Imagine what a wonder they must have been to people not long past learning that the world was round, not flat! Let me show you these.'

He leaned over and turned the page in the catalogue, where there were photos in close-up of some of the detail on the globes. The fat man pointed to one image in particular – in the part of the ocean labelled the Arabian Sea was a wooden sailboat, its decks laden with treasure, rubies, emeralds and draping strings of pearls.

'This illustration is a work of art all by itself,' said the fat man. 'These are pearl-fishers, and from the first time I saw that boat, I wanted to be with them on that ocean. I wanted to be a pearl-fisher, and now I am.'

'You're a pearl-fisher?' asked Sammy, incredulously. 'But there are no pearl-fishers in Greece!'

'Are there shell-fish in these waters?'

'Yes.'

'Where there are shell-fish, there are pearls, and where there are pearls, there are generally pearl-fishers. If I show you something, you must promise to keep it to yourself.'

Sammy nodded. Reaching into his pocket, the fat man withdrew what Sammy assumed was the same matchbox he had seen emptied. The fat man slid off the cover, and held the cardboard tray in the palm of his hand. The tray was filled with pearls of different sizes, some hardly bigger than a pinhead, many the size of young peas, one or two so big, Sammy's eyes widened. Though it was hard to tell their true colours under the street-lamp, some appeared to have a touch of pink, whilst others were graphite grey.

'Are they real?' he asked.

'They are most certainly real,' said the fat man. 'I would be a poor pearl-fisher if I didn't find real pearls.'

'But where do you find them?'

'Shall I let you in on my secret?'

Sammy nodded again.

'Do you know how pearls are made? They are formed by a natural process when the oyster – or mussel, or many other molluscs – finds an irritation inside its shell, a grain of sand or other debris washed inside. As you know an oyster's body is very soft, so to protect itself it forms a hard coating around the irritation of the same substance from which its shell is made – a substance called nacre, or mother-of-pearl, which is the wonderful iridescence we find in mussel shells. Over a period of time – months, or years – the nacre forms a bead, or pearl, like these.'

'But where do you find them?'

'Ah, well.' The fat man gave a knowing smile. 'We pearl-fishers have moved with the times. I have found a very good way of growing pearls which is no trouble to anyone, but which relies on modern technology, helpfully supplied by others.'

'What sort of technology?'

'Fish-farms.'

'We have a fish-farm here in Liteos!'

'Yes, you do. And between us – remember you mustn't tell – I have been making use of it. I find my host molluscs and I plant the seed of my pearls in their shells, by opening them and putting in a single grain of sand. Then I string the shells from the tanks where the fish are growing, and with the fish swimming overhead, they spend their lives hanging from the bottom of the tanks, very much as if they were free in the ocean. And when I judge the time is right – the creatures cannot be rushed, and I have to be patient – I return to the tanks and harvest my pearls.'

'Don't the fish-farmers mind?'

'The fish-farmers don't know. But they don't own the ocean. They use a very small part of it for their own purposes, and I am merely benefiting from the tanks they construct as a framework for my enterprise.'

'Can I touch them?'

'Of course. Hold out your hand.'

Sammy did so, and the fat man let several of the cold, opaque stones fall into his palm. Sammy rolled one with his thumb, marvelling at the rainbow sheen on their smoothness.

'They're wonderful,' he said. 'I've never seen real pearls before.'

'Would you like one? Choose. Which colour do you prefer, the white or the black?'

'Aren't black pearls the rarest? But I think I prefer the white.'

Sammy studied the treasure in his hand. At first he was drawn to the biggest, but then one of the medium-sized ones took his eye; it seemed to glow as though the light of the moon were within it.

'This one,' he said. 'This one is the most beautiful.'

The fat man smiled.

'A very good choice,' he said. 'That one is of excellent quality. If you were to take it to the jewellers over there, he would give you good money for it.'

'I shall keep it. I think it will bring me luck.'

'I think so too. Think of it as a gift from the sea.' Sammy gave back the other pearls, and the fat man returned them to the matchbox, and returned the matchbox to his pocket. 'Now I shall leave you to read in peace, but I shall look out for you when I'm passing again.'

'Why don't you take this?' Sammy offered the fat man his copy of *The Fourth Suspect*. 'I have other books to read. Next time I see you, we can see who spotted the most red herrings.'

'Thank you,' said the fat man. 'That's a good idea. But I warn you, when it comes to red herrings, I am hard to beat.'

Left alone, Sammy played for a while with the pearl in his hand. When the fat man was out of sight, he got up from the bench and wheeled his bike to the *periptero*.

Noula was still tying hooks onto lengths of fishing line.

'*Yassou*, little brother,' she said. 'What are you up to?'

'Can I have a box of matches?'

Noula frowned.

'Why do you want matches? Have you taken up smoking?'

'Nothing like that,' said Sammy. 'I want to light a candle in the church.'

She took a box down from the shelf and laid it on the counter.

'You be careful with them,' she said. 'I don't want the embarrassment of calling out the fire brigade. And you should be thinking about bed.'

'It's early. I thought I'd wait for you.'

'If you want to.'

‘I’ll be reading. You can come and find me.’

‘I’ll be a couple of hours yet. If you get bored, come and tell me before you go home.’

‘I will.’

On his way back to his bench, he passed the litter-bin where he’d first seen the fat man. Noula was absorbed in her work, and wasn’t watching. Sammy slipped the cover off the matchbox and let all the matches fall into the bin, then put his pearl inside the empty box, slid the lid closed, and put the matchbox in the basket on his handlebars.

Five

Almost all his married life, Pericles Kassimis had dreamed of a life on a different island to Liteos: a place of white-sand beaches edged with palm-trees, where the ocean rose in gargantuan waves and a brave man could surf their crests, or even – if he had the skill – ride through the tunnel at their cores; a place where dark-skinned girls swayed their hips in raffia skirts and wore nothing but floral garlands to cover their breasts.

But Pericles had never found that place, and he was too old now, in late middle-age, to mount a surf-board or shin up palm-trees to gather coconuts. It was unlikely, too, that the dark-skinned girls of his imagination would entertain him; he wore his years badly, skinny and blighted by a lack of leisure, a daily excess of alcohol and the perpetual worry of verbal assault from a wife he could never please.

Yet his dream lived on at the Hotel Poseidon, in the terrace bar he'd decorated in Polynesian style, with a roof of palm-leaves and a floor-to-ceiling mural of a surfer riding a tsunami-sized wave. The walls were draped with fishing-nets hung with conch shells; huge pots of banana plants stood sentinel at the entrance, and the background music was the jaunty plink of Hawaiian guitars.

The terrace tables were almost all occupied by guests relaxing with post-dinner *digestifs*. Pericles was sitting on a stool behind the bar, working on a newspaper crossword, and seeing the fat man ascend the steps, he smiled and beckoned him over.

'Hermes! Come and sit over here, my friend. Let me fix you a drink.'

The fat man looked at the comfortable chairs set around the tables, and heaved himself onto a bar-stool with some reluctance.

'What'll you have?' asked Pericles. 'Let me make you a cocktail.'

He handed the fat man a laminated menu featuring photographs of concoctions decorated with paper umbrellas and unnaturally red, sugary cherries: Blue Lagoon, Mai Tai, Cuba Libre, Bali Hai.

The fat man frowned.

'Perhaps something a little less complex,' he said. 'I was thinking of Metaxa.'

'Ah, don't be a stick-in-the-mud!' said Pericles. 'That's an old man's drink! Let me make you a Piña Colada. Rum, pineapple and coconut.'

'It sounds like a dessert,' said the fat man, 'and really, I ate a very substantial dinner.'

'How about one of these, then?' suggested Pericles, holding up his own glass of rum and Coke.

'Is that not a little sweet? How about a Campari soda?'

'Is that not a little bitter? Really, my friend, you should move with the times.'

'Do you think so?' asked the fat man. 'I have always found the times move perfectly well without me.'

Pericles reached up onto the shelves behind him, and took down a bottle of Campari.

'How was dinner?' he asked, pouring a good measure of the red liquid into a glass.

'Indifferent,' said the fat man. 'Indifferent food, indifferent service, though I find the service is always second rate when the food is sub-standard. No-one takes pride in serving food which fails to please. And I was disappointed – no, more than disappointed, I was dismayed – to find no fresh fish to speak of. Here I am in Liteos, in search of the famous golden tuna, and I found nothing but supermarket mullet and Vietnamese squid. Needless to say, I ate neither. The *stifado* would have been acceptable, if it had been made today.'

Pericles lifted the lid on a plastic pineapple, reached in for a pair of tongs and used them to drop several shrinking ice-cubes into the Campari. He opened a can of soda and poured a splash into the fat man's drink.

'The fishing here is over, Hermes,' he said. 'For most, anyway. You should have stayed here and eaten with us. I grilled those bream you caught, and they were excellent.'

'I didn't like to impose,' said the fat man. 'Did you put the fan mussel to soak? It will want a couple of days to clean it, but I'm hoping we can eat it together before I go. The shell will look very attractive here with the others on your walls.'

Pericles pulled a face.

'My dear wife says I have too many in my collection already. If she has her way, the shell will go straight in the rubbish.'

'That would be a great shame. Where is the beautiful Tina, anyway?'

'She's in the office, adding up invoices and subtracting receipts and blaming me for the ocean of difference between the two. I hope you'll dine with us one evening, Hermes. If you work your charms on her, she won't be nagging me.'

He dropped a slice of lemon into the Campari and pushed it across the bar.

The fat man took a sip.

'Perfect,' he said. 'And perfectly civilised. I'll eat with you if she invites me.'

'She won't invite you. She dislikes my friends on principle, though she tolerates you better than most. Speak of the devil, here's a good friend of mine now. Hey, Vaios! Come and sit!'

The Chief of Police was ambling onto the terrace.

'You're late tonight,' said Pericles, as the chief took a stool next to the fat man. 'I was expecting you hours ago. I thought it was your day off.'

'There are no days off,' said Vaios, sitting down heavily. 'I try to have a day off, they come and find me. I'll have a beer.'

'Why did they come and find you?' Pericles opened the freezer, took out a chilled glass tankard and set it under the tap of a barrel of Amstel. When it was filled, he tipped peanuts into a bowl and set them in front of the policeman alongside the beer.

Vaios took a long drink.

'We've got a body,' he said.

The fat man had picked up Pericles's crossword, and was writing in the answer to five down.

'A body?' he asked, laying the newspaper back on the bar. 'That sounds very interesting.'

The chief looked at him with suspicion.

'I don't think I know you,' he said.

'Vaios, let me introduce you,' said Pericles, quickly. 'Hermes Diaktoros, may I introduce Vaios Tsinamis, our venerable Chief of Police. Hermes is from Athens, Vaios. He and I go back a long way. He likes to interest himself in life's mysteries.'

'No mystery here,' said Vaios. 'Do you have any of those pickled capers, instead of these peanuts? My wife keeps telling me I need to lose weight.'

Pericles searched in the fridge for a jar of caper leaves in vinegar, and forked a few onto a saucer.

'So if there's no mystery, whose body is it?' he asked. 'Who found it? Where?'

'It was washed up on one of those little beaches opposite the Holy Unmercenaries,' said Vaios. He put a stalk of the capers in his mouth, chewed and grimaced at their tartness. 'Costas Iordanidis found it.'

'Yiannis's Costas?' asked Pericles. 'I know him. I know his father very well. What was he doing round there?'

'Fishing,' said the policeman. 'So he says.'

'Did he catch anything?' asked the fat man, politely.

Vaios looked at him.

'I really don't know,' he said.

'And who is it?' asked Pericles. 'I mean, whose is the body?'

'We didn't know who it was, at first,' said the Chief of Police. 'We thought we'd got a John Doe case on our hands. Then Maritsa gave me a telling-off for not having called in a priest, so Apostolos sent for Papa Alex. *Panayia mou*, what an error! He sent him down to the basement to give the last rites, and the next thing he knows, there's weeping and wailing fit to wake the dead man if he weren't so far beyond it.' He shook his head. 'Damn me if our John Doe isn't Papa Alex's brother Tassos! Well, I knew Tassos, but I'd never have known him from what was left of his face. Anyway, we've got him at our offices now, being ministered to by the ladies of the church. Poor bastard, what a way to end up! Not pretty, not pretty at all. I reckon he must have been a while in the water.'

He drank more beer, and seemed disinclined to go on.

'I'm guessing he didn't smell too good, then,' prompted Pericles.

'You know, that's an interesting thing,' said Vaios, thoughtfully. 'Though he's been in the water a while, he doesn't smell bad. I thought we'd be getting out the fumigator, but it looks like it won't be necessary. And here's another thing. When we got a close look at him, his top half didn't match the lower. From the waist up, there was a lot of water-damage, but his lower half – with respect to him – looked much fresher.'

'That's not possible, surely?' said Pericles. 'How can one half of him have died before the other?'

'Precisely so,' said Vaios. 'It isn't possible. Anyway, that isn't my problem. The Examining Magistrate's office is sending someone to take a look, so we'll know more when he gets here. In the meantime, I'll have another beer.'

The fat man picked up the newspaper, and appeared to give his attention back to the crossword, and yet the boxes for the clues remained empty. Pericles and the Chief of Police talked on, discussing the performance of the national football team, the corruption of politicians and whether it was more lucrative to grow apricots or peaches, until a customer signalled for Pericles's attention, and he came out from behind the bar to serve them.

'Excuse my asking,' said the fat man, when Pericles was out of earshot, 'but are you seeing anything suspicious in this recent death?'

'Suspicious? In what way?' The Chief of Police put his hand over his mouth to cover a belch.

'Was the man old, or infirm?'

'Not at all. He was in his forties, about the same age as…' The chief was about to draw a parallel in age with the fat man, but glancing at his face, found it suddenly impossible to say how old he actually was, and decided to abandon the comparison. 'Well, I'd put him in his early forties. And he had no infirmities that I know of. He was known to like a drink, but that's no crime. Plenty of us enjoy a drink from time to time.'

'What would you say killed him, then?'

Vaios studied the fat man.

'*Kyrie*…'

'Diaktoros,' supplied the fat man.

'*Kyrie* Diaktoros, I am a long-serving police officer who knows his place in the hierarchy. On the rare occasion we have a body to deal with, I call in the professionals and let them take care of the considerable red tape corpses generate. The man from the Examining Magistrate's office will be here tonight, he'll tell us it's an accidental drowning, there'll be a funeral, and that, as they say, will be that. When you live on an island, you accept that a few will come to grief in the sea.'

'No question in your mind, then, of foul play?'

‘Foul play? What sort of foul play?’

‘Homicide. Murder. Whatever you want to call it.’

Vaios laughed.

‘Spoken like a true Athenian,’ he said. ‘But I’m afraid we’re going to disappoint you. Are you hoping for broken skulls or bullet wounds? I don’t think so, *Kyrie* Diaktoros. What are the chances of a murder happening here?’

Six

The captain of the ferry *Marie-Crysanthe* was offering prayers to St Nicholas for a better end to the voyage than its beginning. Four stops out from their home port of Volos, a broken-down truck had delayed departure for an hour. In the bar, a threesome of bored travellers had used that hour to drink cheap brandy, then got themselves into a fight over a hand of cards, falling over tables and breaking chairs, spraying the other passengers with blood from broken noses and using language so foul, mothers and grandmothers covered the children's ears. The police were called, but no arrests were made; the men were separated – two locked in vacant cabins, the third in a closet with the janitorial supplies – and *Marie-Crysanthe* at last moved on to her next port. Arriving there very late, the crewmen were given orders to hurry the disembarking passengers, and so made a Swedish backpacker hurry too fast. Stumbling under the weight of her backpack, she slid down the saloon stairs and broke her ankle. An ambulance was called to remove the casualty.

By the time she approached Liteos, *Marie-Crysanthe* was almost three hours behind schedule, arriving in those small hours of the morning when only the most committed and most desperate of drinkers remained in the one still-open bar, when the port's back lanes and alleys were the provinces of rats, sneaking philanderers and feral cats.

The officer on watch in the coastguard station had been dozing in his chair. Alerted by a sixth sense to the approaching ferry, he woke and yawned, took his feet off his desk, found his cap and sauntered down the stairs. By the time he reached the dock, *Marie-Crysanthe* had made a turn through a hundred and eighty degrees, and was approaching the harbour-side stern-on.

The few passengers waiting to leave Liteos were bleary-eyed and weary as they gathered up their bags and back-packs and prepared to board. On the ferry's upper decks two crewmen waited, cigarettes in mouths, to throw ropes to those below. On the bridge, the second officer was guiding the vessel to its mooring. The captain switched on the tannoy, and disregarding the fact that most of his passengers were sleeping, made a booming announcement.

'Liteos, ladies and gentlemen, this is Liteos. All passengers for Liteos disembark from the rear deck.'

The ropes were secured to the bollards and the ramp descended, clanging onto the harbour-side. The disembarking passengers made their way ashore, and dispersed into the quay-side's darkness. Those departing hurried aboard, anxious to find a place they could sleep. Within five minutes, *Marie-Crysanthe* was ready to leave.

The captain returned to the tannoy microphone and spoke to his crew.

'Let's go, *pedia*,' he said.

The crewmen fired up the winches to haul in the ropes; gears groaned as the ramp climbed back to the vertical, and the black waters churned as the propellers moved the ferry away from the dock. The pounding of her engines reverberated round the harbour buildings, and her deck lights illuminated the smears of rust below her anchors and in huge red letters along her bows, the name of her operator: Zoutis Lines. Setting her course, she headed towards open sea.

Satisfied his obligations were met, the coastguard officer removed his cap, and stood debating with himself whether to return immediately to his desk, or whether he should alleviate the night-shift's boredom by taking a stroll around the moorings.

Someone touched him on the arm.

She was a slight woman, with black hair styled in a French bob, dressed in a white shirt creased from travelling and the skirt of a soft pink suit, whose jacket was draped round her shoulders. She carried two small cases, one black, one grey.

In the light of the mayor's festive-coloured lightbulbs – decorations never removed after Christmas – the officer thought her attractive, and readied his most winning smile; but another moment of observation told him she was closer to forty than twenty, and he stopped the smile before all his teeth were on show, changing it from warm and welcoming to professionally polite.

'Excuse me,' she said. 'I'm from the Examining Magistrate's office. I believe there's a body you need me to look at.'

He looked her up and down, doubting her suitability for the job.

'It's at the police station,' he said, indifferently.

She raised her eyebrows, encouraging him to say more, but he had made his decision not to take a stroll and was ready to return to his chair.

A trace of impatience crept into her voice.

'So can you show me the way?'

'Along here to the first right,' said the coastguard officer. 'You can't miss it.'

'It's very late, and I'm tired but with a night's work ahead of me,' said the woman. 'If I had fifty drachma for every time someone told me I couldn't miss my destination, I'd be living a life of luxury that wouldn't involve taking ferries which don't get me where I need to go until three in the morning, or whatever time it is now. So just to be sure I don't miss it, maybe you could show me the way? Unless you have more pressing business, of course.'

Her words might have stung, but she softened them with a hint of flirtatiousness in her eyes.

'This way, then,' he said, flatly.

'Maybe you could help me with one of these.' She held out her grey case, and unable to refuse, he took it.

He led the way. Despite her petiteness, the leather soles of her silver slippers rang loud in the stillness of the night. At the entrance to the police station, he stopped and put down her case.

'This is it,' he said.

'Will they be awake? I don't want to interrupt anyone's beauty sleep.'

'These night-shifts are long,' he said, defensively. 'There's nothing to do.'

'Except sleep,' she said. 'And we'd all like to be doing that. Thank you for showing me the way. I appreciate it.'

'It was nothing,' he said, and left her to return to his desk and his dozing.

She left her cases side-by-side at the foot of the stairs, and following an 'Enquiries' sign nailed to the wall, climbed the staircase to the first floor. There were three doors, one marked 'Entry prohibited,' a second 'WC'. On the third door was no sign at all, but taking it as the only remaining option, she confidently pushed it open, and went inside.

The office was of generous size, the stubs of walls still in place from when two rooms were knocked into one. There was no air-conditioning, but all the windows were open to let in a breeze off the sea, which ruffled the papers on the desks. Around the walls were posters held up with yellowing Sellotape, red-bordered appeals for missing persons, each one a grainy-photographed memorial to the long-lost: children, adolescents and adults, some recently disappeared, others gone for over a decade, all with too little hope of ever being found.

A police constable had made himself a bed from six chairs arranged in a line, their backs offset alternately to make sides like a baby's cot and stop him falling off as he slept. He had been snoring before she entered; now he opened his eyes, and taking her to be a member of the public, he sat up quickly, blinking away sleep, struggling to climb out of his bed. His colleague was reading a Western novel whose cover featured a chiselled, Stetson-wearing outlaw pulling the trigger of a hand-gun similar to the one holstered on the policeman's belt. He, too, was startled by the opening of the door, and turned in his chair like a man surprised in a saloon shoot-out.

'*Yassas*,' she said.

The policemen were quickly to recover their accustomed aloof composure. The first had extricated himself from the chairs and, standing up, was smoothing his hair. The second had slipped his book into a desk drawer and drawn a stack of papers close to his elbow, as if official paperwork had been all his night's business.

'*Oriste*,' he said, in a cold, polite tone, which she matched.

'I am Popi Dritsaki, from the Examining Magistrate's office. You put in a call regarding a body, a sudden death?'

The constable who had been sleeping had moved to stand near his colleague, so they formed a short wall of non-cooperation.

'What of it?'

'I'm here to perform an examination of the body,' she said. 'To determine if a death certificate can be issued and the body released for burial. You know the drill, I'm sure.'

'We were expecting Dr Skandamis. That's what the chief said.'

'Dr Skandamis is away, enjoying a relaxing holiday with his family,' said Popi. 'Under those circumstances, they send me.'

'Do you have identification?'

Popi's eyebrows lifted.

'Is that a joke?' she asked. 'A woman walks in here at three in the morning asking to see a dead body, and you ask for identification? I think you should consider two scenarios. Either – and I suggest this is most likely – I'm who I say I am, namely a disgruntled, tired examiner trying to do her job. Or secondly, I'm a very strange individual with a fetish for necrophilia who happens to have got word you've got a body here and I've come hot-footing over to take a look. Which seems more likely to you? As a matter of fact I do have identification, but who you'll check it with, I don't know. I suppose we could all sit around until the court's offices open in, what? Five, six hours, and you could ring them? Or you could let me get on with the job in hand so we can release the body to the family as quickly as possible, hopefully before breakfast. Which shall we do?'

The policemen were silent, each waiting for the other to answer.

'So,' said Popi. 'Can I see the paperwork? Then maybe you can take me to see – him, her, which is it?'

'It's a male,' said one of them, going through the papers on his desk. 'He's downstairs, in the archives.'

'In the archives?'

The policeman frowned.

'Yes. Why not? It's quite secure.'

'And who ordered him taken there?'

'The chief.'

'And did it not occur to your chief – or to any of you – that it might be difficult for me – or for Dr Skandamis, for that matter – to work in the archives? I don't mind for myself, as long as you don't mind cleaning up afterwards.'

The policemen looked at each other.

'It might be better if you went to the medical centre,' said one.

'I think that's a very good idea,' said Popi. 'The two of you could carry him for me. Is it far?'

'I don't know if we should move him without the chief's say-so.'

'As you wish,' said Popi. 'Please, wake him and ask him.'

'I meant we should wait until he comes into the office in the morning.'

'When lots of people are about to see you with the body, and the medical centre's full of sick people and there's no spare room? Is that what you mean by waiting?'

'We don't have anything to move him on.'

'Don't you have a stretcher? If you don't, I'm sure your friends at the coastguard office do. One of them is there now. I've just spoken to him. He could help you carry the body. And don't forget we'll be needing a sheet to cover him, if you don't already have one.'

The policemen seemed to accept the need for action at last, and left her. Popi made her way downstairs, and found the room which housed the Liteos police's archive in near darkness. The air was musty and dusty and sweet with the smoke of incense; the walls were lined with shelves of cardboard boxes bulging with manila files, some so overstuffed only string bindings prevented them bursting. At the centre of the room was a long table, from which more overstuffed boxes had been removed and stacked behind the door to make space for the body of Tassos Hardouvelis. Lying with candles at his head and feet, he was draped in a white sheet, which was, Popi noted, drawn up to cover his face, contrary to tradition. Beside him sat two elderly women, one on either side in mirror images, watching over the body like *lampades*, Hecate's mythical torch-bearing companions of the underworld.

'*Kali spera*.'

The women nodded to acknowledge her.

'Ladies, forgive me,' said Popi, 'but I have to ask you to break your vigil.'

'Break our vigil?' asked one. 'This poor man needs our watchfulness for the sake of his soul!'

'We gave our word to the Chief of Police,' said the other. 'We said we would stay with him until the family could be here. They wouldn't let us wash him, though. That still needs to be done.'

'I'm afraid in circumstances such as these, there are other things which must be done first. Examinations which must be performed, to establish the cause of death.'

In the candlelight, the women blinked. Shadows caught in the hollows of their eyes.

'He drowned,' said one. 'No need for any examining.'

'Another one lost,' said the other, making crosses over her heart. 'The sea is a cruel mistress.'

'You may be right,' said Popi. 'Even so, I must do my examination. With it being so late, I'll ask one of the officers here to drive you home.'

The prospect of a ride in a police car seemed to offset the disappointment of their truncated vigil. With dignity, the two women rose, and wished Popi a good night.

Popi stood beside the covered body and offered prayers, to St Panteleimon to guide her in her work, and to St Michael for Tassos's eternal soul. Then she took one of the chairs vacated by the old women, and waited in silence until the peace of the place was broken by the policemen's return.

∞∞∞

The policemen and the coastguard officer carried the body with an air of furtiveness, avoiding the quickest route which would have taken them past the still-open bar, weaving instead through the back-streets in hushed disagreement as to which way they should go. They passed new lovers in a doorway, who, inebriated by desire and alcohol, might never have noticed them go by, except the girl, hearing footsteps, opened her eyes mid-kiss. Her eyes widened in shock, and she was about to cry out; but following the men with her black and grey cases, Popi put a finger to her lips requesting silence, and the girl closed her eyes again, giving herself up to her lover, and to lust.

At the medical centre, one of the cleaners was waiting with the key. When she saw what the men were carrying, she crossed herself, handed over the keys and hurried away. As they carried the body into the reception area, Popi switched on all the lights. The place smelled of bleach and antiseptic, and of the lemony white geraniums growing on the window-sill.

Breathing heavily under the weight of the corpse the men waited while Popi opened doors. In one of the examination rooms were a gurney and a sink, and a dispenser of surgical gloves on the wall.

'In here.' With relief, the men laid the body on the gurney and wiped the sweat from their foreheads. 'It's not ideal, but it will do. I'll need one of you to stay here, to keep guard. I'd hate anyone to walk in on me.'

The policeman who stayed behind was glad to do so; there was a TV in the reception area, and a kitchen to make coffee where Popi found a bucket and cloths. Using the cleaner's keys she let herself into the doctor's office and helped herself to kidney bowls and an Anglepoise lamp.

Back in the examination room, she opened her black case and took out laundered scrubs, overshoes, a case of instruments, a notebook and a camera. She loaded film into the camera, found a clean page in her notebook and headed it with the date, the place, and the significant details from the police paperwork she'd brought with her, then transposed the same details onto an official five-part form, pressing hard with her pen to make all the copies legible. When she had changed into the scrubs, she pulled on a pair of latex gloves and removed the sheet from Tassos's body.

Walking round the gurney, she studied the corpse from every angle, making notes of her first impressions, which were confused. The planes where Tassos's face had been appeared smooth, almost as though he was wearing a featureless mask, or a sculptor dissatisfied with his creation had chipped away the eyes, nose and mouth. The ears, too, were no more than stumps, and very little hair remained on his scalp, only a few tufts of black curls here and there. His shoulders, face and neck all showed signs of the damage she would expect from immersion in sea-water and the action of marine scavengers, fish or crabs; yet from the sternum down, the damage was much less, and below the waist the corpse seemed perfectly preserved. Whether he had been bald or not in life was impossible to say, though plainly he had been a hirsute man, and his undamaged skin was still thick with hair which would have covered all his upper body.

She stood back to take photographs. Tassos had lain initially on his back – his blood had pooled in his calves and the backs of his thighs, in his underarms and buttocks – but that made the severe damage to his face with all its hallmarks of being immersed in water the more puzzling. She leaned down to his chest and sniffed, but there was no smell of decay, a fact which was again in contradiction to the apparent beginnings of putrefaction. Bending over him she peered more closely, trying to determine the reason for the border between the blanched, damaged flesh and the well-preserved, and there, just below the sternum was a puncture wound, a yellow-edged split well hidden by Tassos's chest-hair. Running her fingers over his torso, she found another, then a third, then more, spread all over his upper chest and stomach.

Popi had seen such wounds before, though rarely in such numbers. Without doubt, Tassos Hardouvelis had been subjected to a frenzied knife attack.

∞∞∞

The beds at the Hotel Poseidon were comfortable, and the fat man slept well, waking as dawn brought its early radiance to the sky, masking the last few stars and gilding the teal-blue sea.

He left his bed, put on the white cotton robe which was hanging behind his bathroom door and went barefoot onto the balcony. There was a welcome coolness in the early morning. Amongst the houses on the hillside, cockerels were crowing a fugue. The book he had from Sammy was open face-down on the table, and he sat down and began to read.

Out at sea, the fishing boats were heading home, and distracted by them from the adventures of Inspector Bekas, the fat man watched them approach. The men at their helms were steering straight for the port, no doubt dreaming – as he was – of coffee, and hearing the rattle of cutlery from the floor below as breakfast was being laid, he went inside and rang down to reception to order a Greek coffee without sugar.

Returning to his chair, he again picked up his book, but he had read barely two pages before his attention was caught by a small boat leaving the harbour, sailing in opposition to those port-bound. Its captain was known to the fishermen, or at least they were known to him; to each boat he passed, he waved. The boat headed in the direction the fat man had taken on his fishing trip the previous day, but the captain was no professional fisherman. He was wearing the hat and robes of an Orthodox priest.

There was a knock at the door, and the fat man rose from his chair to let in the waiter who had brought his coffee. Back on the balcony, he took a sip of the tarry brew, and lighting a cigarette, at last gave *The Fourth Suspect* his full attention.

∞∞∞

When Popi had finished her examination, she covered Tassos's body, cleaned the implements she had been using and washed her hands. Removing her stained scrubs, she folded them and placed them inside a polythene bag before returning them to her black case and dressing again in her skirt and blouse.

In the waiting area, the police constable was sleeping. Popi turned off the TV, and the silence woke him.

'I need you to find something for me,' she said. 'I need an air-conditioning unit in here to keep the body cool.'

The policeman looked askance.

'Surely we're going to hand him over to the family?'

'Not yet,' said Popi. 'Not until I say so.'

'So what did he die of?'

'That's confidential for the time being. Please go and get an air-conditioning unit, or he's going to start to smell.'

'We don't have air-conditioning at the station.'

'Then I suggest you find somewhere that does, and requisition a unit from them. You could try a hotel.'

'I'm sorry, *kyria*, but it's the end of my shift. I should go home at seven.'

'Go home with my blessing. But first make sure someone's bringing me an air-conditioning unit.'

Scowling, the constable left. Popi returned to the doctor's office and took a seat at his desk ready to write up her notes, but her pen remained still in her hand, and the page before her remained empty. For a while, she sat deep in thought; then she stood up and returned to the room where Tassos lay, turned back the sheet and peered again at the puncture wounds on his torso.

On the other side of the window-blinds, the world was coming to life. A moped buzzed by, swerving round an over-laden donkey; there was spattering on the pavement as a woman sluiced down her courtyard and let the dirty water dribble into the street. A chain rattled on a hoisted anchor, and metal feet scraped on cobbled stones as a cafe owner set out his tables. She smelled hot bread and pastry from the baker's, diesel fumes and the saltiness of the sea, and as Popi re-covered Tassos's face, she felt anger that for him, these mundane sensations had been snatched away, and were forever lost.

Seated again in the doctor's chair, she yawned, and knew tiredness was undermining her clear thinking. Maybe she would be wise to sleep a while, and return to her report refreshed. Hearing the street-door open, she glanced at her watch, and assuming it was still too early for the medical centre staff to arrive, she waited to hear the rattle and clatter of an air-conditioning unit and the voices of the policemen carrying it in. But there was only the door closing, and footfall crossing the waiting area before a man appeared in the doorway.

He was gaunt and dishevelled. Freeze-framed in his surprise at seeing Popi, he stood with one hand still on the door-handle, a black case much like her own in the other, and an unlabelled bottle of *tsipouro* lodged under his arm. He looked at her, and she looked back at him, taking in his faded t-shirt with its logo of a German beer, the jeans that were only held up by his belt, his lank white hair in much need of a wash, cut and comb, his untrimmed toe-nails poking from his salt-water-marked sandals. From his Adam's apple to his cheek-bones his beard grew lush, silver except for the amber nicotine stains under his nostrils. Narrowing his eyes in a squint, he seemed unable to make sense of what he was seeing, and glanced up at the nameplate on the door – *Dr Nikos Vatopoulos* – to reassure himself he was in the right place. Then he gathered himself.

'Who the hell are you?' he demanded. 'Get out of my office! I'm calling the police!'

Popi stood up and went towards him, holding out her hand. When she was close to him, she caught the whiff of stale alcohol and the stink of old sweat.

'You must be Dr Vatopoulos. I'm Popi Dritsaki, from the Examining Magistrates's office. And there's no need for the police. I'm here with their full knowledge and consent. I apologise for intruding without your permission but we thought it would be inconsiderate to wake you in the small hours.'

He didn't take her hand.

'And I think it was inconsiderate to let yourself in here without my permission,' he said, angrily. 'This is my private office, not a public facility.'

'I suggest it is a public facility, since it's owned by the Department of Health. And I'm sorry we didn't ask, but there was an emergency situation. Why don't you let me show you?'

'Is there a patient I should be attending to?'

'Not exactly.'

She walked past him, but he didn't immediately follow her, instead taking his time to put his case on his desk and the bottle of *tsipouro* in the glass-fronted cupboard behind it, tucking it away amongst the meagre stocks of antiseptics and dressings.

'So,' he said, finally joining her. 'What have you brought me?'

She led him into the examination room, giving him his first sight of the covered corpse.

'Who is it?' he asked.

'In life, he was Tassos Hardouvelis,' said Popi. 'Maybe you knew him.'

'I do. I did.' He put out his hand to lift the sheet.

'I should warn you,' said Popi, 'he is not at his best.'

The doctor glared at her.

'I've been practicing medicine for over forty years,' he said. 'You'll find there's very little I haven't seen before.'

He peeled back the sheet, and Popi watched the blood drain from his face. The doctor took a deep breath.

'Poor bastard,' he said. 'He's been dead a while.'

'Actually, I don't think so. His upper torso suggests decomposition, but on closer examination...'

The doctor wasn't listening.

'What the hell happened to his face? Poor bastard! How did they identify him?'

'From the notes I've been given, he was identified by Papa Alexis Hardouvelis. Is that his brother, his father?'

'His brother,' said the doctor. 'Is he sure? His own mother wouldn't know him.'

'His clothes probably helped, though he was wearing very little. His build and his hands, too. People who know people well can usually identify them from very little.'

'Are you patronising me?' As he turned to her to speak, his breath was a sour gust of alcohol and onions.

'I wouldn't dream of it,' said Popi. 'I was only saying...'

'What did he die of?' asked the doctor, fumbling in the back pocket of his jeans for a packet of cigarettes.

'I'm afraid I have to ask you not to smoke,' said Popi. 'The risk of contamination...'

'Not smoke, in my own office?'

'Respect for the dead, then.'

He put the cigarettes away.

'So what was it?'

'To be honest, I'm not sure,' said Popi. 'There are some inconsistencies in my findings. I want to give it some thought before I write up my report.'

'Has someone told the family to come and pick him up? I'll be starting my morning surgery within the hour.'

'That's my point. They can't pick him up until the cause of death has been firmly established, and I'm not yet in a position to be sure. The police are bringing an air-conditioning unit to keep him cool, so I can have another look at him if I need to.'

'Probably drowned, wouldn't you say? Plainly he's been in the water. He liked a drink, and his business was with fish. He was bound to fall in one day.'

'No water in the lungs,' said Popi. 'So no, he didn't drown. And the knife wounds...'

'Knife wounds? What knife wounds?'

'There are a number of them, eleven in all,' she said, pointing them out. 'Here, here.'

The doctor's eyes grew wide in exaggerated astonishment.

'My God, I don't believe it!' he said. 'You people! The man was murdered, and you're talking about writing reports! Whoever did this will be long gone by now, hiding up in the hills and claiming sanctuary! We must get the Chief of Police onto it straight away!'

‘Wait a moment, please,’ said Popi. ‘I’m not sure ... ’

‘Women are never sure,’ he said. ‘When did you ever know a woman able to make up her mind? You should have called Chief Tsinamis as soon as you saw these wounds! My God, do I have to do everything myself?’

He had already reached the street door, and she called after him.

‘Dr Vatopoulos! Wait!’

‘You’ve waited too long already!’ he called over his shoulder. ‘Leave this to me now, and please vacate my office!’

Seven

Despite rising so early, the fat man was late down to breakfast. Most of the other guests had left for the beaches or tours of the island, or settled themselves with sun-cream and entertainment – books, magazines and foreign-language newspapers – by the pool.

Pericles was behind the bar, re-stocking the shelves with bottled beers and juices.

'*Kali mera*, my friend!' he called out. 'Here you are at last! I was beginning to think I'd missed you, that you'd beaten us all to it and gone fishing.'

'No, no,' said the fat man. 'I had my head in a book, one of those detective books that grab you so you don't want to put it down. I was so keen to find out who was the killer, I couldn't leave it until I'd finished.'

'And did you guess the solution? Was it clear to you from page one who was the guilty party?'

The fat man frowned.

‘I’m sorry to say that it wasn’t. Though I think the writers of these things take huge liberties. They omit the most salient facts, which if given to the reader would immediately make everything clear. And they scatter distractions everywhere, littering the pages with little details which might or might not be pertinent. Which is a clue, and which a distraction? All too often, it’s impossible to tell.’

‘I see you’re disgruntled,’ said Pericles, emerging from behind the bar. ‘Someone has got the better of you, and you’re unhappy about it. A good breakfast will put the world to rights. Take a seat, and I’ll get your coffee.’

As Pericles headed towards the kitchen, the fat man looked around the terrace. Most of the tables had been used and not yet cleared, and the remains of croissants and sweet rolls lay amongst coffee cups, crumpled napkins and honey-smeared knives. One table, though, was still occupied, by a woman alone sipping coffee, cutting and eating small pieces from a slice of marble cake. She wore a pink skirt and silver shoes, and her eyes were hidden behind sunglasses with bold white frames. There was a clean table alongside hers, and the fat man took a seat there.

As he sat, he thought he’d caught her attention, though with her eyes hidden by the sunglasses’ copper lenses, it was impossible to say. He smiled, regardless.

'*Kali mera sas*,' he said. 'Forgive my sitting so close, but all the other tables ... ' He waved his arm to show the remains of others' breakfasts.

'Not at all. I'm glad not to be the only latecomer at the party.'

'Have you been staying here long?'

She shook her head.

'I arrived last night, or rather this morning, very early. Hence my late breakfast.'

'Are you on holiday?'

She shook her head.

'I'm here on business. You?'

'A little work, a little relaxation. May I ask what line you're in?'

'I'm afraid I work for the government. My business is official.'

'What a coincidence! I also work for the authorities.'

'What a mysterious pair we are!' she said, and gave him a delightful smile. She brushed cake-crumbs from her fingers, and offered her hand.

'Popi Dritsaki.'

The fat man rose from his chair and leaned over to clasp hers.

'Hermes Diaktoros, of Athens.'

'I knew from your accent you weren't from here,' said Popi. 'And Athens! I'd love to be there now, instead of marooned in this backwater.'

'You're not a fan of the islands?'

'If I have a swimsuit and a companion, of course! But to be here alone, working when everyone else is at play ...'

'I understand how hard it is. I spend too much of my working life by myself. Would you think me impertinent if I offered to remedy the situation, for one evening at least? Would you consider dining with me? That is, if you expect still to be here this evening.'

She glanced at her watch, drained her coffee cup and stood up. Her figure was attractive.

'I must go. But I do expect still to be here. The business I'm dealing with has taken a turn for the complicated. And yes, company over dinner would be most welcome. As long as you think we shall have common ground for conversation.'

'We can tell each other horror stories of the dubious places we have stayed in,' said the fat man. 'I have enough of those for several evenings of dinners, without the need for you to say a word.'

'We shall have a competition, then, for the most miserable experience. I've plenty to offer myself.'

'Do you have any preference for the type of food you'd like?'

'I prefer it to be edible,' she said. 'Beyond that, I put myself in your hands.'

'In that case, I shall take advice from my friend. He owns this place, which is thankfully much better than many. Should we meet here, in the bar? We could have an aperitif before setting out.'

She gave him another charming smile

'That would be lovely,' she said. 'I shall look forward to it.'

ꝏꝏꝏ

As Popi left him, the fat man went to scrutinise the remains of the breakfast buffet. The yogurt bowl was empty and the apricot and cherry compotes were nearly gone, but towards the back of the table the cheeseboard was almost untouched. He helped himself to several pieces of Graviera over which he drizzled a teaspoon of honey, took a sesame-seed encrusted roll from the bread-basket and, as an afterthought, added a piece of marble cake to his plate.

As he returned to his seat, Pericles was bringing out his coffee.

'I see you introduced yourself to our new guest,' said Pericles, placing the petite cup by the fat man's arm. 'I don't think Vaios will be very pleased they've sent a woman.'

'Who has sent her?' asked the fat man. 'And why should the Chief of Police not be delighted? I found her quite charming, charming enough to take to dinner this evening.'

Pericles laughed, and clapped the fat man on the back.

'Still working that old magic, eh, Hermes?' he asked. 'Good for you. But charming or not, she'll cause a stir at the police-station. They'll have been expecting that crusty old curmudgeon they usually send from the Examining Magistrate's office, and instead they've sent her! Our Chief of Police really isn't one for equal opportunities. I'm sure he won't like the idea of a woman interfering with his body.'

The fat man looked quizzical.

'His dead body,' clarified Pericles. 'Won't that put you off your dinner? The thought of where her hands have been?'

'She struck me as very bright, and I'm sure she's more than capable of doing her job. And it could make this evening very interesting. I shall be intrigued to hear how she's getting on.' He broke a piece of the Graviera with his fork, dipped it in the honey and put it in his mouth. 'That's very good,' he said. 'Just enough salt to off-set the sweetness.'

'My brother-in-law makes it,' said Pericles. 'He's a Cretan, and he knows his cheese.'

The fat man speared another bite-sized piece.

'What are they saying about the dead man?' he asked. 'I'm sure there were plenty of experts on the case at the bakery this morning.'

'They're saying it's a scandal your dinner-partner won't let him be buried. Dr Nick, our home-grown medic, is making it his business to try and get the body released, but without your friend's signature on the right piece of paper, poor Tassos is going nowhere.'

The fat man split his bread roll with his thumbs.

'What kind of man was Tassos Hardouvelis?'

'You have a fantastic memory for names, Hermes. Tassos was part-owner of the fish-farm over towards the Holy Unmercenaries. Probably you saw it when you were over in that direction yesterday.'

'I did. What did he farm?'

'Bream,' said Pericles. 'A good cash-crop. He should have been doing pretty well for himself.'

'I agree,' said the fat man, eating his bread. 'Farming bream seems very enterprising, especially given how over-fished our waters have been the last decade or two.'

'You would think so. But the truth is, the business hasn't been going well. Tassos and his business partner, Orestes Stangos, had big ideas. They were talking of exporting to Italy and even further, but big ideas need a work-force, and our fishermen weren't ready to sign up. What were they to do, abandon their trade and their independence to work for someone else? It's harder and harder for them to make a living from the sea, but they've all been too stubbornly proud to surrender their licences and become wage-slaves.'

'That must make life hard for the fish-farmers.'

'I think it did. I heard they were working crazy hours. Or at least Orestes was. Tassos, they say, wasn't pulling his weight. He was drinking too much, and drinkers as a rule don't like early mornings. There had been a couple of arguments, one or two very public. Last I heard, Tassos was saying he was going to buy Orestes out, and Orestes was saying the same about Tassos.'

The fat man tried his cake.

'This is good,' he said. 'One of Tina's, I suppose? It sounds to me as if the fish-farmers' partnership was on the rocks.'

'I'm sure it was. Orestes certainly didn't want buying out. He wanted to go into business with his cousin. They had offered Tassos hard cash, but he wasn't letting go so easily. But lack of labour wasn't their only problem. Some of the fishermen were angry at the pollution they claimed came from the farm. The residue from the feed was drifting close to shore and poisoning the water, letting algae grow and de-oxygenate the water. That's been killing – so they say – all the fish and shellfish that are left. Some have been taking matters into their own hands. If the fish-farm was killing off the wild fish stocks, they said they were owed recompense. So there's been sabotage.'

The fat man's expression encouraged Pericles to go on.

'They cut the nets by night. Hundreds, maybe thousands of fish escaped. Suddenly catches of bream were up, and the price – here in Liteos at least – was through the floor. Tassos and Orestes were furious. It was never their intention to fund an upswing in the local fishing trade. All over the island, the people are eating cheap bream.'

'Hence my catch yesterday,' said the fat man. 'So it wasn't down to my skill after all.'

'More down to the fresh stocks in the water,' said Pericles. 'There was another incident a few nights ago, another tank let loose. The fish-farm is in serious trouble. That's what I heard.'

'Unsurprising, given there were others making a living at Tassos and Orestes's expense.'

'Indeed. When the nets were cut the second time, they agreed a plan of keeping watch, taking turns to spend the night over there until the stock was harvested. Then Orestes spotted Tassos in one of the bars when he should have been on watch. There was a fight, and things were said. Now Tassos is dead.'

'Does the Chief of Police know all this?'

'Everyone knows.'

'So why did he tell me there was no question of foul play? It seems to me this story has every element required for resentment and bad feeling, and those are fertile breeding grounds for violence.'

'Do you really think so?' asked Pericles. 'It seems a bit extreme. Nothing ever happens in Liteos.'

'Places where nothing ever happens are where wounds fester deepest.'

'You're tending towards assuming there's been a crime, then? More likely he just slipped and fell overboard from the fish-farm, don't you think?'

'Maybe,' said the fat man. 'But if that's happened, it would be awfully convenient for Orestes. Suddenly he has free access to one hundred percent of the business.'

'Are you thinking of taking an interest?' asked Pericles. 'Because if you are, you'd do best to begin at the fish-market, and the gentlemen at the fish-market don't work very late.'

'That seems an excellent place to start. I shall finish my coffee and make my way there.'

The fat man had eaten his cake, and Pericles reached across to take his plate.

'My compliments to your good lady on her baking,' said the fat man. 'By the way, may I make further use of your boat? I may decide to do a little more fishing.'

'By all means. But didn't you say it had engine problems? You can't rely on being conveniently rescued if it breaks down again.'

The fat man smiled.

'Don't worry about me, old friend,' he said. 'I'm confident there'll be no mechanical problems today.'

Eight

A strong smell of fish led the fat man the last hundred metres to the market. The building was a monument to Turkish occupation and a grandiose construction for its modest purpose, a Byzantine-style rotunda whose dome rose in a pinnacle like a sultan's cap. A bicycle with a book in its handlebar basket was propped against the outer wall. Three steps led up to the market floor, around which ran a stone bench set at intervals with porcelain sinks, their water supplied through brass taps in the forms of spitting dolphins.

The market's hub was a vast, round stone table, where the fishermen had laid out their catches. The fishermen themselves were gathered to one side, sitting on upturned crates and dilapidated chairs discarded by the cafés and tavernas. The men were loud and laughing, scruffy and stinking, all burnt mahogany by the sun and sea-winds. They were relaxing with coffee and retsina and a smoke, and when they finished their cigarettes, they ground out the butts under the heels of their sandals and kicked them into the wet gutters.

A hosepipe was attached to one of the dolphin taps with a faulty connector, which despite being lashed round with gaffer-tape was leaking so badly, only a very little water was reaching the hosepipe's end. With this meagre flow and a soft-bristled broom, Sammy was doing his best to sluice away the leavings from the cleaning of fish – the scales which had scattered everywhere, winking as they caught the light, the purple entrails and the blood which ran when the fish were gutted, all rinsed away into the dark hole of the drain. The fishermen took no notice of Sammy, though he was listening to what they were saying, and at one moment paused in his work, ready to offer a remark. Then he thought better of it, and went back to his sweeping.

Given the poor performance of the hosepipe, there was a remarkable amount of fishy water spreading onto the street, and in the morning's heat, the piscine smell was unpleasant. Anxious for his white shoes, the fat man took great care where he put his feet as he climbed the steps onto the market floor.

He wished Sammy kali mera. The fishermen affected to be unaware of him, but they watched him from the corners of their eyes, their laughter growing louder and their banter more animated to mask their interest in an affluent-looking customer. At first, the fat man feigned disinterest in them too, gazing up instead at what had been, once, a splendid ceiling, now mostly ruined by the ingress of rain so only scraps of ultramarine pigment and traces of gilding remained.

When he gave his attention to what the men were selling, the display was disappointing: a few pipe-fish, too young and thin to make a good meal; a scorpion fish, ugly and dangerous with its porcupine spines; a heap of whitebait with blasted stomachs, illegally caught with dynamite. The rest were bream and there were many of them, all of similar weight, laid out in wooden boxes of crushed ice, which was melting fast and adding to the slurry on the floor.

'Gentlemen, kali mera sas,' said the fat man.

He peered at the fish. One of the fishermen drained a coffee-cup of retsina, and jumped to his feet. He wore a beard of many days growth, and a ragged checked shirt with only two buttons left tucked into his filthy trousers. Sammy was in his way, and the fisherman pushed him aside.

'Move,' he said, under his breath. 'Koproskilo.' To the fat man, he gave a broad smile. 'Kali mera, kyrie. All fresh, all very fresh, caught today.'

He went to one of the boxes, and lifted out a silver-scaled bream, displaying it on the palm of his hand, the fish wide-eyed as if dead from shock.

The fat man glanced at the fish and shook his head.

'I'm bored of bream,' he said. 'Is there nothing else?'

Hearing the fat man's accent, the fisherman narrowed his eyes.

'Where're you from, friend?'

'I come from Athens.'

'I was there once,' said the fisherman. 'The fish-market in that city! Fantastico! Here, the sea is empty. We've nothing left.'

'There's bream,' called out another of the men. 'Whatever price he offers you, I'll give you better.'

The fisherman holding the bream shot him a threatening look.

'The truth is,' said the fat man, 'I'm not looking for fish, but for a particular fisherman. Orestes Stangos.'

Realising there was no sale to be made, the fisherman laid the bream back in the box, sauntered back to his seat and refilled his coffee-cup from the bottle of retsina under his chair.

The men were all quiet.

'Don't any of you know him?' asked the fat man. 'I'm sure you must.'

One of the men nudged another.

'Hey, Vassilis!' he said. 'The gentleman's looking for your cousin.'

'I know him,' said Sammy.

The fisherman stood up and carried his retsina to one of the dolphin taps to dribble in a little water. As he passed Sammy, he poked an elbow into his back.

'Do your work, malaka,' he said, 'or you'll get no pay.' He took a drink, and looked at the fat man. 'You asked for a fisherman. Orestes Stangos is no fisherman. He runs a factory.'

'And quite successfully,' said the fat man. 'Are these bream not from his factory?'

'What's swimming in the sea is ours to catch. We all have licences. Don't we, lads?'

The fishermen all muttered their agreement.

A younger man spoke up.

'If you're looking for Orestes, you should try the Neraida cafe. He'll be there, drowning his sorrows.'

'Over what?' asked the fat man. 'The loss of his partner, or the theft of his stock?'

The men fell back into sullen silence. The fat man clapped Sammy on the shoulder.

'How are you, son?' he asked. 'You're working hard, in this heat. Tell me, have you still got the pearl I gave you?'

'Of course,' said Sammy.

'May I see it for a moment?' asked the fat man. 'I'm worried it may have a flaw. Since I gave it to you as a gift, I would not forgive myself if it were imperfect.'

Sammy leaned his broom against one of the sinks, and with the slight limp his physical condition caused, hurried down to his bicycle. One of the seated men snickered.

The fat man followed Sammy, who rooted in the basket of his bicycle until he found his matchbox. Sliding off the lid, he took out his pearl and handed it to the fat man, who held it up to the sun, allowing the light to play on its lustre.

From the shade of the rotunda, the fishermen were watching.

The fat man gave a nod of satisfaction.

'I was wrong to be concerned,' he said. 'Your pearl is perfect. Keep it safe, my boy. There are always those who would steal the things we value.'

As the fat man walked away, Sammy returned the pearl in its box to his bicycle basket. When he went back to his work, the fisherman with the retsina beckoned Sammy over.

'What do you have there, lad?' he asked, and for once there was no malice in his voice. 'That looked like something pretty.'

Sammy was reluctant to speak.

'Come on, you can tell me,' said the fisherman, coaxingly. 'No secrets amongst us sea-dogs. We're a band of brothers who work under this roof, aren't we?'

Still Sammy wouldn't answer. He picked up the hose-pipe, and held its dribbling end over the wet gutter. When the fisherman grabbed his ear, he yelped, and the fisherman squeezed Sammy's earlobe until he yelped again.

'Tell me,' he said, 'or I'll take my knife to you, and split you like one of those fish!'

'It's a pearl!' The fisherman squeezed harder. 'Please! Leave me! He's a pearl-fisher, and he gave me a pearl!'

Abruptly, the fisherman let him go.

'A pearl-fisher? He's having you on, *malaka*! There's no such thing as pearl-fishers in these seas.'

‘Yes, there are,’ said Sammy, rubbing his ear. ‘He grows them using fish-farms. He’s even growing them at the fish-farm here.’

‘Is he, indeed?’ asked the fisherman, glancing at the table of unsold fish. ‘Well, I’ll be damned!’ And taking a long drink of his retsina, he returned thoughtfully to his chair.

Nine

The fat man made his way around the harbourside, observing the people busy with the business of summer. The old-style *kafenions* were filled with local men catching up on each other's affairs; the contemporary cafés were serving iced coffee, ice-cream and late breakfasts to tourists preparing for days at the beach. A tour-bus behind time for a rendezvous was stuck behind a group of meandering Germans, and the driver blew his horn, cursing them for being in the road; but the Germans, who had been his passengers the previous day, thought he was being friendly, and waved at him, still meandering and blocking his way. A pair of Greek matrons dressed head-to-toe in black tutted at the beautiful Italian girls browsing, all but naked, hand-crafted ceramics, the exotic scent of coconut oil rising from their glistening skin. As the fat man passed a group of people waiting to board a taxi-boat, a baby half-asleep on his mother's shoulder opened his eyes and watched his departing back, smiling in delight as if he had witnessed some wonder.

Towards the harbour's end where the road narrowed, the people were fewer. Outside a tourist office, the fat man paused to study the boards advertising scuba-diving lessons, and looked up from the photographs of the underwater world to see a grey-robed priest hurrying towards him.

'*Yassas*,' he said, as the priest went by, but the priest responded distractedly, throwing a mumbled response over his shoulder.

The Neraida café had once been a private house, set on a flat, rocky outcrop so it faced the sea on three sides and its rear door was only metres from the water. Before the war, there had been a garden bounded by a low wall with an implanted iron fence; the wall remained, though the railings had been put to other uses decades before. A pair of grandiose gateposts formed plinths for two plaster mermaids, whose upturned tails were turquoise and whose long hair was yellow blond; they wore painted pearl necklaces around their necks and smiled with dark ruby lips, each holding out a scallop shell in the cup of their hands.

The café's decor was a shrewd mix of shabby tradition and fashionable touches. Barnacled amphorae on the terrace bloomed with scarlet geraniums, and there were chrome lanterns by the door; the tables were hand-made and rickety, but the chairs were woven wicker, made comfortable by canvas cushions with a nautical motif. A stranger would take it as a long-established business with an entrenched and devoted clientele, and indeed almost all the terrace chairs were taken. A murmur of conversation mingled with the soft sound of the sea on the rocks close by the customers' feet.

By the open doorway, a sign bore three words: *Coffee, Ouzo, Telephone*. The fat man went inside, into a high-ceilinged room generous enough to have once been a grand *salone*. Now, it was the Neraida's kitchen, decorated in a shade of mint-green which had discoloured almost to khaki from winters of smoke leaking from the chimney of a decrepit wood-burner. There were posters on the walls – a panoramic view of Manhattan, Rome's coliseum taken from the air, and Christ overlooking Rio de Janeiro – that had been there a long time, with marks on the glossy paper from several replacements of sticky tape which had lost its glue. In one corner, an ice-cream fridge hummed, and a refrigerated glass counter held a few cans of lemon and orangeade, bottled beer, retsina and water. On top of the counter was a selection of ouzos and a plate of heavily sugared, ridged pastries deep-fried like doughnuts, but everything was shadowed by a magnificent stainless-steel coffee machine, and a fire-brigade-red industrial coffee grinder whose wooden base formed a drawer from which coffee could be spooned. On the floor beside the grinder was a hessian sack of roasted coffee beans with a brass scoop planted in the top, and the rich scent of coffee was overwhelming.

Behind the counter, the patron was boiling Greek coffee, holding the long-handled *kafebriko* a little higher over the gas flame than was conventional. He was a tall man, striking for his height but also for his white hair which he wore in a long ponytail down his back. That, along with his white beard and eyebrows, gave him an ecclesiastical appearance, but his clothes – an orange t-shirt emblazoned with *Miami Beach,* cut-off denim shorts and leather sandals – were far from priestly. Down his arms and on the skin visible at the neck of his t-shirt, he was covered in fantastical tattoos, twisting snakes and fire-breathing dragons, a pirate ship, a tiger's head and a bloodied dagger, all intertwined with exotic flowers and multi-coloured leaves, making the man into a beautifully executed work of art.

'*Kali mera*, friend,' he said. 'Welcome to my modest enterprise. What can I get you?'

'Your coffee smells excellent,' said the fat man, 'and you have an impressive display of ouzos, so maybe I should have both.'

'You're my kind of customer. The coffee's straight off the plane from Brazil. I roast it myself, and grind it as I need it. And I would say you're a Greek coffee, no sugar.'

'That's an astute guess. My preference would be for Samos ouzo, if you have it.'

'Of course.'

Finally satisfied with the coffee he was brewing, the patron poured it with a flourish into a waiting cup.

'How about one of these?' He indicated the pastries on the counter. 'Churros, a speciality of South America. On the house.'

'I've only very recently finished breakfast,' said the fat man. 'But since I've never tried one, I think I will say yes.'

'Eh, Elias!' The shout came from the terrace. 'Where's my coffee?'

'Eh, *malaka*!' shouted the patron. 'I'm coming!' He gave a shrug. 'I like to take my time making the coffee,' he said to the fat man. 'The beans deserve it, and I find if I boil it more slowly, the flavour has more time to develop. Stands to reason. So please, find yourself a seat, and be assured I won't forget you.'

'I'm in no particular hurry. But I am in search of a particular person – Orestes Stangos.'

'He's out there talking to the holy man,' said Elias. 'Papa Alex.'

'The priest has left. I passed him as I arrived. Was he the priest whose brother has died?'

Elias scrutinised him closely.

'You're well informed, for a stranger.'

'This place is small. People talk, and a man can't help hearing. The alternative would be to walk around with cotton wool in my ears.'

'Yes, that was him. His brother was a customer of mine. Papa Alex and Orestes were sitting together under the window. You'll find Orestes by the glass on his table. He's broken with tradition this morning, and ordered himself an ouzo. He isn't usually a drinking man.'

'I was told he might be drowning his sorrows.'

'Who told you that?' Elias looked at the fat man for his answer, but the fat man seemed not to have heard the question, so Elias went on. 'I think he's more likely to be celebrating.' He placed a churro on a saucer, grabbed a glass of water and placed it with the churro on a tray, and adding the coffee he'd just made, came out from behind the counter. 'It's not for me to say, of course,' he said, over his shoulder as he carried the tray outside. 'I shouldn't like to speak ill of the dead.'

The fat man followed him out onto the terrace. There was, as Elias had said, only one man drinking ouzo, at a table holding two coffee cups and an uneaten churro.

'May I sit here?'

On his way back to the kitchen, Elias deftly removed the empty cup and the churro, leaving a vacant place for the fat man. With no good reason to refuse, Orestes Stangos gestured without interest at the empty chair. Despite a recent unkemptness and swelling around his eyes from lack of sleep, he was a handsome man, with the same rugged tan as the fishermen in the market, but still young enough for sun and wind not to have stolen his good looks.

'Please, sit. I'm leaving anyway.' He began to rise from his chair.

'Before you go,' said the fat man, himself sitting down and tucking his hold-all under his seat, 'may I speak with you a moment?'

'I'm not good at conversation,' said Orestes, 'and I'm especially bad at it today.' He put his hand in his pocket and threw money onto the table, enough to cover his ouzo and two coffees.

'I wanted to ask you a few questions about Tassos Hardouvelis. A minute or two, that's all. Please, sit down.'

Orestes looked down at him.

'Do I know you? What's Tassos to you?'

'I represent the authorities,' said the fat man. 'I promise I will only take a few minutes of your time.'

'What authorities?' asked Orestes, but the mention of authority was enough to make him retake his seat.

'I should introduce myself. I am Hermes Diaktoros, of Athens.'

'Athens? What does Tassos have to do with anyone from Athens?'

Orestes seemed distracted, his eyes moving not over the café terrace but beyond it over the sea. Through the window behind them, an internal door caught by a breath of breeze slammed, and Orestes started nervily, not noticing in his distraction that the fat man hadn't answered.

'You were Tassos's business partner. You must have known him very well.'

'I've known – I knew – Tassos for many years. He and I were at school together. We haven't been in business together long, though. Just a couple of years.'

'You have the fish-farm. That's very enterprising of you.'

'Enterprising maybe, but it's necessary. There's no way to make money from conventional fishing in Liteos anymore, so it made sense to look in a different direction. It made sense to me and Tassos, anyway. Not everyone sees it as a good thing. I don't see it as such a good thing myself, these days, not the way things are turning out.'

'And how is that?'

'Vandalism, and being robbed blind. A partner who lacked ...'

He stopped, and looked closely at the tables around him, to gauge if anyone was listening.

'Lacked what?'

Elias brought out the fat man's coffee with a churro, a glass of water and a measure of ouzo, and picked up Orestes's money. He tucked a receipt under the ashtray, and that seemed to trigger a thought in the fat man, who reached into his pocket for his cigarettes and offered them to Orestes.

Orestes looked at the box and took one.

'I gave up last year,' he said. 'Looks like I'll be starting again.'

The fat man lit their cigarettes with his gold lighter, inhaled, exhaled and tried his coffee. Its quality was exceptional, smooth and mellow, so good he immediately took a second sip.

'The patron knows his business,' he said, and poured a little water into his ouzo, turning the clear liquid milky white. He tasted the ouzo too, and nodded in satisfaction. 'Many people prefer Lesvos ouzo over any other, but I hold my preference for Samos. Which did you have?'

Orestes's attention had again wandered.

'I'm sorry,' he said. 'I didn't hear you.'

'I was asking about your preferences in regard to ouzo.'

Orestes shook his head.

'I have no preference. I'm not much of a drinker. But today ... ' He held up his cigarette. 'Today isn't any old day.'

'You were talking before I arrived to Papa Alex. Tassos's brother.'

'I was. He came to find me, to let me know what's going on. It was considerate of him. He said there'll be a delay in holding the funeral because of the post-mortem, that the Examining Magistrate's office ... Poor bastard!'

'Why did he come all the way down here to tell you that? Couldn't he have telephoned your office?'

'Maybe he tried, but I'm not there, am I? I think there were things he wanted to get off his chest. A priest confessing to me, imagine! He was upset about the fight he'd had with Tassos. It must be hard when your last words to someone are unkind.'

'A fight? What had they fought about?'

'I don't know, I'm not sure. He said money, then he said a family matter. Maybe he couldn't remember himself. When you're angry with someone, words come from nowhere and anywhere.'

'Did they fight often?'

'I don't think so. Papa Alex is a very easy-going man. At least I've always thought him so. But you can't know what a man is like in his own home.'

'You were talking about Tassos lacking something. I know you don't want to speak ill of him – I can see you're a respectful man – but what did you mean, exactly?'

Orestes sighed.

'Commitment. That's what he lacked, recently. Tassos wasn't a bad guy. Why would I have gone into business with him if I thought that? But his interest in the business seemed to be fading away. Things were difficult, and he wouldn't discuss our situation. He just kept telling me everything would be fine and walking away. There was something immature about his attitude. He had big ideas and some of them were good ideas, but they were ideas way beyond us at the moment. Like the packing-plant he wanted us to build. Up to now it's always been just me and him packing the fish. It takes a while, but we get through it. It isn't hard when most of your stock is lost. And he thought we should expand our sales area, look at the Italian market. We weren't ready for any of it, but he insisted we should expand. He said if I wouldn't go halves with him, he'd raise the money for a packing plant himself. I couldn't make him see we had to walk before we could run. Things were rocky between us, these last few weeks. In fact they've been so bad, I offered to buy him out.'

'And what did he say to that?'

Orestes had smoked his cigarette to its end. He stubbed it out.

'Typical Tassos! He said that if I didn't want to keep working with him, he'd buy me out, which was an absurd idea. Where was he going to get money to buy me out?'

'Forgive my asking, but where were you going to get money to buy him out?'

'I have a cousin who's keen to go into business with me. He fishes traditionally at the moment, but he can see opportunity in what we're doing.'

'Did Tassos know that?'

'As it turns out, yes. We had a big argument, right here in fact. When I found out we'd been sabotaged again, I was so angry! The bastards cut the nets, and all our market-ready fish swam free, every last one gone, while he was supposed to be on watch. We had an agreement, one night on, one night off, watching the farm. It's not ideal – you don't sleep well over there – but it's a deterrent. So I took my turn, and did my bit. But on all the occasions the saboteurs have struck – three, with this recent one – Tassos has been missing from his post. I found him right here, and what comes out? That he'd spent the evening drinking! Yes, there was a fight. Yes, I was held back from punching him in the mouth. So of course now I'm expecting the police at any moment, asking me if I killed him.'

'Killed him? What makes you think he was killed?'

Orestes looked at the fat man.

'Why else would he be dead? He was fit and healthy. Why should he just die?'

'People have accidents. Maybe he fell into one of your tanks.'

'That's not possible. We cover them with nets to keep off the thieving gulls and gannets. But I know these people. Some of them don't like what we're doing, and some of them are jealous, and if the Chief of Police hasn't heard about our fight by the end of the day, I shall be very surprised. In fact I'm thinking of going and telling him myself.'

'Maybe you should. Better to come from you than from someone else.'

Orestes considered.

'You know what?' he said. 'You're right. Elias! What do I owe you?'

'One more question, before you go,' said the fat man. 'The saboteurs – how would they know Tassos was absent from his post, that the fish-farm was unguarded?'

Orestes shrugged.

'Anyone might have seen him ashore. This is a small place, and small places have many eyes. Maybe they went to look for themselves if the coast was clear. They cruise by whilst they're out fishing, and if there's no-one there, out come the knives. It wouldn't take long.'

Elias came to stand by Orestes's shoulder.

'Four fifty,' he said.

Absently, Orestes hand him a five hundred drachma note, and waved away change. Elias left them, and as Orestes stood up, the fat man asked, 'So now he's gone, what happens to his share of the business?'

'I don't know.'

The fat man smiled.

'I doubt the truth of that. You have everything invested in your enterprise. Isn't there a clause in your partnership contract to cover this eventuality? Does his share of the farm come to you?'

'It's more complicated than that.'

'But essentially?'

'Essentially, yes.'

'So you're a beneficiary from Tassos's death to the tune of half a business that you were wishing to acquire. That being the case, I think your idea of going to the police voluntarily is a very good one.'

ooooo

After Orestes's departure, the fat man sat for a while, drinking his excellent coffee, enjoying the sweet, crisp churro, sipping the aniseed ouzo and watching the sea. As the sun rose to its mid-day peak, the other customers were drifting away, and Elias came to sit at the fat man's table, wiping his hands on a cloth.

'This is a magnificent spot you have here,' said the fat man. 'You must do very well. Especially if you charge all your customers twice.'

Elias frowned.

'I refer to Orestes,' said the fat man. 'He put money on the table when I arrived, and paid you again as he was leaving.'

'Did he? When it's busy, I lose track. I'll make it right with him when I next see him. I do all right without robbing my customers, as you've seen. But it grieves me because I could do so much better. If I could knock this old place down, I could build something new and exciting, something architecturally interesting that would attract a younger crowd. This place could be at the forefront of a new nightlife for Liteos, with DJs and music and a video wall. I'm overwhelmed with ideas!'

The fat man looked dubious.

'I have to say I am a fan of the traditional, and I think it would be a great shame to knock this place down. How old is it? A hundred, two hundred years old? Yet I am a believer too in the benefits of attracting a younger clientele. While it may not be my taste, we must be open to diversification in our tourism. But if you have ideas, why have you not executed them? Have the planners interfered?'

Elias shook his head.

'Not the bureaucrats, no. The problem is, I don't own the place, I only rent it. And to everything I propose, the woman I rent it from has always said no – even to re-painting the walls. If I had my way, we'd have vibrant colours, oranges and reds, the really modern, but no. Every time I ask, no. So I tried to buy it, she said no. Still, the rent is cheap, and my customers seem to like the place as it is.'

'But you are not so happy with your customers.'

Elias spread his hands and slapped his thighs.

'Eh! What can I do? It's steady trade, but aren't they dull, these men playing *tavli* and gossiping about what's for dinner and the best way to cook octopus? In the capitals of the world, coffee shops are places where revolutions begin, where poets and writers debate philosophy, where the boundaries of morality are challenged!'

'You'll forgive the observation,' said the fat man, 'but if you're looking to challenge the boundaries of morality, I think Liteos is entirely the wrong place. You should try Athens. You'll find plenty of people at the boundaries of morality there.'

'I know Athens, my friend. I'm a man who's travelled the world, and the part of the world I loved the best was South America. Such a lively, vibrant place, the people always smiling, dancing, the women so much more free ... And they know their coffee! That's where I learned to make coffee, during my time in Brazil. Still, this place has, for the time being, two big advantages. Firstly, the rent is cheap. And secondly, when there are no customers, I can cast a line from where that far table is, and see what I can catch.'

'Do you catch many bream, by any chance?'

Elias smiled.

'You're well informed. Are you by any chance with the police?'

The fat man laughed.

'I? No. Though my path does cross that of policemen from time to time, and I do take an interest in police matters, on behalf of different authorities. I should introduce myself. Hermes Diaktoros, of Athens. If you're wondering at my name – Hermes Messenger – I was given it by my father. He's a great scholar of the classics.'

'Ah, so you're from Athens, eh?' Elias wafted a fly from in front of his face. 'So what brings you so far from the city?'

'Fish,' said the fat man. 'I came to try the golden tuna, but I've been out of luck so far.'

'All gone,' said Elias. 'Fished to extinction by a bunch of greedy fools. Now we're reduced to farmed bream. Liteos and its tuna is a very sad story, my friend, a very sad story indeed.'

'Tell me.'

The fly that had been bothering him landed on Elias's knee, and he slapped at it, but missed.

'The first golden tuna was landed by a man fishing for swordfish. He was working alone, so when he came back with that great golden fish, he was quite the celebrity for a while. Stathis, they call him, Stathis Rigopoulos. He made very good money from that fish, sold it within an hour of bringing it home to a foreigner for the Japanese sushi market. Well, that was the beginning of a tuna bonanza. Almost every week in the season, one or other boat came back with one of those beautiful fish, and the restaurateurs were falling over each other to buy them. Premium fish, premium prices.

The TV cameras were here, famous chefs and gourmets from all over the world. And when there wasn't tuna, they wanted other fish. The fishing boats were never in the harbour. They were out there taking whatever they could find, using whatever methods they thought best, legal or illegal, dynamiting, lamping, anything to catch something they could sell. No surprise at all, the day came when someone noticed catches were down, first by ten percent, then by twenty, thirty, until they were catching almost nothing at all. It's been three years now since the last golden tuna was caught.'

'It's not every day a new species of fish is found,' said the fat man. 'Where did they come from?'

Elias shrugged, and swatted again at the troublesome fly.

'If you ask me, they were big-eye tuna, strayed from waters where they should have been. There's some very deep water round these shores, and maybe it was cool enough for them to stay comfortable. Doesn't really matter now, does it? What's gone is gone, sold and lost.'

'Maybe not,' said the fat man. 'You never know what's swimming below the surface.'

'Indeed you don't. You see my two girls there?' Elias pointed to the plaster statues on the gateposts. 'They're pretty things, made to show what we think mermaids should look like. But a mermaid isn't a pretty wench at all. I say that, and people look at me as though I'm mad. How should I know what a mermaid looks like? But let me show you something.'

He rose from his chair and went into the kitchen, returning a moment later with a round cardboard box which had once held Turkish delight. He retook his seat and lifted the lid, removing a piece of tissue paper to reveal what was inside.

'Look at that,' he urged. 'You take a look at that.'

Lying on another piece of tissue was a spear-head the size of a pencil-stub, finely made of slender bone and carved into a sharp point. Along its length was mounted a trio of barbs made from what appeared to be the round and spiny vertebrae of some fish.

'What is it?' asked the fat man, intrigued. 'I see it is some kind of spear, but who made it?'

'Who indeed?' asked Elias. 'I can't answer that with absolute certainty, but I can tell you what I believe. I found this spear-head myself, in the flank of a fish that I caught in a net when I was staying with my brother in Albania. The fish – a good-sized snapper – was already dead, which was no surprise given how deep the spearhead was buried in its side. It seemed I had caught what was, by rights, someone else's catch. When I showed it to my brother, he said he'd seen such things before, that fishermen on that coast had from time to time caught dead fish the same as me. He advised me to take myself to a church and have myself blessed, that to catch such a fish invoked a curse, stealing as it was from the mouths of mermaids.'

The fat man raised his eyebrows.

'Yes, indeed,' said Elias. 'That's what the people there believed. My brother introduced me to a man who swore he'd taken one of the creatures in his nets, and how terrifying she was – a fighting, spitting harpy of a thing, with sharp teeth and claws whose single aim seemed to be to get herself back into the water and take that fisherman down with her.'

'What did he do?'

'What would any sane man do? He bundled the nets overboard as fast as he could, started his engines and made for the shore. And he never once put to sea again, after that.'

The fat man picked up the spearhead very gingerly, and held it up close to his eyes.

'What's it made of?' he asked.

'I showed it to a marine biologist, who said it was probably a sting-ray barb,' said Elias. 'The smaller bones, the round ones fitted over it, could be from many fish, maybe grouper or gurnard. It's so finely worked and delicate, it looks as if a child's hand must have made it. But mermaids, who knows?'

The fat man laid the spear-head carefully back in its box.

'I've heard many tales, over the years, similar to the one you tell,' he said. 'But I've never seen one of these. And a fish killed by it... Who threw the spear with such good aim? I have seen photographs of what was claimed as a mermaid skeleton found in Italy, some years ago now. No doubt it was a hoax, but it was a good one. And maybe there are logical explanations for the strange things men come across far from shore, but it's certain that they do come across strange things. The sea is a lonely place and maybe the mind plays tricks, but I've met people who believe they've seen fantastical, mythical creatures that couldn't possibly exist. I once knew a man who swore he'd seen Poseidon's trident held up above the waves, when he was miles from the nearest shore and the sea was at its deepest. Was it a mirage? He knew it was impossible, and yet his story never changed. Who can ever know what will swim or crawl into nets we cast into the oceans? In the remote parts of the planet new species are discovered every day, though most of them are not new at all, but very ancient.'

As Elias re-covered the spearhead with its tissue, three men were walking through the gate. They were venerable old men of the island, in no hurry and with nowhere to go, one berating another in a loud voice.

'You're making a mistake there, a bad mistake! He's a thief, and he'll rob you blind!'

The man receiving the advice seemed unconcerned. He led his companions to a waterside table, and called to Elias for three ouzos as they sat down.

Elias left the fat man to pour his customers' drinks, while the fat man listened to the old men's discussion become more heated.

'*Áde, malaka!*' one was saying. 'He's taking you for a fool, and that's what you are, an old fool!'

Elias carried a tray out to their table, and laid out the glasses of ouzo, a jug of water and a dish of salted almonds, for which all three of them made a grab at the same time.

'Put this on my bill,' said one of the old men, but his instruction was rescinded by another.

'I'm buying,' insisted the second. 'And there's an end to it.'

Elias ambled back to the fat man's table against a backdrop of the old men's bickering. As Elias sat down, the fat man pointed to the box holding the mermaid's spear.

'Tell me about Tassos,' he said. 'What did he make of strange objects pulled from the sea?'

'Ah, Tassos.' Elias smiled. 'You know, I think I might have myself a spot of ouzo. Can I get you another?'

'Thank you, no.'

Elias fetched himself a drink, and placed a dish of the salted almonds on the table.

'*Yammas*,' he said, raising his glass. 'Tassos didn't believe in mermaids. He was always practical and down-to-earth. It's his brother who's the mystic in that family. Papa Alex is a decent kind of priest, a believer in the faith, not in it for the money, like so many of them. Alex loves the church and Tassos was a man who loved the sea, a born fisherman. Which was remarkable, because his father was a landlubber. He was postmaster here for many years – a good, steady job where he never even got his feet wet. But Tassos, from what I heard, was out fishing from being a boy. He was one of those who cashed in on the bonanza in a small way. He never owned a big boat, never went for tuna or swordfish, but he did all right for himself with squid and lobster, same as many others. Then he went away, and when he came back, the damage was done and the sea was pretty much empty. That's when he came up with the idea of the fish-farm, and found a partner in Orestes.'

'With whom he fell out, in the end. Did you witness their argument?'

'I did. Harsh things were said. Orestes accused Tassos of being more interested in drinking than in the business.'

'And was that true?'

'No. Tassos was a man maybe like yourself. He liked his ouzo – he considered himself a bit of a connoisseur – but I never saw him drinking to excess. Maybe the last few weeks he drank a little more, but he was under pressure, and which of us doesn't drink more under pressure?'

'So if he wasn't a drinking man, why was he here with a glass in his hand when he should have been watching over the bream?'

Elias took a long drink of his ouzo.

'You take great interest in his affairs, man of Athens. Why should that be?'

'It's an interesting occurrence, the unexpected death of a man in his prime.'

'Too true. He had his reasons for being here. Let's leave it at that.'

'Before we leave it, did Tassos strike you as someone who might take his own life? Was he brought low enough by his troubles to have done himself violence?'

'I don't think so. But who knows? We go from euphoria to despair in a heartbeat, especially if we've had a drink too many. It's the human condition.'

'That sounds like the voice of experience.'

'Euphoric, despairing and dead drunk.' He laughed. 'Which of us has never been in all of those conditions?'

The old men were calling for more ouzo.

'Let me pay you what I owe,' said the fat man. Elias named his price, and the fat man handed over a bank-note. 'Keep the change. One more question, if you will. Where would I find Stathis Rigopoulos? I should be interested to hear his story of that first tuna.'

'He keeps his boat in the small harbour beyond this one. You might find him there.'

'Thank you. No doubt I shall be seeing you again.'

Elias gave a low bow of his head.

'I thank you for your custom, man of Athens,' he said, and as the fat man walked away, he carried the Turkish delight box back inside.

Ten

Papa Alex made his way home via a longer route than usual, following the lesser-used pathways and alleys. At the bottom of the lane leading up to the house, a police-car was parked in the shade of the Tasty souvlaki house. One of the junior officers he had seen at the police station was behind the wheel, head back and eyes closed, his arms folded over his stomach as he dozed.

Papa Alex hurried up the lane. The garden gate stood open. Cicadas were chirping in the plum trees; a neighbour's radio was playing a love song filled with regret. For a few moments he listened, trying to hear over the music what was happening inside the house, but he could make out nothing but indistinct male voices.

His father Lambros was in the *salone* with the Chief of Police. Lambros had opened the shutters and windows, but the staleness of settled dust could not be swept away by the influx of light. Until his mother's illness, the delicate glasses and bottled liqueurs on the silver-plated salver were dusted daily, and the lace doilies under the vases of artificial flowers were laundered every week, so the scent of starch used to vie with incense and the smoke of the lamp burning before the icon of St Anastasia.

The lamp had not been lit today. His father was sitting at one end of the hard-seated sofa, opposite the Chief of Police on a formal dining chair. Very little in the room was new; almost every piece of furniture was an heirloom, none of it with any cash value but all of it cherished for its history – great-grandmama's china, great-grandmama's linen, and great-grandmama's dining table, where in the coming days, they would lay out Tassos's body. The only new piece of furniture in the room was a cheap pine bookcase filled with paperbacks, most written by foreign authors, which overflowed from the shelves into stacks on the chair alongside.

Papa Alex glanced at the clock on the mantel – another heirloom, an ugly, hefty piece of green onyx – which suggested it was later than he'd thought, but then he realised that the clock was stopped, a heresy to all the clock's previous owners.

'Come in, son, come in,' said Lambros. The rings under his eyes were dark as the bruises on his forearms, and there was a tremor in his hands he was trying to hide by resting them on his knees. Grey stubble was already appearing on his cheeks; the last time he had grown a mourning beard, its dominant colour had been black. 'Have a seat.'

Papa Alex crossed the room and took a seat near the Chief of Police, then immediately stood up again. He cast an anxious glance in the direction of the bedroom.

'Forgive me,' he said. 'Mama is incapacitated but she would never forgive our not offering you coffee.'

Vaios shook his head, and waved the suggestion away.

'I don't want anything, thank you,' he said.

Vaios was wearing his full uniform and was turning his cap in his hands, the motion emphasising his discomfort at intruding.

'How are you, Papa?' he asked. 'I didn't want to disturb you, and I wouldn't have come, but it's important.'

He looked across at Lambros and gave a small smile intended as reassurance.

'The Chief has something to tell us you won't want to hear,' said Lambros, as Papa Alex re-took his seat. 'For myself, I can't take it in.' The old man touched his heart as though it pained him. 'I don't understand it! I don't understand!'

'What is it, papa?' He reached out for his father's hand, squeezed it and held it between his own. 'What's going on?'

Vaios bowed his head, then looked Papa Alex in the eye.

'Your brother,' he said. 'As you know, the pathologist has arrived to look into the cause of his death. To be honest, I thought we were looking at something very straightforward. It's difficult for me to speak plainly. I don't want to cause you any distress, but I have no choice but to be honest. It was my belief that some accident had befallen your brother, and I expected the pathologist to confirm that. Yet she has found something rather unusual. Your brother appears to have been stabbed.'

'Stabbed?'

'I don't understand,' said Lambros again. 'How is it possible? I don't understand!'

'Hush a moment, papa,' said Papa Alex. 'Stabbed, where stabbed?'

'In the chest.'

Papa Alex shrugged.

'So why does that make it not an accident? Might his – his body not have caught on something in the water?'

'He was stabbed several times with a knife, Papa,' said the policeman, and the old man groaned and pulled away from Papa Alex's grip to bury his face in his hands.

The priest looked steadily at Vaios.

'You're saying somebody stabbed him.'

'Yes.'

'That he was deliberately killed.'

'I think we have to say so, yes.'

Lambros's shoulders shook with a sob.

'This changes everything.'

'Yes, it does.'

'What about the body?'

'It will be released to you, just as soon as ...'

The *salone* door opened. Agni Hardouveli stood before them in a black winter coat, a flower-sprigged nightdress visible below the hem. She wore no stockings or shoes; her toe-nails were long and in need of cutting; her long, grey hair was loose, falling on the shoulders of her coat, tangled where she had slept on it.

She looked round at them all with blank eyes, with no more recognition in them for her husband and son than there was for the policeman.

'I'm going to collect the eggs,' she said. 'Yorgia will be here to fetch them at four.'

Papa Alex jumped to his feet.

'I've already done it, mama,' he said. 'And Yorgia won't be coming till much later. Papa and I will take care of it. You go back to bed, and I'll bring you some tea.'

'I don't want tea,' she said. 'There are bugs in it. I'd better put the soup on. They'll be here this afternoon, and everyone must eat.'

Vaios looked questioningly at Lambros, and Lambros gave a slight shake of his head. Papa Alex put his hands gently on his mother's shoulders, and turned her round to guide her from the room.

'You don't need your coat, mama,' he said. 'It's hot today. Here, let's take it off.'

He led her away; Lambros and the Chief of Police could hear her slow shuffling and objections as she was taken through the house, the sound of mother and son climbing the stairs.

‘She doesn’t know us,’ said Lambros, dejectedly. ‘We’ve had no chickens for as long as I can remember, but every day she wants to collect the eggs. Yorgia was her aunt. She’s been dead more than twenty years.’

‘I’m sorry,’ said the Chief of Police. ‘It must be very hard.’

‘You can’t imagine how hard. But it’s a blessing she understands nothing about Tassos.’ Tears filled his eyes, and he rubbed them away with his fist. ‘He was a good boy at heart, a good boy! A knife, you say? I don’t understand! Why a knife?’

‘I realise it’s upsetting,’ said Vaios. ‘But we will find whoever did it.’

There were footsteps overhead, the creak of floorboards and Agni’s querulous voice becoming louder as she grew enraged. The reasons behind her complaints were muffled, but then she shouted very clearly, ‘Don’t touch me!’ and there was the sound of something being knocked over, a cup or glass.

‘I’m sorry,’ said Lambros, ‘I should go and help him. It takes two of us sometimes to persuade her to take her medication.’

The Chief of Police nodded his understanding and rose from his chair.

‘I’ll be in touch, of course, when there’s more news. And we’ll be needing to ask you some questions, you and Alex, about Tassos’s associates.’

‘You mean you’re looking for the names of those who might have had a motive.’

‘Yes, I do mean that.’

'Maybe it was an accident.'

Vaios shook his head.

'I'm sorry,' he said. 'It wasn't an accident.' Overhead, Papa Alex was pleading with his mother. 'As I said, I'll be in touch.' Vaios offered his hand, and Lambros took it expecting a brief shake, but Vaios held on to it and ran his eyes over the bruises on Lambros's forearm. 'Looks like you've taken a few knocks.'

Lambros pulled back his hand.

'They're nothing,' he said. 'Sometimes she gets frustrated, over-excitable. It's nothing we can't cope with.'

For a long moment, Vaios looked at him.

'Well, you take care of yourself,' he said.

After the Chief of Police had left, Lambros stood a few moments at the foot of the stairs. There was, for the time being, calm. Papa Alex was singing a song to his mother, a childhood song of butterflies she used to sing to him.

Lambros went into the kitchen. The place was a mess, the table littered with unwashed dishes, the remains of a meal a feast for flies. He picked up the chopping board and the knife he'd used to cut tomatoes, and scraped the scraps from the plates into the waste.

A bottle of pills was on the shelf. *Agni Hardouveli*, read the label. *Take 1 tablet three times daily. Do not exceed the stated dose.*

Lambros unscrewed the bottle cap, and tipped two of the tablets into his hand.

ꝏꝏꝏ

The police station was quiet, and just one officer was manning the enquiry desk and the phones. Orestes Stangos hesitated in the doorway, and seeing the chief wasn't there, was ready to leave, but as he turned round, his movement caught the officer's eye.

'May I help you?'

'I was looking for the Chief of Police. I thought I should come and talk to him. My business partner has died, and I don't want to end up a suspect.'

'A suspect?'

'I've come voluntarily to be interviewed.'

The officer looked baffled.

'There's no-one but me here at the moment,' he said. 'And I'm not qualified to ask you any questions. What do you want to be interviewed about?'

'The death of my partner, Tassos Hardouvelis.'

'So what are you saying exactly, that you want to make a statement?'

'A statement?'

'A written statement. Your version of events.'

'There were no events. That's what I want to say.'

'So you want to make a statement to say you have nothing to say?'

'I want to make a statement to say I had nothing to do with his death.'

The policeman smiled, sarcastically.

'So shall we expect the whole island to come and tell us they have no involvement either?'

'Tassos and I had an argument. I'm sure it's already been mentioned?'

'Not to my knowledge. Should it have been?'

'It had nothing to do with him dying, so no.'

'I'm sorry, *kyrie*, I'm not sure why you're here. Just to be clear, you've come to tell us you had nothing to do with the death of Tassos Hardouvelis. Is that right?'

'I had nothing to do with his death, but I had a connection to him. Wouldn't you be coming to interview me?'

The officer pulled a face.

'I don't think so. If the chief were here we could ask him, but he's out on a call. Are you a relative of *Kyrie* Hardouvelis?'

'No. I told you. I'm his business partner.'

'That doesn't mean you're not related.'

'We're not related.'

'Then I'm sorry, *kyrie*, I can't discuss this matter with you any further.'

At the door, Orestes turned back.

'Will you tell the Chief I was here?'

'If you tell me who you are.'

'Orestes Stangos. He knows me well enough. Tell him I'll be calling in again. Voluntarily.'

Eleven

The dog was refusing to eat, and hadn't eaten a good meal in nine days, according to Stathis's counting, though his counting was suspect – he couldn't have said if today was Wednesday or Sunday or somewhere in between. She lay alongside the sofa on the bare linoleum, her head on one of Stathis's discarded sandals, as if she had misjudged the space she needed to lie down in and, having made the error of judgement, now lacked the energy to stand up and move to put it right.

On the sofa, Stathis lay in his own inertia between dozing and waking, trying to calculate the time from the light in the room. The TV was on, the volume turned low, and the film was the same one that was beginning when he first closed his eyes. He watched the black-and-white images playing on the screen. A young man sprinted laughing down a back-street, pursued by an angry older man in a suit; a pretty girl was waiting for the young man in a café, wearing feline-eyed sunglasses and the kind of full-skirted cotton frock Panayiota used to wear. The young man grabbed her hand and pulled her up from her chair to run with him, and she looked back anxiously towards the older man, her father. Being young, of course they easily lost their pursuer. The scene changed, and the young man picked up a bouzouki, plucking a tune as the young woman smiled her admiration.

He had been like that young buck, once – black-haired and fast on his feet, too sure of himself and his immortality. And Panayiota had been like the actress – lovelier, even, with a prettier smile and more curves. Stathis had no interest in the young man's song. He reached down to touch the dog's head, and she raised her soulful eyes to his and sighed. He ran his hand down her back, feeling the nodules on the bones of her spine under her soft, grey fur. Despite the heat, she was shivering.

'Ach, Circe,' he said. '*Koukla mou.* What can I do with you?'

Behind the lace curtains, flies buzzed. Time was, when he woke from his siesta, it would be to the smell of brewing coffee, and Panayiota moving in the kitchen. If he wanted coffee now, he made it himself, but somehow it never tasted quite the same.

Stiffly, he got up. Circe watched him but didn't follow. In the kitchen, he searched amongst the dirty cups for the cleanest, and rinsed it carelessly at the tap. A brown line remained, the tide-mark of the dregs which had stood in it for days. He rinsed the *kafebriko* too, pouring its dregs over the plates in the sink before refilling it half-clean. The greasy water the plates were soaking in was beginning to stink. He'd have to wash them soon, or risk poisoning himself. The cutlery drawer was open and empty but for cake forks and a ladle, and he searched the table for a teaspoon, hunting under newspapers and utility bills, finding one at last amongst the empty dog-food cans. There were stains on the plastic tablecloth, and no space for the vase of flowers Panayiota always kept at the centre of the table – geraniums when nothing else was blooming, wildflowers in the spring, fragrant roses from the garden in the summer. In place of flowers there was a bag of almonds brought by a neighbour, last almond season. Soon it would be almond season again.

When Maritsa had brought his lunch, she'd cleared space for his plate, rinsed him a knife and fork and covered everything with a clean cloth she'd brought from home. She'd lit the candle-lamp in front of the photograph on the dresser of her mother in her prime, and its light fell too on the photograph beside it: Stathis proudly displaying the great golden-scaled fish, Liteos's first golden tuna. It had become Stathis's habit to lay the picture face-down; it was Maritsa's habit to pick it up and put it back on display.

She said the same thing almost every day.

'Come on, papa, you can't live like this. You've got to make an effort. What would mama say? And that dog should be outside. Let me at least help you clean.'

'I'll get round to it in my own good time,' he'd snapped today. 'I thought once your mother was gone there'd be no more nagging.'

He regretted the words the moment they were said. The hurt showed in her face though she tried to hide it, unnecessarily rearranging the cloth over his food.

'The offer's there, when you're ready,' she'd said.

'I'm doing fine just as I am,' was his reply.

As he put the coffee-pot on to boil, Circe came and stood by his feet, skinny and shivering. He lifted the cloth from the food: chicken stew, fresh bread, sliced tomatoes. The stew smelled good, but it roused in him no desire to eat. He tore off a small piece of chicken breast and held it out to the dog, but she turned her face away without even sniffing it.

'You not hungry either?' He dropped the chicken back on the plate. The dog, seemingly exhausted, lay down where she stood. His coffee was coming to the boil; he turned off the gas and poured it into his cup, but it lacked colour and fragrance, and he felt no relish at the prospect of drinking it.

He sighed.

'Maybe we should take ourselves a little walk, see if we can work up an appetite.'

Maritsa had left him clean shirts in the cupboard, but Stathis sniffed his armpit and thought the one he was wearing would do. He called to Circe but she wouldn't get up, so he filled her bowl with fresh water and left her to sleep.

He walked slowly down the road to the waterfront, hands behind his back. His old friend Dinos was sitting outside his house in the shade of a voluminous vine. Decades ago, Stathis and Dinos had sat next to each other at school; they had been best man at each other's weddings. Dino's wife had her lap full of peaches which she was splitting, skinning and stoning, the good fruit going into a large glass jar, the stones and the overripe, bruised fruit dropped onto newspaper spread by her feet, where wasps were crawling. She was missing all her teeth, and her lips curved inwards, the way Stathis remembered his grandfather. He thought how old they were looking, white-haired and frail, then realised he was a fool for thinking he looked any different.

Dinos called out to him.

'Hey! Hey, stranger, where've you been hiding? Come and have coffee!'

Stathis waved his hand.

'Another time. I've things to take care of.'

'So come and play *tavli* later on. It's been a while since I whipped your hide. I'll wait for you at the Neraida. Loser buys the drinks.'

For that moment, the idea seemed a good one.

'All right,' said Stathis. 'Don't forget your wallet!'

But he regretted the commitment as soon as it was made. He didn't think it mattered. Dinos would understand when he didn't turn up.

He went the route he always went, like the bereaved beating a path to a grave. Leaving the main road which led to the port, he took instead the narrow passage between a bakery and an empty apartment building, then followed the downhill twists in the lane to a beach with a half-moon quay. At the end of the quay was the old customs house, derelict and roofless with political graffiti spray-painted on its walls. Here was where foreign vessels used to load and unload, and it was still called the Turkish quay, but there was no commercial traffic these days. The Turkish quay was a backwater dock for boats with engine problems, boats up for sale, boats in need of repair, where the mooring fees were cheap and sometimes not collected at all.

Stathis made his way along the shingle beach, past the boats languishing in eternal dry dock, deteriorating year by year with no chance of ever again putting to sea. Amongst these forlorn corpses he stepped over paint cans and brushes, tossed-away cigarette butts and a mound of desiccated seaweed, brought in by the last storm of spring and left to dry there all summer.

The *Panayiotissa* was moored near the quay's end. Her dilapidation had been slow and accidental: first, some damage to the deck-rail, hastily repaired and never properly fixed; next a crack to the glass in the wheelhouse, mended with tape and the pane never replaced; then a fault in the bilge-pumps, so she carried more water in the hull than she should, and the smell of damp became unpleasant and all-pervading. A navigation light failed, and then another; the VHF no longer functioned reliably; the engine became tricky to start, and it was too long since the algae and barnacles on the hull had been removed. Some of the inflatable fenders protecting her hull disappeared in the night, so her paintwork developed scrapes and grazes.

But Stathis still came to visit often, as if she were a beloved relative past her prime, shaking his head at each new problem, regretful of her decline. Today as always, he climbed aboard and unlocked the door to the wheelhouse. The air inside was overheated, but still harboured the stink of damp, and he fastened the door back to allow the cooling late afternoon air to circulate. He laid the keys on the dashboard, and out of habit opened the small coffer which had contained the holy relic, and although it was no surprise, sighed to see it wasn't there.

The water moved in a slight swell as the wash of a vessel far out to sea finally reached the shore, and several waves broke splashing on the beach. Stathis was no longer confident in his sea-legs, and as the boat rocked, he held onto the dashboard, regretting once again the unserviceable state of the fenders and fearing more damage as *Panayiotissa* knocked against the quay. He glanced up at the photograph of himself and Mikey – still hanging there, though there were spots of mould behind the glass – and decided it was long past time to act.

On deck, he made an assessment of the fenders, checking the prow and to port and starboard to find those which might still provide some protection for the hull. Finding two or three which might do, he struggled with the knots which tied them to the rail; the rope had decayed and hardened, and couldn't be unpicked. Taking out his pocket knife, he began to saw through the rope binding the first.

'*Yassas*, captain!'

Stathis hadn't noticed anyone else on the quay when he arrived, nor had he noticed anyone approach, but the fat man was standing alongside *Panayiotissa*, looking her up and down.

Stathis looked at him, taking in his pale linen suit, his hold-all and his white shoes, and wishing him a brusque *Yassas* in return, gave his attention back to his task.

The fat man moved closer to *Panayiotissa*, so close that if he reached out his hand, he could have touched her.

'Some people say, when you get a little sea like that, there's a mermaid swimming under the boat.' He stepped back and made a show of checking the water to prow and stern. 'But I don't see any here. If there were mermaids in this harbour, I dare say you would have noticed.'

Stathis didn't answer, but carried the fender he had cut loose to where the hull most risked contact with the quay, and tied it in position.

'I think you may be the man I'm looking for,' persisted the fat man. 'I assume from your boat you're a tuna-fishing man.'

Stathis stood back from the deck-rail. The fender was half-flaccid, but the hull would be better protected than before.

'Sword-fisher, first and foremost,' he said. 'And not a fisherman of any kind, for some time.'

The fat man laughed.

'I don't believe that,' he said. 'There isn't a Greek man alive who, given a hook and line and a position near water, won't drop in a line and see what comes out. I know men who'd even be tempted in a bath-tub.'

Standing back, he read *Panayiotissa*'s name aloud, and Stathis was suddenly ashamed of how badly the lettering was faded, remembering the painstaking pleasure he had taken repainting it every spring when he and Mikey were a team.

Now the fat man was holding out his hand over the deck-rail, so Stathis was obliged to shake it, or be objectionably rude.

'Hermes Diaktoros, of Athens. *Chairo poli.*'

Stathis transferred his knife to his left hand, and shook the fat man's with his right.

'Stathis Rigopoulos.'

Returning to the fenders, he began to cut a second rope.

'She looks like a vessel with some service behind her.'

Stathis heard the fat man's words as a compliment, and felt a moment of pride.

'It was in this boat,' he said, 'that I caught the first golden-scaled tuna ever landed in Liteos.'

The fat man's admiration showed in his face.

'That was an impressive achievement,' he said. 'I'm honoured to meet you. One of the main reasons for my visit here is to taste the famous fish.'

'I wish you luck, then,' said Stathis. 'That was a long time ago, and there are very few left now, if any at all. The people went mad for them, hunting them down as if they were made of gold, not flesh and blood. They took too many, of course. There hasn't been a single one caught in three seasons.'

'That must make you sad.'

'It makes no difference to me. Like I said, I'm out of the business.'

'But this was the very boat where it all started. If she could talk, she'd tell some stories, I'm sure.'

'Oh aye, she'd tell a few stories.' Suddenly despondent in the face of her decay, Stathis went into the wheelhouse to end the conversation, but the fat man called after him.

'Would you allow me aboard? I'd relish the chance to have a look at her.'

'Please yourself. There's little enough to see.'

Leaving his hold-all on the harbour-side, the fat man climbed onto the deck, and stood behind Stathis looking over his shoulder at the view of the sleepy harbour.

'You'll forgive me for saying, but this is rather a backwater,' he said. 'What are these boats doing here? That yacht, for example, gives its home port as Hamburg.'

'It was owned by a German,' said Stathis. 'He lived on it for a while, and was going to make his home here. But then he needed parts, flew home to buy them and we've never seen him since. The coastguard towed it round here when his mooring fees weren't paid. Who knows what happened to him? Illness, maybe, or death.'

'Or maybe he came into a fortune and bought something bigger, and sailed away to see more of the world. What about that little cruiser? What's her history?'

Stathis shrugged.

'Who knows? Found drifting, abandoned. Folks said a suicide, a man jumped overboard when his business went bad.'

'When people know nothing, they must invent, and usually they invent what's miserable,' said the fat man. 'Maybe there was romance involved, a meeting at sea of star-crossed lovers and a girl whisked away to a life of happiness.'

'I think the suicide's more likely,' said Stathis, 'though they never found a body. Deep as our waters are, that's no surprise.'

'And what about the caique there?' The fat man pointed to a wooden boat, beached and lopsided on the shingle. 'She looks a good age. How old, seventy, eighty years? What's an old lady like her doing unloved and uncared for? She could be restored to her former glory with a competent craftsman's touch.'

Stathis looked across at the caique as if seeing for the first time her peeling paint and the tattered tarpaulin draping her wheelhouse.

'Now, she was a beauty, in her day,' he said. 'I remember her from when I was a boy. She used to be a cargo boat in a small way, and she must have covered some distance in her time. Sturdy in the water, she was, and built for winter. Then she put in a few years as a tourist boat, trips round the island and that nonsense, until the guy who had her bought something new and flashy, a fibreglass boat that goes fast and doesn't need re-painting every year. And do you know, the tourists all complained! Turns out they like to go slow, and they love a bit of character.'

'And what about your boat?' asked the fat man. 'How come the brave, hard-working *Panayiotissa* has ended up here?'

Stathis was at a loss for an answer. He stroked the dashboard with a forgotten affection.

'Aye, there'd be life in the old girl yet,' he said. 'I had someone take an interest in her only recently, someone wanting to put her back to work, but the work wasn't dignified. He wanted something reliable to take him backwards and forwards from that damned fish-farm, since he needs to be out there every day, whatever the weather, feeding those poor creatures. Let them go, I said, and they'd feed themselves. He was talking about spending a bit of money on her, a re-fit he said. I asked him what for, if all he wanted to do with her was motor between the harbour and a place you could find with your eyes shut.'

'You didn't accept his offer, then?'

'I did not.'

'Why not?'

'Because I'm a sentimental old fool. I should have taken his money and let her go, but I didn't want to see her at sea with someone else at the wheel. We have history, she and I.' He pointed to the damp-damaged photograph. 'You see this picture? That's me, on the left. You wouldn't recognise me now, I don't suppose. And that's my cousin, Mikey. Like a brother to me, he was. We grew up together as boys, we worked together as men. That fish we'd taken there was the biggest swordfish ever caught on this coast, and we held that record for nearly five years. Ah, Mikey and I, we had some good luck on this boat, and some good times too. It was never the same, after he was gone.'

'What happened to him?'

'What happened to him? Mikey did something stupid. He threw our luck away.' He tapped his finger on the brass coffer beside the wheel. 'We used to have in here a relic beyond price, a vial of the blood of St Nicholas himself. We had it from my uncle, Mikey's father, and it kept him safe at sea for more than fifty years. Of course it would! What sailor wouldn't be protected by the blood of our patron saint! But there was a season when we couldn't find any fish, and we'd had three trips to sea and come back empty, three wasted trips that cost us money we couldn't afford. And as we sailed back into port after that third time, so out of pocket we didn't know where we'd get the money to refuel this old girl, there off-loading at the quay was another boat weighed down with two great fish!

'Mikey was angry and disappointed in himself. We'd told ourselves the fish weren't running, that they weren't there to catch, and here we saw the evidence of our bad luck. He was beside himself, in tears. I told him we'd do all right next time, but he wouldn't listen to me. And what did he do but take the saint's blood from that box, and throw it overboard! Oh, it broke my heart to see it gone! But not as badly as it broke my heart to lose Mikey.'

The old man wiped away a tear.

'*Hasta*,' he said, looking at the photograph. 'I don't like to remember. Not two weeks had gone by, and he and I were still trying to put together the money to make another trip. I'd taken a few days' work with my father-in-law, fencing some land he had up at Ayia Triander. Mikey was taking out the dinghy, a little launch we used to have for going ashore when the water was too shallow to get *Panayiotissa* in close. He was after squid and mullet, whatever he could sell to make a few drachma. So off he went one morning, and that evening, his daughter brought the message that he hadn't come home. We set out to look for him without knowing what direction he'd taken, and it was no surprise we didn't find him. What use was it, us blundering about in the dark? So we went out again at first light, but it wasn't until noon we found the launch, drifting keel-up far south of here. There was not a sign of Mikey. Plainly something had upended the boat, and that would have been the end of him. Mikey was a seaman all his life, but he never learned to swim.'

The water rippled, as though unseen hands were rocking *Panayiotissa* from below.

'What do you think happened to him?'

Stathis looked over the prow towards the horizon.

'Mikey would have said the mermaids took him, but I've no belief in them. Maybe he leaned too far over the side, or got surprised by a freighter's wash. But he's down there still, and that breaks my heart. Sometimes when I was out there, I used to think I heard him call. I couldn't sleep at nights, thinking he might be somewhere below me in that black water, angry because I wasn't looking for his bones. I got to where I didn't want to be out there by myself, but no-one would go with me. They thought by his throwing away the holy relic, this boat was cursed.'

'Hardly cursed,' said the fat man. 'You caught the first of Liteos's golden fish.'

'I did,' agreed Stathis. 'And I caught a few more too, but by then I wasn't alone. I used to take my Panayiota with me, and you know there's supposed to be no worse luck than that, a woman on a boat. But I enjoyed her company. She didn't swear or snore, and she was happy to do the cooking. She wasn't strong enough to do the heavy work, but she could turn the handle on the winch, and steer a straight course when it was needed. She and I did all right together, but now she's gone, too.'

'Maybe you should look for a new mate.'

Stathis shook his head.

'Not at my time of life. Shall I tell you my intention? I'm thinking I should take this girl to some quiet cove, and put a match to her, give her an honourable end.'

'It would be a great shame to burn her, when she might still be out there catching tuna. Your knowledge is vast, and you could teach someone a great deal.'

'There are no more tuna. Those fish are gone, and that's that.'

'Maybe the fish are simply growing wily. Maybe you need to try new bait. In fact, I've been thinking maybe I should try for myself. I have a rendezvous this evening, but might I buy you a drink first? I'd like to hear the full story of what happened when you got that first bite.'

The thought of a drink and company for once sounded tempting. Stathis locked up the wheelhouse, and walked with the fat man from the Turkish harbour to the port, telling him as they went how he had landed the first fish, what he had learned subsequently about the tuna's habits and tastes, how he and Panayiota had worked as a team.

The fat man was leading in the direction of the Neraida, but when they reached the *periptero*, Noula was sitting outside, tying more hooks onto more lines.

The fat man wished her *kali spera*.

'*Kali spera, kyrie!*' she said. 'Where are you going?'

'I'm taking this gentleman for a drink,' said the fat man. 'I'm sure you know him?'

'I know Stathis,' said Noula. 'Stathis is famous in Liteos.'

'Noula is that rarity, a woman who fishes,' said the fat man.

'Only in a small way,' said Noula. 'Just here, inshore.'

'May I see that?' Stathis held out his hand for the hook she was tying, and when she gave it to him, held it up to his eyes.

'Not bad,' he said.

'They're just for tourists,' she said. 'I sell plenty, and the bait to go with it.'

'I've heard about your bait,' said Stathis. 'I've heard rumours about secret ingredients.'

Noula laughed.

'Not really secret,' she said. 'I have my inspirations, and my brother's a reader. He passes on information he finds in his books. But I sell plenty, so I'm guessing it works. I've never had the chance to try most of it for myself. None of the men here will take me out. Even those that are willing, their wives won't let them.'

'Eh, Stathis!' Dinos was making his way along the harbour-side, heading for the cafe. 'Have you brought your wallet?'

'I'll be late,' called Stathis. 'This gentleman is buying me a drink.'

'Go,' said the fat man. 'Join your friend. You and I can have a drink another time.'

'It's been an honour to talk to you,' Noula said to Stathis. 'You're a hero to me.'

'Me?' asked Stathis, shaking his head as he walked away. 'I've been called many things in my time, but never once in all my years a hero.'

Twelve

'I wonder if we might have a mutual acquaintance.' The fat man was escorting Popi along the harbour, walking at her side at a leisurely pace, diverting his attention from time to time to look into the water at the fish swimming just below the surface, or pausing to admire one of the foreign cruisers with their opulent interiors of chrome and polished wood. Popi had put up her hair, applied makeup and changed into a white cotton dress, but she still wore her silver slippers. 'Professor Pantelis Maglinis. He used to head the Department of Pathology at the Athens Medical School, but it's some time since I spoke to him. I don't know if he is still there?'

Popi looked at him in surprise.

'You know Professor Maglinis?'

'Quite well, actually,' said the fat man. 'I have helped him out on several matters in the past. We occasionally dine together when I'm in Athens. He has a house outside the city where he keeps goats.'

'Professor Maglinis keeps goats? I find that highly improbable.'

'Improbable or not, it is the case. He and his wife make excellent goats' cheese. I believe they have won several prizes.'

'As far as I'm concerned, Professor Maglinis is one of the sternest, most terrifying people I've ever met. He lectured once or twice while I was in training, and his books on pathology are standard university texts.'

'The sternness, I assure you, is nothing but a front. I've always found his company very entertaining. Shall I send him your regards?'

'He'd have no idea who I am.'

'Really? Well, perhaps that should be remedied. I think this is the place Pericles recommended.'

The Amalthea restaurant was small and intimate, hidden down a backstreet away from the harbour-front bustle. There were four tables for two on the pavement, all candle-lit and laid with linen cloths and napkins, and water-bottles and wine goblets made of blue glass; all were occupied but one, which held a *Reserved* card. The outside walls of the Amalthea were painted sky blue, and using that as a backdrop, a clever artist had created a wonderful garden of bright flowers and trees bearing a harvest of oranges, peaches and lemons, with exotic birds nesting in their branches. Over the diners' heads jutted a wooden balcony overladen with pots of trailing green ferns and flowering plants – gardenia, jasmine and rose – whose perfumes drifted down to the tables like the very scent of heaven.

The fat man waited until Popi was seated before sitting down himself. Popi took her napkin from a blue goblet, shook it open and laid it across her lap, pulling the skirt of her dress straight beneath it. A tendril of black hair had escaped from her loosely pinned French knot, and she tucked it behind her ear.

The fat man placed his own napkin on his lap, and smiled at Popi.

'May I say how lovely you look this evening?' he said. 'Your earrings – may I see them? They're very beautiful.'

She leaned towards him, and the gold earrings glinted in the candlelight. They were formed of two bees touching, almost kissing, around a drop of golden honey, and from their extended wings dangled three golden orbs.

'You know the original, of course,' she said, leaning back in her chair. 'The Minoan bee pendant from Malia. I saw it on a trip to Crete and fell in love with it. I bought the earrings as a tribute to the craftsmanship of that piece. They remind me of what we can achieve, even under the most basic of circumstances.'

'I know the pendant very well. I have visited the museum in Heraklion on many occasions, and I think the bee pendant is one of its finest treasures. I don't know if you're aware how it was made? They used a process called faience, where tiny beads of gold are soldered to the base. The Minoans learned the technique from the Syrians, with whom they were close trading partners.'

Popi smiled.

'You're very well informed, *Kyrie* Diaktoros.'

'Please,' he said, 'call me Hermes.'

A young man appeared by their table.

'*Kali spera sas*,' he said. 'Welcome to the Amalthea. Have you eaten with us before?'

The fat man shook his head.

'No. We are here on the recommendation of my old friend Pericles Kassimis. He made our reservation.'

'If you'd like to come into the kitchen and see what's available this evening, you're welcome to do so,' said the waiter. 'Or many of our customers prefer us to surprise them. I could bring you out a few small plates to begin with, and we could take it from there.'

'I love surprises,' said Popi.

'Surprise us both, then,' said the fat man. 'And surprise us with the wine, too. Something Greek, of course, but apart from that I leave it up to you.'

'So,' he said, as the waiter left them, 'how have you been finding your time here in Liteos?'

Popi sighed.

'I don't want to spend the evening talking about the business of death. But in truth, after spending a lot of last night with my hands inside a corpse, I spent much of today arguing about the cause of his death with a man who knows nothing about pathology, but who is a man and so must undoubtedly know more than me on any subject you care to name, including any matter on which I am an expert.'

'I'm afraid that is the nature of men,' said the fat man, sympathetically. 'Are you at liberty to tell me what is the source of your disagreement?'

'Not really. Anyway, I'd rather talk about something else. The name of this restaurant, for example. Who was Amalthea? Wasn't she someone in mythology?'

'I don't want to lecture you.'

'But you do know?'

He smiled.

'Yes, I know. Amalthea was nurse to the infant Zeus, in many accounts a goat who suckled him on her milk. When her services as nurse were no longer required, he was said to have made her tanned hide into his thunder-shield and endowed one of her horns with the boon that it would fulfil the wishes of whoever possessed it, thus making it the origin of the horn of plenty.'

'That seems a grisly fate for someone who's suckled you with their own milk.'

'Other versions of the tale say he turned her into a constellation to live forever amongst the stars.'

'Better. But still probably not the kind of reward poor Amalthea was hoping for.'

The waiter brought out a bottle in an ice-bucket and showed the fat man the label.

'Malagousia,' read the fat man. 'A very interesting choice.'

'From a producer in the north who's reviving the grape very successfully,' said the waiter. 'Would you like to try it?'

Uncorking the bottle, he poured a little into the fat man's glass. The fat man swilled it round, sniffed and tasted it.

'Excellent,' he said. 'A nuance of peach and honey, and a little dryness in the finish. Popi, you must try this.'

The waiter filled their glasses and replaced the bottle in the ice-bucket. The fat man raised his glass to clink it with Popi's.

'*Yammas*,' he said. 'To new friends.'

'New friends.'

Popi took a sip of the wine.

'It's wonderful,' she said. 'But did you notice? There was a perfect example of what I was saying. Who did he ask to taste the wine? You – a man – or me, a mere woman? He didn't ask. He made the assumption the choice of wine was down to you.'

'Ah, Popi! You are that most daunting of creatures, an independent woman!'

'I don't mean to be daunting. I merely ask for respect, and a seat at the same table as the men. Sadly I rarely get it.'

'You have it from me,' he said. 'I promise you that.'

The waiter brought out the first small plates: tiny whole shrimps pan-fried with ouzo, aubergine dolmades filled with spiced pork and rice, vivid beetroot hummus with home-baked pita bread. They talked for a while about the food they were eating, then about delicacies they'd eaten elsewhere; the fat man mentioned the *kleftiko* he'd eaten in the town of Dendra and the *mezedes* in the village of Vrisi, and Popi spoke of lobster on the island of Spetses, the spiced sausages she'd tried in Crete.

The waiter cleared away the first plates and brought three more: crispy courgette fritters made with mint and sheep's cheese, slices of wild boar salami, haricot beans cooked with rabbit and mountain herbs. He poured them more wine, and left them to eat.

'So tell me a little about yourself,' said Popi. 'What about your family?'

The fat man speared a slice of salami, and took his time chewing.

'There's very little to tell,' he said, when his mouth was empty. 'I travel a lot – too much, in truth – so there's never been time for a wife and children.'

'What about your parents?'

'Oh, they're still with us. They have a place north of Athens. What about you?'

Popi held up her right hand to show her empty ring-finger.

'Divorced,' she said. 'For the reasons you might expect. I didn't make time to wear an apron and put food on the table, or spend half my life starching shirts and ironing bed-linen. So he found someone who did. And I never wanted children. I'm too exposed to the underside of life, and I see too many sudden deaths and tragedies. Every one of my clients, if I can call them that, is somebody's child. Sometimes as I'm falling asleep, all I can hear are the pitiful wails of heartbroken mothers.'

'Now I must challenge you on your sexism. In my experience, men feel the loss of their children quite as much as women.'

'You're right, of course. In fact I think the bond can be stronger between a father and daughter. Mothers and sons, fathers and daughters, those are the bonds that are hardest to break.' She smiled, a little sadness in her eyes. 'Listen to me, talking about death again. What a miserable dinner companion I am!'

He reached out, and for a moment laid his hand over hers.

'Please, don't worry. I think what's happened today has troubled you, and we tend to speak what's on our mind, whether we wish to or not. If you want to say more, you'll find me an interested listener, and very discreet. As a stranger here, I'm hardly likely to repeat to anyone what you say. And maybe I can even offer a little advice. In my time, I have seen many instances of sudden death, and have been at the heart of many investigations into its causes.'

'So when you said you work for the authorities, you were referring to the police?'

'No, I wasn't. I think the best way for me to put it is that the authorities I work for are overseers of the police.'

She looked at him quizzically and was about to ask more, but the waiter appeared again, and picked up the empty plates.

'Shall I bring more?' he asked.

'For me, most definitely,' said the fat man.

'The food is fantastic,' said Popi. 'Keep it coming.'

She let the question around the fat man's background lie unanswered, and seemed to give her attention to the music playing quietly in the background, an island lament of death in patriotic war.

'You're thinking of life's sorrows,' said the fat man. 'But there are two sides to every coin. Light always follows dark, and dark light.'

'Not for Tassos Hardouvelis,' said Popi. 'His light won't be rekindled. Which is why to me it's so important the right person pays the price. It's a terrible thing to take a life.'

'You think someone killed him?'

Popi was about to answer, but the waiter reappeared.

'Octopus baked with orzo pasta,' he said, laying the dish on the table. 'Tart of Swiss chard and feta. Duck braised with Metaxa, milk-fed goat with lemon and juniper and a warm salad of green beans and toasted almonds.'

'Good heavens,' said Popi, leaning back from the table. 'So much food!'

'We shall eat slowly, and do it justice,' said the fat man, 'Would you bring us another bottle of wine?'

Popi raised her hands to object.

'I mustn't drink too much. I have a battle to fight tomorrow.'

'Maybe we can make that battle disappear,' said the fat man. 'Tell me what you've seen, and we'll put our heads together.'

She laid down her fork, deciding whether or not to trust him. He seemed not to notice, but broke the buttery pastry of the tart with his fork and tasted it, showing his approval with his expression as he chewed.

'You must try this. The only pastry I've had as good as this is made by an aunt of mine. I shall tell her when I see her she has a rival. She makes an excellent tart during the spring months, with eggs from her own hens and wild greens from the banks of the river Arachtos, which she says are blessed with levels of flavour and nutrients you can find nowhere else.'

'The river Arachtos? Doesn't the bridge at Arta span the Arachtos?'

'Indeed it does. Such a dark tale. Do they still teach the story in schools, I wonder? It always seemed extraordinary to me that a story of human sacrifice was considered suitable for young minds. "A score of masons and forty boys, two wagons and a carter, three times three hundred days they worked, upon the bridge at Arta." The fate of that poor woman troubles me to this day. They walled her up in the bridge to make it strong, and she went to her death with such dignity. No-one was ever brought to justice for her death, and a wrongful death unavenged is anathema to me.'

'And it was the chief mason's wife, of course, rather than the chief mason, who was sealed up to die, women being expendable,' said Popi. 'But the practice of human sacrifice was commonplace then. Almost every bridge more than two hundred years old has some poor soul under its foundations. I suppose no-one regarded it as a crime. Like in the story of the bridge at Arta, it was just a necessary act to ensure the bridge stood strong. These days they content themselves with a rooster or a pig, but even that is too much blood for me.'

'Thus the sacrifices to the old gods continue, even under the benign mask of the Orthodox church. But I don't believe the old gods ever demanded the blood of beautiful young women such as she was.'

'You sound almost as if you knew her.'

The candlelight flickered in his eyes.

'That would hardly be possible, would it? But I have been familiar with the story for many years, as no doubt have you. If you ever cross the bridge, you'd swear you hear her weeping. I have only walked over it once, and I shall never do it again, out of respect to her. Blood sacrifice without consent is murder. Of course there have been countless examples throughout history of brave souls who have given their lives for the good of others, and countless small acts of sacrifice are made every day. I'm not saying all forms of sacrifice are wrong. Self-sacrifice – the sacrifice of position or possessions or even liberty for the benefit of another is at the other end of the spectrum, and one of the noblest deeds a man – or a woman, of course – can perform.'

Popi drank more of her wine and picked up her fork.

'This is more morbid talk for two strangers over dinner,' she said. 'And it puts me back in mind of what happened today.'

'If you would tell me what is troubling you, you will find me more than ready to do what I can to resolve the situation. I realise you're bound to confidentiality by your professional code. But if you trust me, maybe I can use that information to find Tassos's killer, if indeed he was killed.'

She took a piece of the tart.

'That's my dilemma,' she said. 'So if I say more, consider yourself sworn to absolute secrecy.'

The fat man placed his hand over his heart.

'My most solemn word.'

'This is a very confusing case. At first glance, the body appears decayed. The upper torso has the appearance of having been submerged in water for some time – at least two or three days – and has suffered significant damage from being eaten, most likely by crabs. The head is very badly damaged, and that's distressing for the family. But from the ribcage downwards, the story is different. The corpse is in good condition, and gives the appearance of more recent death, definitely within the last forty-eight hours.'

'Which must be the case,' said the fat man. 'I have met people who spoke to him within that time.'

'So, that is the first issue – a body which appears to have died at two different times. Then my internal examination threw up another interesting facet. In my professional opinion, this man died of shock, a shock so intense it stopped what had been a heart in pretty good health.'

'He didn't drown, then?'

Popi shook her head.

'Most certainly not. There was no water in the lungs, and no evidence I can find that he has been immersed in water at all, except superficially on the upper torso, as I've just said.'

'So he was frightened to death.'

'Maybe. Shock can take many forms. But whatever it was, it must have been dramatic. Most men of his age and health can withstand significant levels of psychological trauma.'

The fat man took a piece of duck.

'So if you know what he died of, why have you been having problems today?'

'Ah, well.' She sipped more wine. 'There's more. He'd been stabbed.'

'Stabbed? Where?'

'In the stomach and around the liver, I'd say with a knife, a smallish knife. I found eleven separate wounds. They would have been enough to kill him, if he hadn't already been dead.'

'Post-mortem stab wounds? Why would anyone do that?'

'You're the investigator, Hermes. My job is to report what I find. My mistake was to bring the stab wounds to the attention of this island's so-called medical professional, a certain Dr Nikos Vatopoulos, or Dr Nick, as he likes to be known. Not a man with much time for women in the medical profession, and not a man with much time for facts, either. As soon as I showed him the stab wounds, he was off and running with the idea of murder by knife. Now, I'm not saying this isn't murder – it may or may not be – but certainly Tassos wasn't killed with a knife. The problem is, by the time the doctor and his police buddies had got together, there was no room for the opinion of me, a mere woman. They're all fixated on this erroneous idea, and everything I say is falling on deaf ears.'

'Have you filed your official report?'

'Not yet. I shall have to do so tomorrow. We need to release the body to the family. I put a call in to my immediate boss to advise him what's going on, but he was out of the office. It's summer. People keep short hours.'

'I want you to do me a favour,' said the fat man. 'In the spirit of summer, could you be missing in action when your boss calls back? And I know it's a difficult thing to ask of you, but could you leave the police and the doctor under their misapprehension for the time being?'

'I'm very reluctant to do that, to be honest. The family must come first.'

'I have an idea that by delaying, you will be putting the family first. Please do this, for me. Lose yourself tomorrow morning. Go and find a beach, sleep and swim, have a long, leisurely lunch. If you can give me that time, I may have some answers for you.'

'It seems wrong to do that. I have my professional reputation to think of.'

'I guarantee that whatever happens, your reputation won't suffer. You have my word on it.'

'All right,' said Popi. 'But just until lunchtime. Beyond that, I can make no promises.'

'I hope we will be further on by lunchtime,' he said. 'Have you had enough of these wonderful *mezedes*? If you have, maybe you'd let me buy you some dessert. Pericles tells me there's a little place not too far away where they make the most excellent ice-cream.'

ꝏꝏꝏ

When Stathis's game of *tavli* was over, he wandered slowly home, jangling his winnings in his pocket. The shops were beginning to close, and the butcher had just stepped outside to fetch in his advertising board.

'*Yassou*, Stathis,' he said.

Stathis was struck by a thought.

'Do you have any lamb's liver?' he asked. 'Fresh, not frozen.'

The butcher weighed him a quarter-kilo and wrapped it in waxed paper. Stathis carried the package home, afraid of what he'd find there, but Circe was where he'd left her, and wagged her tail weakly when he came in the door.

He crouched down and stroked her head.

'How are you, my girl?' he asked, and bent down to her so she could lick his face. 'See what I brought you.'

He took one of the dirty dishes from the table, and with his pocket knife cut a slice of the bloody liver into pieces. Crouching down again, he offered a morsel to Circe. She sniffed, and turned her face away.

'Come on, *koukla*,' he said, offering it again. 'It's tasty, and good for you. It'll make you strong.'

The dog sniffed at it again, and gently took it from him.

'That's my girl,' he said, offering another piece. 'That's my good girl.'

Circe ate almost a whole slice of liver, and drank a little water. Seeing her improvement – and his win at *tavli* – had given Stathis some appetite too. The chicken stew Maritsa had made was waiting. Tearing off a piece of bread, he began to eat.

ထထထ

Papa Alex could smell burning.

Although he had tried to stay awake by making himself as uncomfortable as possible in the armchair, the stiffness in his neck and the soreness in his back had not stopped sleep from overtaking him. He had left a cigarette burning in the ashtray. By the lamp-light, he could see the long snake of ash lying in the base, and the burning stub had dropped onto the bedside table, leaving a tarry scorch-mark on the varnished wood.

Shocked at his carelessness, he jumped up from his chair, and began to search for the source of the burning – the rug, his robe, the chair itself – but there was nothing. At least, not in his room.

Opening the bedroom door, he hurried onto the landing, where the smell of smoke was drifting up from below. Switching on the light, hitching up the skirt of his robe, he ran downstairs.

The kitchen door was ajar, the light blazing. Still fogged with sleep, he checked the hall clock: almost three hours after midnight.

There was a frying-pan on the stove. The pan was full of sliced onions sluiced in olive oil, but the pan was cold. The gas-burner beneath it was unlit, but the burner behind it was on full, the blue flames generating enough heat to singe a doily draped over the cooker-hood, which was nearing ignition point and ready to burst into flames. The skins of the onions were on the table, along with the knife which had cut them.

His mother was barefoot in her nightdress, standing at the table sifting flour into a bowl and oblivious to the smoking doily.

Papa Alex pulled the cloth from the cooker hood and dropped it into the sink. He turned off the burner.

His mother, unconcerned, gave him a smile which had nothing of her in it, a vacant smile such as one might offer a stranger. The flour she was sifting had spread everywhere, even to her face.

'Mama,' he said, quietly. 'Mama, what are you doing?'

'They'll be here soon,' she said, tipping more flour into the sieve. White clouds billowed. 'I'm making a cake. But I can't find any eggs. I thought Yorgia brought them, but I can't find them.'

'I know where they are,' said Papa Alex, gently. 'Why don't you leave it to me to finish that? You go back upstairs, and get some rest. You don't want to feel tired when they get here, do you?'

She looked at him as if she couldn't see who had spoken, her eyes mal-focused. Then, a flash of recognition.

'Alex,' she said.

'Yes, it's me, mama,' he said. 'You can trust me to finish it. Come, I'll help you up the stairs.'

The moment of lucidity was gone, and with it the manic energy which had animated her. She looked old, and very weary.

'Don't forget the vanilla, then. It's in the cupboard over ...'

She looked around at all the cupboards in the kitchen, the ones under the sink, the ones on the wall, and not able to remember where she might keep the vanilla, waved a vague hand.

'Let me help you upstairs, mama,' he said.

'No!' She was suddenly angry. 'I shall take myself!'

She left him, and he was unwilling to let her see him following, so he kept his distance, hiding behind the door. In the hallway, she was unsure which way to go, and he called out to her softly.

'Up the stairs, mama. Your bed's upstairs.'

She climbed the stairs with difficulty, clutching the banister with two hands as though the house were a rocking ship on a stormy sea, as if the stairs could not be trusted not to trick her and throw her off. When she reached the landing, she hesitated again, but only the door to her room was open, and that was the one she chose.

Back in the kitchen, Papa Alex found a cloth to clean up the table. When he was done, he opened a cupboard, and took his mother's pills down from the shelf.

Thirteen

A mosquito had found its way into the fat man's room. The night was hot, and even with the balcony doors open, it was hard to sleep; but it seemed whenever he found himself dozing, he would hear the malicious creature whine by his ear, and needed to pull his sheet round himself to protect himself from its bite. After a few hours of broken sleep, in the hour before dawn he was fully awake. Climbing from the bed, he closed the balcony doors before turning on the light, anxious to avoid intrusion from any more insects.

He dressed himself in shorts and a shirt, and then searched in his bag for a bottle of shoe-whitener. Barefoot, he took it and his shoes out onto the balcony, but as he was about to sit down, a flicker of movement caught his eye. A gecko – a tiny albino lizard – was scuttling on the balcony wall.

'Well, my friend,' said the fat man, stretching up to examine it. 'I have a job for you inside.' Lightning fast, he gripped the gecko by its tail between his finger and thumb, and carried it wriggling into his room where the mosquito had settled over the bedhead. 'There is your breakfast,' he said, and placed the gecko on the wall, where its sticky feet carried it scuttling upwards in search of its meal.

Back out on the balcony, the air was pleasantly cool. A crack of dawn was showing at the horizon. His shoes showed up well in the semi-dark, and the fat man took his time applying the whitener, taking extra care where there were scuff marks or stains. When he was satisfied both shoes were as white as they could be, he put them under his chair to dry, and seemed content to watch the world emerge from the fading darkness. The sky's slate grey became amethyst, then muted coral, then blazed titian red, and the first of the morning fishing fleet was heading in, motoring slowly towards the port.

As the fishing boats drew close to their moorings, another boat was heading out in the direction of the fish-farm and the Holy Unmercenaries. In the brightening dawn, its captain was easy to identify by his priest's hat.

The fat man slipped on his shoes and left his room. As he crossed the terrace, the Hotel Poseidon was silent, the kitchen staff not yet arrived to make breakfast. At its mooring, Pericles's boat rocked on the gentle swell. The bucket Costas Iordanidis had borrowed was in its bows. The fat man started the engine and hauled up the anchor, and casting off the mooring rope, took his seat at the tiller to follow in Papa Alex's wake.

ꝏꝏꝏ

The monastery of the Holy Unmercenaries was in the loneliest of places, set on a promontory the local people called Ammoglossa – Tongue of Sand – where the wind always blew. The waters were too shallow to fish and too featureless to attract sea-creatures, and the vast sandy beach was littered in all seasons with waste from the sea – dried seaweed and driftwood, cans and bottles and all the odd rubbish tossed into the water by crews and passengers aboard boats which by-and-large by-passed the island. In winter, strong northerlies fetched the garbage high onto the beach, leaving a tide-mark which remained until the storms of the following autumn. In summer, the sand dried to abrasive white powder, which – no matter what precautions were taken – the wind insidiously deposited into hair, eyes and mouth, and with no shade from the sun or natural windbreaks, it was impossible for anyone to relax there. With so few visitors, it was worth no-one's while to clear the rubbish, and so despite the place's original beauty, Ammoglossa had become ugly, smeared with treacly marine oil, the bleached butts of castaway cigarettes and remnants of plastic and polystyrene blowing over the shore.

The monastery of the Holy Unmercenaries stood beyond even the winter reach of the sea, on a terrace of fissured bedrock half-buried in blown sand, surrounded by sharp spears of aloe-vera. The monastery itself was small, no more than a squat, conical-roofed chapel with quaint outbuildings. Many years ago, it had been a two-monk penance of a place with a long, long walk to civilisation and gardens too salt-besieged to grow anything but a few stunted vegetables. The isolation was hard work even to habituated holy men, and the view of passing boats was a regular temptation to desertion.

The buzz of Papa Alex's outboard motor was loud above the sounds of wind and sea. To avoid the long walk from the jetty to the chapel, he headed instead for the beach, and as he reached the shallows, cut the outboard engine and lifted the propeller clear of the water, allowing the boat under its own momentum to run aground on the sand. Removing the leather sandals from his bare feet, he threw them high up the beach away from the lapping waves and picked up a cotton bag from the seat beside him. Holding up the hem of his robe, he stepped over the side of the boat into the shallow water and paddled ashore.

Indifferent to the sand clinging to his soles, he slipped his sandals back on, and holding a hand to his face to keep the abrasive wind out of his eyes, he made his way towards the chapel.

The chapel walls were in need of care; the whitewash had not been refreshed after the winter rains and was spoiled by green stains of algae and stormborne dirt, and in places had fallen away to leave the stone exposed. The arched iron gate was also in need of new paint; it stood under a carved Maltese cross which had once been gilded, but the gold had faded long ago, and the cross itself was becoming indistinct, as if retreating back into the stone.

The gate was ajar, and as the priest put out his hand to open it, it swung open in the wind, squealing on its un-oiled hinges, banging back against the stone arch. Papa Alex was disconcerted. Usually the gate caught at its base and needed pressure to open it.

He went through the gateway and down the three steps into the courtyard. The walls held back the wind, and without its blustering, the place had an ethereal near-silence, a stillness in keeping with its holy purpose. To his left, the wooden doors into the chapel were set in an ornate stone frame, at whose head was a portico, and above that, further stone carving in the Eastern style, as though the door were wearing a pointed turban. Terracotta urns standing sentinel by the doors had once held flowers and herbs – Papa Alex could remember rosemary and basil – but they were empty now of all but dry earth and the stalks of dead weeds.

Despite its intended purpose as a place of worship and devotion, the monastery had recently been a home. A step-ladder was propped close by the chapel door with a screwdriver on its top step, as though someone had abandoned a repair to the bulbless lamp which should have lit the entrance. Across the courtyard from the chapel, an area between an outhouse and the outer wall had been covered in a makeshift roof of scaffolding planks and tarpaulin weighted down with bricks and breeze-blocks, and under this shelter was an outdoor kitchen – a sink with a modern mixer tap which seemed unlikely to produce a flow of water, and a domestic touch below the sink of a gingham curtain strung on fishing wire to screen whatever was stored behind it. A dish-rack held several coffee cups and a plastic-handled knife; a length of red Formica made a worktop, though the veneer was lifting from rain damage; on the outhouse wall was a kitchen cabinet of the same Formica, supported by ugly grey brackets with insufficient screws. An umbrella stand was filled with ecclesiastical candles as tall as a ten-year-old's head, and all around were icons of St Cosmas and St Damian, the Holy Unmercenaries, the lamps before them dirty and neglected. Beyond the kitchen shelter, a faded duster was pegged to a washing line fixed between a nail in the wall and an apricot tree, whose branches were weighed down by a crop of golden fruit.

Papa Alex left the cotton bag by the outdoor sink and went to the chapel door. The iron key was waiting on top of the architrave. He unlocked the door and pushed it open, letting light into the dim interior, letting out the smokiness of burned-out candles, the dusky scent of incense and the cool dampness which never left the place even in summer. A raised stone marked the threshold, and for no reason he could name, Papa Alex was suddenly reluctant to cross it and leave the world of the new morning for the shadows within. Persuading himself there was nothing to fear, he breathed deeply and stepped through the door.

From the walls around him and from the iconostasis, the eyes of the usually benevolent saints Cosmas and Damian seemed cold and assessing, as if he had intruded where he was unwelcome. He bowed to each icon in turn, and crossed himself. No-one, it appeared, had been here since his last visit; there were no burned-down candles in the sand-box, no sign that any lamps had been lit. He made the lamp-lighting his first job, then lit a censer and paid his full respects to the icons, one by one. When that was done, feeling overcome with tiredness, he sat in one of the choir stalls and closed his eyes.

When he emerged, he left the chapel door open, thinking the morning air and a little warmth would do something to disperse the air of gloom inside. Blinking in the sunlight, it took a few moments for him to realise he was no longer alone.

The fat man was sitting on a rickety, cane-bottomed chair in the shade of the apricot tree. There were three ripe apricots in his lap, and the stones from three already eaten were in his hand. He raised that hand to the priest in cheerful greeting.

'*Yassas*, Papa,' he said. 'You have caught me consuming church property, for which I apologise.' He looked up into the tree's branches. 'But the tree is over-laden, and if I don't eat these, they'll be windfalls and good for nothing.'

He stood up and tossed the stones of the apricots he had eaten onto the roots of the tree.

'Forgive me,' he said, offering his hand. 'I haven't introduced myself. I'm Hermes Diaktoros, of Athens.'

The priest shook his hand.

'Alexis Hardouvelis.'

'I know who you are,' said the fat man. 'Even though I have been in Liteos only briefly, I'm aware of the tragedy regarding your brother. I'm very sorry for your loss. May his memory be eternal.'

The priest nodded his thanks. The fat man noticed the fatigue in his face, the redness of his eyes.

'It's none of my business, of course,' he went on, 'but I'm surprised to see you here, when your family is going through such a crisis.'

'You'll forgive me, *kyrie*,' said Papa Alex, 'but as you say, my family's business is my family's business and no-one else's. I'm a man of the church, and the church's work is unrelenting.'

The fat man moved to where he had a view out to sea, across the array of round tanks which made the fish-farm.

'Those structures out there – was that not your brother's farm?'

'It was.'

'And he was found, I gather, in the cove – we can just about see it, I think – over here to the right?'

He pointed across the water. Papa Alex looked at him.

'You're taking a great interest in my brother,' he said. 'Did you know him? You're a stranger to me, and my brother and I were close.'

'No, I didn't know him,' said the fat man. 'But I am, by profession, an investigator, and I would like to offer my help to find out who killed him, if you will accept it.'

'An investigator? You're a policeman, then?'

The fat man smiled.

'No, no, Papa,' he said. 'They have their methods, and I have mine, and they find my methods a little unorthodox. Your brother was a man in his prime, and would seem to be gone before his time. That makes it a matter of interest to the authorities.'

'No doubt you'll have all the information you need from the Chief of Police, then. I'm sure you'll understand that it's distressing for me to discuss it. My coming out here is nothing more than a diversion, a chance to gather my thoughts. The time I need for contemplation might as well be used, I thought, in doing some useful work.'

'This chapel is under your care, then?'

'All the chapels on Liteos are under my care.' He picked up his bag and began to take out its contents – a six-pack of matchboxes, a bundle of candles tied with rough string, a bottle of sunflower oil. 'This chapel is dedicated to the healers Cosmas and Damian, the Holy Unmercenaries, and as such it is of importance to the people of the island.'

'It is a long way to travel to ask their help.'

'Of course its remote location makes access difficult, and its care is difficult, too. We were lucky for many years in having a resident custodian, for the summer months at least. She made a bedroom in one of the storerooms, and lived to all intents and purposes a monk's life, though they used to live here in pairs. It wasn't an easy life, for her or for them. There used to be a garden, but that apricot tree is all that's left of it.'

'It would take a strong person – man or woman – to live here.'

'She was hardier than most. She took up residence when she was praying for her baby daughter, who was born with a condition which went undiagnosed until she had suffered what was feared would be permanent damage to her sight. The custodian prayed to the Unmercenaries for her daughter to be healed, and promised to devote her life to the saints if she were. The child was taken to Athens for treatment which was by and large a success, and the custodian was as good as her word, and lived here ever after – her husband and daughter with her, until the daughter grew up and moved away.'

'Why was she undiagnosed?'

'Dr Nick was only newly qualified then. A young and inexperienced doctor must be forgiven for not identifying a rare disorder.'

'It is easier to forgive such an error when the damage can be put right. Modern medicine gives us much to be grateful for.'

'Do you think so? You sound like my brother. He set great store by modern medicine. I put my faith in the power of prayer.'

'But which of those cured the woman's daughter?'

'I suppose we must say elements of both. Her life grew harder again when her husband died, and without him to man the boat which was their lifeline, she was dependent on passing fishermen to bring her life's essentials. She became a little touched towards the end. She died quite recently, and so the place has lost its carer. I come when I can find the time, to light the lamps and tidy the place.'

'It has a kind of beauty,' said the fat man. 'Maybe she learned to content herself with that.'

'Maybe she did. Or maybe her mental state was a welcome cushion from hard reality. Sometimes it is so, and sometimes it's a wall which steals us from our loved ones before our time. Is it for the beauty you've made the journey, or are you here to petition the saints? The chapel is open, as you see. I've brought candles, but there are some in there already, and a box for donations.'

He reached up to take the faded duster from the washing line, and lifted down one of the lamps to clean.

The fat man wandered into the chapel, passing from the brilliance of early morning into the dimness of the interior. The candles Papa Alex had lit flickered. Rather than approach the icons with reverence, the fat man bit into one of his apricots, and chewed it whilst examining the intricate paintings, shaking his head at the sombre expressions on the faces of the two saints. Quickly losing interest in them, he began instead to inspect the walls, the flag-stoned floor and the vaulted ceiling where gold-painted stars had all but vanished behind the grime of candle-smoke. In the end, it was in the seaward-facing window he found what he was looking for. At its apex was a carving in a different stone to the rest of the chapel, fixed by what means he couldn't see. The carving was pitted and weathered as though it had spent many years outside, in contrast to the well-preserved stone inside the chapel, but the symbol the mason had worked could still be made out: a three-pronged trident.

Eating the last of his apricots, he made his way outside. Papa Alex was standing in the courtyard gateway, gazing across the beach towards the sea and the fish-farm in the distance.

'I found what I was looking for,' said the fat man.

The priest turned away from the water, and his expression was of unmistakable grief. Tears were running down his cheeks. In one hand, he was running his thumb over the blade of his whittling knife, and in the other was the part-carved thrush, as if he had tried to work on it but had abandoned it in the face of his anguish.

'I'm sorry. I shouldn't disturb you further.'

Papa Alex closed the knife and put it in his pocket along with the carving. He wiped away his tears with the sleeve of his robe, and their wetness darkened the grey cloth.

'You're entitled to be here,' he said. 'This is God's house, not mine. Stay as long as you like. But if you're finished in the chapel, I shall go and spend some time there myself. I feel the need for prayer and forgiveness.'

'Forgiveness? What have you done that needs forgiveness?'

Papa Alex shook his head and covered his face.

'If only!' he said, his voice muffled by his hands. 'If only!'

'Please,' said the fat man, concern in his voice. 'Come and sit for a few moments. Let me get you some water.'

He led the priest to the chair under the apricot tree. Papa Alex seemed glad to sit, and laid back his head, closed his eyes, and repeated his words.

'If only!'

The fat man touched him lightly on the shoulder.

'Take heart,' he said. 'Are you berating yourself over some business left undone with your brother? If so, you shouldn't. When the hours of a man's life are at a sudden end, it's natural to wish that there had been more time, that all loose ends had been tied up, all goodbyes properly said. But please, take it from me, very rarely is that how it happens. One life ends, but those around it continue. Only a man who has known of his approaching death has time to put his affairs in order, and that luxury brings its own curse, the time to fear death and live with the sadness, sometimes the terrible despair, of parting with loved ones. Your brother's sudden death brings you pain, but perhaps for him it was more of a blessing than you know.'

Papa Alex once again hid his face.

'We quarrelled,' he said. 'I was angry at him, and he at me. Our last words to each other were shouted. He left the house in a black mood that I caused, and that will lie forever heavy on my soul.'

The fat man frowned.

'What did you argue about?' he asked. 'Might it not have been something quickly forgotten?'

'His drinking,' said Papa Alex. 'It had begun to take over his life, make him forget his responsibilities. He was bringing shame on the family.'

'I'm sorry to hear that. I gather on the evening of his death, he spent some time in the Neraida cafe. Probably drinking, as you suggest, but the proprietor there, Elias, whom you know, intimated he and your brother had some business to discuss.'

'I expect Tassos was asking for the rent. No doubt to pay off his bar bill.'

'Rent?'

'The Neraida belongs to my mother.'

'I see.'

Papa Alex began to weep again.

'The fact of his death was bad enough, but now Chief Vaios tells us he was attacked with a knife. A knife! Who could have hated him enough to do that? It makes me sick to think of it!'

'A woman can wield a knife. Was your brother not married?'

'He was divorced. He was married to a Swedish woman, but she went back to Sweden several years ago.'

'Before they discovered the knife-wounds, what did the police tell you he had died of?'

Papa Alex looked unsure.

'I don't remember,' he said at last, shaking his head. 'I don't know whether they told us anything. The shock, you know – it takes your wits away.'

'What did you assume, when you saw the body?'

'I suppose I thought he had drowned. The way he'd been found suggested it.'

'Did you know him to be a swimmer, then?'

'My brother loved the water.'

'So would it have made any sense to you, his drowning?'

'If he had been drinking, I suppose. Or suffered a cramp. He might have been hit by a passing boat.'

'They have told you, I suppose, that he was found on a beach?'

'Yes, of course. You can almost see the place from here.'

'Then, forgive me, how would it have been possible he could have drowned and yet crawled from the water to lie dead on the beach?'

'I don't know,' said Papa Alex, vigorously shaking his head. 'And now it turns out that he'd been stabbed! His life was not easy or happy, and now he's gone. Sometimes the will of God is a baffling thing.'

'Sometimes what you call the will of God is nothing more than the circle of life. You may find comfort in your god, Papa, but the only true comforter is time. I'm deeply sorry for your loss. I shall leave you to your prayer and contemplation, but no doubt we shall meet again.'

As he turned to go, he seemed to be struck by a thought.

'I am forgetting,' he said. 'A very small thing. I have a book of yours, *The Fourth Suspect*. Sammy lent it to me. He thought you wouldn't mind if I read it.'

'I don't,' said Papa Alex. 'Please, read it at your leisure. Keep it.'

'Of course I shall return it. But crime novels seem an unusual choice for a priest.'

'I've loved them from being a boy. My uncle kept a book-shop in Thessaloniki, and he used to send them to me. Not to me, actually – to my mother. But she was never a reader, nor my father either, but I read them all. They inspired me with the ambition to be a policeman – not an everyday policeman like Vaios, but a detective. I was ready to move to Athens, or Volos, anywhere I thought there might be murder and serious crime. I even thought of emigrating, trying for citizenship in Australia or America and joining a police force there. But my mother was desperate to have a priest in the family, so in the end I put on the cloth. My uncle still sends me books, and I still enjoy my detective novels, and the challenge of the puzzle. Really, you're welcome to keep it.'

'I couldn't help but noticing it's a first edition,' said the fat man. 'No doubt your uncle sent it as a special gift. I wouldn't feel right in keeping it.'

'Leave it anywhere, then. Any chapel or church on Liteos, and I shall eventually find it.'

ooooo

The sea was ruffled under the morning breeze, and the prow threw up spray whose droplets were cool and refreshing. The fat man went slowly, turning the small boat into the biggest of the waves to ride them more easily. At one point, he looked back towards the chapel. Papa Alex was standing in the gateway, watching where he was headed. The fat man raised his hand in farewell, and gave his attention back to his navigation.

Pericles had given him clear instructions on how to find the cove where Tassos Hardouvelis had been found. The beach was sheltered on the north side by a trio of rocks jutting out from the water, the middle one shorter than the others and giving the impression of an armchair, so people called it the Mermaid's Throne. As those rocks came into view, he could see they resembled a chair, and the romantic image of a fish-tailed maiden seated there to comb her hair was almost believable. At closer quarters, the illusion was dispersed. The rocks were of volcanic origin, and far too sharp to make a seat for anyone.

He cut the engine, and steered the boat to moor it in the same place as Costas Iordanidis when he'd brought his *gomina* here. He dropped the anchor, checked it had found purchase and looped the prow rope around a rock. Taking off his white shoes, he jumped down from the boat into the shallow water.

There were no crabs here now. The water was warm to his feet, the shingle squeezing between his toes a pleasant sensation. Hands on hips, he stood and surveyed the little beach. Two tall men lying head-to-toe would cover its breadth; four would cover the distance from the water's edge to the back of the cave. He took note of the water, of the maximum distance the waves ran up the beach, and the line where the water had reached with the wash of a passing boat. The shingle was disturbed, dimpled by booted feet. He looked up at the rocks overhanging the beach to confirm the apparent impossibility of accessing it that way, and then bending his head, made his way towards the back of the cavern, looking for any access through the rear. There was none, nor any trace of the body that had been here, no detectable corpse smell.

And yet, there was something.

Sniffing, he followed his nose. Close to the back of the cave was a whisky bottle, a half bottle of Johnnie Walker Black, the cap screwed on but empty. He crouched down and picked it up carefully with his fingertips, and sniffed again. The smell of whisky was on the bottle, and the label when he touched it was damp, not with water but with Johnny Walker. He scooped up a handful of the shingle where the bottle had laid and held it to his nose. The shingle too smelled of alcohol. Dropping the shingle and rubbing off the particles sticking to his hand, he cast his eyes around the cavern for anything he might have missed. Satisfied there was nothing, he stood a while looking out at the scene from the beach – the chapel of the Holy Unmercenaries almost directly opposite, and in the middle distance, the tanks of the fish-farm.

Returning to the boat, he climbed aboard, and laid the empty whisky bottle on the bench. As he hauled in the anchor, he glanced across again at the Holy Unmercenaries. Papa Alex was still in the gateway, watching, as it seemed, the fat man's every move.

Stathis stood in the wheelhouse of the *Panayiotissa* and looked out to the harbours end, where the blue water expanded into possibilities. New talismans were hanging where Mikey's garlic used to be – a blue glass eye, and a small icon of St Nicholas, a cheap facsimile of an ancient painting, but still a tribute to the saint.

He ran his hand over the dashboard to wipe away dust, then turned the key in the ignition and fired the magnetos.

Panayiotissa's engine started up as if it had been running only yesterday.

Fourteen

When he returned to the port, the fat man tied up the boat outside the Hotel Poseidon. Most of the guests had left for the beaches, and the terrace was quiet. A single table was occupied by a Scandinavian family, waiting in glum silence for the boat which would take them away from Liteos, their packed suitcases by their feet. A few others lay on sun-beds at the far end of the terrace, and the fat man recognized the girl who had been with Costas, wearing a tiny bikini and sunglasses, bored with her magazine, watching the water and the passers-by.

He didn't go inside the hotel, but made his way instead around the harbour-side, his hold-all in one hand and the empty whisky bottle held with two fingers in the other. At the fish-market, the fishermen were hawking their catches, most of it bream. Sammy moved among them, desultorily washing down the place with a trickle of water from the leaking hosepipe, but he didn't see the fat man as he passed.

At the police-station, the fat man followed the 'Enquiries' sign to the first floor. The office door was wedged open with an off-cut of cardboard, and the smell of coffee leaked onto the stairs. The office, too, smelled of coffee. A young constable was making himself a *frappé*, and turned round from spooning sugar into a glass to wish the fat man *kali mera*. Two other officers, a man and a woman, were seated at their desks, heads down and apparently deep in concentration on the paperwork in front of them. A man in civilian clothes sat relaxed and amused at a desk in the back corner, his feet on a chair as if he were of importance, listening to the row between the Chief of Police and Tassos Hardouvelis's business partner, Orestes Stangos.

The fat man put his holdall between his feet, and crossed his arms to listen.

'This can't go on!' Orestes was shouting. 'The coastguard say it's your responsibility, you say it's theirs, and in the meantime, neither of you does a damn thing! Everyone in Liteos is eating my fish for free! That's stolen property, and I say it's down to you to get out and find out who's ruining my business! It won't be difficult! I'll give you a list of names!'

The Chief of Police had stood up to be eyeball-level with Orestes, who was red-faced and so enraged, there were tears in his eyes. His fists were clenched in tight balls and trembling; the veins on his neck stood out above the collar of his t-shirt. The Chief's expression was polite, but there was annoyance there too;

his arms were folded defensively, and from time to time his eyes flashed to the fat man, as if he were displeased to have a witness to this scene yet fully aware Orestes was too angry to be interrupted.

'I don't need a list of names from you,' he said, firmly. 'I'm well aware whose names are on your list, and they'd be on mine too, except, as I keep saying, the cutting of your nets is a matter for the coastguard. It isn't under my jurisdiction. What is my remit is the death of your partner, and it may surprise you to know that in cases of...' He hesitated, and glanced at the fat man. 'In cases of sudden death like his, we are woefully under-resourced, but we are making that death our top priority, as I'm sure you want us to. Which, after all, is most important, Orestes? Tassos's death, or the loss of your fish? How do you think his family would feel if we put a few bream before him?'

Orestes ran his hand over his head in exasperation.

'For God's sake!' he said. 'Can't you see the two are connected?'

'Connected? In what way, connected? What proof do you have of that?'

'Well, it seems a hell of a coincidence to me! What's the obvious explanation? Tassos caught them at it, cutting the nets, and one of them went too far to shut him up!'

'You think your fish are a motive for murder?'

The man in civilian clothes smirked, and took a sip from a plastic cup he was hiding under the desk.

'How much do you think those fish are worth? Eh?' demanded Orestes. 'Do you have any idea?'

The chief shrugged.

'Twenty thousand? Fifty? A hundred? What difference does it make? Fish are fish. A man is dead, and that's where we're focusing our attention.'

'I can see where your attention is, since you're all here sitting in your comfortable chairs when you should be out there asking questions!'

The chief looked at him coldly.

'With respect,' he said, 'if you weren't here shouting at me, I would currently be engaged in conversation with Dr Nick, discussing his findings regarding the body.' He nodded towards the man at the back. 'So you see, coming here and making a scene is helping nobody.'

'You'll give yourself a coronary,' said the doctor, plainly amused, 'and then where would you be?'

'The same place I am now,' said Orestes. 'Going bankrupt.'

'When I am done with the doctor, I will speak to Apostolos and see what's happening with the coastguard investigation. And when I have anything to report, rest assured you'll be the first to hear it.'

'And in the meantime, I continue to be the island's laughing stock, with every fisherman and every taverna raking in the profits from my investment.'

'To make someone a laughing stock is not a crime,' said the chief. 'And anyway, not only your investment, surely? Who gets Tassos's share of the business, now he's gone?'

'How the hell should I know?' demanded Orestes. 'It should be no-one. He was in the process of selling to me!'

'We've only got your word for that, though, haven't we? If I were you, I'd expect to be dealing with a new partner. Or were you thinking that with Tassos out the way, you'd have a free hand in the business and the profits?'

'Oh, for God's sake, don't be absurd!' Orestes was shaking his head as he was heading for the door. He caught the fat man's eye. 'Expect nothing from these clowns,' he said. 'They're good for nothing but speeding tickets. Anything else is beyond them.'

They heard Orestes running down the stairs. Dr Nick was smiling. The chief of police closed his eyes and turned his face to the ceiling.

'*Panayia mou!* He blames us for Androutsos's buck-passing!'

'You can't blame him for blaming somebody,' said the doctor. 'What he says is true. The whole island's eating fish at his expense. He says he knows who's done it and probably he does. Probably we all do. I know where I'd put my money.'

Vaios circled his shoulders to release the tension there.

'Thinking you know who's responsible and proving who's responsible are not the same thing. No doubt Androutsos has the same names in mind, but he'll have to catch them in the act before he can do anything. So, there goes one unhappy citizen. Let's see if we can do better with the next. Tomas, make me coffee.' He gave his attention, at last, to the fat man. 'Ah, my old friend's friend! How are you enjoying your holiday? What can we do for you?'

'It's more what I can do for you,' said the fat man. 'I've brought you something which I think will be of interest in the Tassos Hardouvelis case.'

'Really?' Vaios glanced across at the constable, who was again spooning sugar into a glass. 'Make it *metrio*, not *glyko*,' he said. 'My wife says I'm putting on weight.' His attention went back to the fat man. 'And what's your interest in the Hardouvelis case, *Kyrie*... I'm sorry, I've forgotten your name.'

'Diaktoros, Hermes Diaktoros.'

'*Kyrie* Diaktoros, that's right. From Athens, as I remember. So, your interest is what, exactly?'

'I think any citizen would regard it as his duty to help the police in their investigation of a death, if it were in his power. Let me be honest with you and tell you I am aware this death may not have been due to natural causes.'

The constable placed the coffee glass under the *frappé* maker and switched it on, and whilst it was running, the chief made no effort to speak. When the constable was satisfied with the foam and consistency of the coffee and was confident it would meet with the chief's approval, he switched off the machine. At the back of the room, the doctor took another surreptitious swig of his drink.

'I appreciate honesty,' said the chief, at last. 'But I can't agree with you about the average citizen and his sense of duty. I've been in this job for the best part of two decades, and I've never found it any easier to get information out of our citizens than it is to get blood out of a stone. The average Greek, friend, is not often minded to voluntarily help the police-force in its work. On the contrary, for the most part he will cross the street to avoid us. Yet here you are, aiding us with our enquiries. Does that mean I should make enquiries about you?'

'You are welcome to do so, of course,' said the fat man. 'And no doubt you will ask Pericles about me, when you see him. He will vouch for me, I'm sure, and there is nothing suspect about my motives. It is only that I have what you might call an over-developed sense of justice, and I am keen to see that in the Hardouvelis case, the right conclusions are drawn. Which is why I brought you this.' He placed the whisky bottle on a desk. 'I found it this morning on the beach where Tassos's body was found. No doubt it's appeared there since the body was removed, or the officers who retrieved the body would have picked it up at that time and brought it in as possible evidence. I have been careful in handling it, and I don't think I will have done any serious damage to what's already there, in terms of fingerprints.'

'Fingerprints?' The chief's tone was scornful, and the constables and the doctor took no trouble to hide their amusement. 'It's just an old whisky bottle, washed up there.'

‘Hardly,’ said the fat man. ‘It was a good way up the beach. Was Tassos a drinker? I have heard rumours that he was, and others say he wasn’t.’

‘And whose prints would you expect us to find on the bottle, if we were to look?’

‘I think you might find that Tassos’s brother has handled it. Papa Alex.’

‘What on earth makes you think that?’

‘From my balcony at the Hotel Poseidon, I have an excellent view of the comings and goings from the harbour. On the last two mornings, I have seen the priest take a boat in the direction of the Holy Unmercenaries. This morning, I found him at the chapel, but he was only arriving there as I was, despite having a significant lead on me. Where had he been in the meantime? I wonder if he went to the beach where his brother was found, and left this bottle.’

‘But why would he do that?’ asked the chief. ‘With respect, you’re not making any sense.’

‘To me, it is obvious,’ said the fat man, ‘but I don’t want to influence your thinking. I suppose he knew you would be going back there at some point to take measurements and have another look over the scene, and that’s when he intended you to find this. I have saved you the trouble, and brought it to you.’

‘And what am I supposed to do with it?’

‘As I say, I suggest you have it checked for fingerprints. If you find any of Papa Alex’s, you might begin to think about what that means. This bottle carries a message, and it is up to you to interpret it. By the way, Tassos was stabbed, was he not?'

'How did you know that?'

'Papa Alex told me himself, this morning. And I did wonder ... Still. I mustn't take up any more of your time. Though he did seem very distressed, very distraught.'

'What are you trying to say? Since you claim a duty to speak out.'

'It's nothing, I'm sure. The man is a priest, and the dead man his own brother. It wouldn't be possible.'

'What are you saying?'

'I'm sure there's nothing to it. But Papa Alex was very distracted, and he was playing with a knife.'

∞∞∞

At the fish-market, flies were landing on the boxes of unsold bream. Hours past the time they'd usually be home, the fishermen were still touting for sales, growing tetchy as they undercut each other's prices and still found no buyers.

The fisherman who had spoken to the fat man wandered away from the others to the far side of the market, and beckoned to Orestes's cousin Vassilis to join him.

'What is it, Dinos?' asked Vassilis. 'Don't tell me you've had another good idea.'

'Smoke?' Dinos offered his cigarettes, but Vassilis declined, and Dinos put them away. 'Yes, I've had an idea. How much have you made today?'

Vassilis spat on the floor where Sammy had recently swept.

'Nothing,' he said. 'By the time I've paid for my fuel, less than nothing. What have we done but flooded the island with fish we can't sell?'

'We could sell it elsewhere,' said Dinos. 'Pack it up and take it to another island.'

'Don't be stupid,' said Vassilis. 'We don't have enough to make it worth our while.'

'Maybe we should look at other products, then. Leave the fish to these *malakes*, and catch ourselves something else.'

'Something else? What something else?'

'You saw what that man gave Sammy. You saw the pearl in that box. They're out there for the harvesting. The boy said so.'

'You're mad.'

'It's worth a look, surely? If you're not prepared to take a look, I'll find someone who is. It's a less risky business, anyway. There's no theft in harvesting directly from the sea.'

'You and your bad ideas. You're crazy.'

'Are you in, or out?'

'What about the fish?'

'Put it in the freezer, bring it out when the stock levels fall. We could go over there tonight.'

'And if we're caught?'

'Like I say, friend, there's nothing to be caught for. It's not a crime to pull oysters from the sea.'

Fifteen

The further the fat man walked from the harbour, the more the streets and lanes ran into each other and at cross purposes, petering out at cultivated gardens where tethered goats nibbled on sparse, dry weeds. Neglected dogs, demented with boredom and frustration, barked furiously at the end of chains staked in the hard-baked ground. There was the smell of roses, of frying vegetables and over-perfumed laundry drying on lines; there were sounds of hammering, of children shouting, of cicadas in the trees.

There were no nameplates on the roads, so the fat man asked directions of an old man leaning breathless on a stick, resting in his return journey from the local bakery, his bag of bread-loaves standing on the road between his feet.

'Left, left and left again,' said the old man. 'The house is painted green. You can't miss it.'

The old man was right. The house the fat man was looking for was an anomaly in the neighbourhood, where the others were conventional shades of ochre, or plain white. The courtyard gate stood open, but was blocked by a child's tricycle with only two wheels, whilst the tricycle's owner sat, glum-faced, on the step, a plaster over a cut on his knee and his elbows yellow with iodine. Costas Iordanidis was crouched down tinkering with the lost wheel, trying to fit it back into place.

'You should be more careful,' he was saying to the child. 'If you ride so fast, you're going to keep breaking it.'

'I can't win if I don't go fast,' whined the child. 'What's the point of racing if you can't go fast?'

'I don't see Leonidas with his knees in ribbons and his bike in bits,' said Costas, tightening a nut on the axle.

'That's because he didn't win,' said the child.

'The boy has a point,' said the fat man, coming to stand over Costas. 'It would seem he's prepared to make necessary sacrifices for the honour of coming first.'

Costas looked up at him.

'You,' he said, and he glanced anxiously towards the house and the child. 'What are you doing here?'

'I wanted to thank you for returning my bucket, and to ask you a question,' said the fat man, turning his face so the child wouldn't hear him. 'Why not walk with me to the end of the lane, and you can give me directions back to the port from there.'

Costas hesitated, then dropped the spanner, which fell with a clatter to the ground.

'The gentleman's lost, and needs directions,' he said to the child. 'Wait here. I shan't be a moment.'

He stood up, and together he and the fat man strolled towards the end of the lane.

'Why have you come here?' asked Costas. 'I thought we understood one another. My situation is delicate.'

'I don't want to bring you any trouble, and I shall be gone quickly. But I didn't realise when we met that you and the young lady had found a body. You both made a good job of being composed.'

'I don't see it had anything to do with you. I don't see it now, unless you're going to tell me differently.'

'I'm taking a professional interest in Tassos Hardouvelis's death. I presume someone has told you that's who you found?'

Costas shook his head.

'No, no-one's told me anything. I asked them not to bother me unless it was urgent, for obvious reasons. Do you know how he died?'

'Not yet. There seems to be some doubt. You did know Tassos, though?'

'Yes.'

'I gather he was the rightful owner of the bream I caught. Did you know that at the time?'

'I knew there was a good chance of it. He and Orestes have been doing an excellent job of re-stocking these waters.'

There was a hint of amusement in his voice.

'Not willingly, of course,' said the fat man. 'Since you were out that way with your lady-friend, I should ask if you had anything to do with the fish-farm's latest trouble?'

'Me? Absolutely not! Why would I spend my time with a girl like that hanging around the fish-farm?'

From behind them, the child shouted.

'Costas! Hurry up!'

'I have to go,' said Costas. 'They'll be wondering why I'm talking to you. My fiancée's mother's visiting.'

'Just tell me about the body,' said the fat man, 'and I shan't trouble you anymore. Think back to how Tassos was lying.'

Costas shrugged.

'Like the sea had washed him up there, on the beach.'

'His feet were in the water, then?'

Costas frowned, thinking back.

'No,' he said, shaking his head. 'He was well up the beach, come to think of it. He was under the overhang of the rock. And his head was towards the water.'

'So it would have been a big wave to put him up on the beach.'

'Yes, I suppose it would.'

'So if I ask you again, do you think the sea had washed him up there to where you found him?'

'I don't think it could have,' said Costas. 'It's summer, and the sea is calm.'

'Did he look, in fact, as if he had been in the water at all?'

Costas nodded.

'Part of him, definitely, yes. The top half of his body looked like he'd been in the water for days. His skin…I don't want to remember it. But his legs, his lower half, I wouldn't have said so, no. You might have said he'd been strung up by his feet and dangled half in and half out the water. That's a horrible thought, isn't it?'

'Yes, it is.'

'Do you think that's what happened? Maybe he got his feet caught in something, a rope or a net, and was suspended in the water until he drowned.'

'An accident, you're thinking. It's possible, but not likely. Tassos didn't drown.'

'But I assumed…'

The child called out again, louder.

'Costas! Come on!'

A woman appeared in the doorway and spoke to the child, who pointed to where Costas and the fat man were standing, and the woman looked curiously towards them.

'My mother-in-law-to-be,' said Costas, pointing vaguely as if he were giving directions. 'One of the nosiest women you'll ever meet. She'll be quizzing me for hours on who you are. I have to go.'

'I have one more question,' said the fat man. 'Was there anything else on the beach? Anything lying about?'

Costas was distracted, looking back towards the house.

'I don't think so,' he said. 'Just masses of crabs.' He shuddered at the memory.

'No bottles or rubbish?'

Costas shook his head.

'I don't remember anything else. And we spent plenty of time looking at our feet, trying to find somewhere to put them that wasn't infested. I have to go.'

'Before you do, I wonder if you'd mind a stranger offering you a little food for thought. I assume you're not marrying for love, since I saw you with that rather beautiful young woman yesterday. In my considerable experience, young men in love don't entertain other women.'

Costas looked sad.

'My fiancée's a nice girl,' he said. 'And the family has property. I shouldn't like to embarrass her by not going through with it.'

'And maybe you like the idea of the property. But your fiancée will be far more embarrassed once you're married and people start telling her about your inevitable dalliances and adulteries. I have a feeling that if you have the courage to be honest now and back out of this contract, you will both find partners to make you much happier. You should talk to her, ask her how she feels, be honest with each other. And life is shorter than you think, Costas. Given a choice between property and happiness, very few old men would choose property. I saw the girl you were with this morning, at the hotel. I wondered if she was waiting for you. Of course I'm not suggesting she would be a serious love-affair, but until she and other beauties like her cease to tempt you, I don't think you have found the right woman to have your children and share your life. I offer that for your consideration, in appreciation of the help you have given me. I shan't trouble you again unless it is absolutely necessary.'

ꝏꝏꝏ

Costas had, in the end, given no directions, but the fat man's way was clear enough. The sea was visible from certain vantage-points between the houses, and he wandered in that general direction, taking his time to admire the prettiest and most productive gardens. He passed a bakery, where the window was filled with pies and pastries, and bought himself a *bougatsa*, accepting the baker's wife's offer of extra cinnamon and icing sugar, which she shook over the pastry with gusto.

Outside the bakery was a bus-stop with a bench, and the fat man sat down to enjoy his snack at leisure. The pastry was crisp and buttery on the outside and unctuously chewy beneath the outer layers, and he bit into it with relish, savouring the combination of the creamy custard filling with the extra sweetness of the added sugar. When he was done, he balled up the paper bag the pastry was supplied in, dropped it into a lop-sided and battered litter-bin, and drawing a silk paisley handkerchief from a pocket, wiped the stickiness from his hands.

The sun was hot, and the harbour was still some distance away, so he decided to rest before carrying on. Within a few minutes he saw a bus approaching, and standing up, put out his hand. The oversized minibus was dilapidated, its side-panels loose and rattling and apparently held in place by the advertising for Fix beer on its sides. Clouds of black smoke billowed from its underneath, and it carried a hefty roof-rack more than adequate for the luggage of a Himalayan expedition. The automatic doors weren't working, and the driver signalled to the fat man to push from his side.

When the doors flew open, the fat man greeted the driver with a smile.

'*Yassas*,' he said. 'Are you going to the harbour?'

'We are, friend,' said the driver, cheerfully. 'Jump on.'

The passengers already aboard watched him with interest. The fat man handed over his fare, and asked the driver if he went near the Hotel Poseidon.

'I can go there, for a paying customer,' said the driver. 'No extra charge.'

'Excellent,' said the fat man, and he chose a seat next to a window to watch the sights of Liteos as they went by.

ထထထ

Spoiled on a diet of raw liver, Circe was almost her old self. When Maritsa arrived with her father's meal, the dog ran barking to the door, wagging her tail as Maritsa unloaded dishes onto the kitchen table.

'What's that dog doing in here?' asked Maritsa. 'You should tie her up outside. And what's happened to you?' She kissed her father on both cheeks. Stathis had shaved, and smelled of lemon cologne. He'd washed his hair, and combed it back with a daub of oily pomade. 'What's happened in here? You washed the dishes! Well, about time. I'm very glad to see it.'

'I'm just going out,' he said.

'Aren't you going to eat your lunch?'

'I'll eat it later. I have a rendezvous to thrash someone at *tavli*.'

When he left the house, Circe was at his heels, and he walked slowly to allow her to keep up. On the way to the Neraida cafe, he went via the *periptero*, where Noula was reading a magazine about fishing.

'*Despinis, kali spera*,' said Stathis.

Noula put down her magazine.

'Uncle, *kali spera*. How are you? Is that your dog?'

'This is my beautiful Circe,' he said. 'She's been unwell, but I think she's on the road to recovery.'

'She looks very thin,' said Noula. 'Does she like biscuits?'

Without waiting for an answer, she took a packet of Petit-beurre biscuits from the shelf, opened it and offered one to the dog. Circe took it without hesitation.

'Have you been fishing today?' asked Stathis.

'I went for an hour or two this morning, but I didn't get much. The water's too warm. All the fish are further out.'

'I was thinking of maybe going myself, today or the next day. Maybe the day after.'

'That's good.' Noula offered Circe another biscuit.

'At my age, I worry about going alone. If something happened to me out there ... But I should like to catch another fish or two, before my time's up. So I was wondering if you'd be interested in going with me. We wouldn't go too far, but I reckon I know a few places we might try. You could bring the bait. I'm very interested in your bait. You might be too busy, of course.'

Noula smiled, and rubbed Circe's head.

'Thank you for asking me, Uncle. I'd love to go,' she said.

ꝏꝏꝏ

Lambros sat at the balcony table in the shade of its awning, a well-read newspaper and a sheet of paper by his hand. The paper had the look of a legal document, closely typed and spaced in numbered paragraphs, but it had, at some time, taken a soaking, and the fibres of the paper had matted when wet.

The typed lettering had survived quite well and was, for the most part, readable, but the signature at the foot of the page was a blur of blue.

With a pen, he drew a stroke on the blank margin of the newspaper. The colour was, he thought, a good match for the signature's ink.

He tried again to smooth the rippled page, but it was hopeless. The paper would never return to its original state. Regardless, he placed the tip of the pen at the beginning of the signature, and traced it as best he could, following the lines of someone else's hand.

When he was done, he sat back and looked at his work. There was no point in deluding himself. His fresh blue writing stood out plainly as a forgery, and any possibility of salvaging the document was gone.

He tossed the pen across the table, and picking up the document, crumpled it into a ball and threw it after the pen. It skidded off the table, and came to rest against the balcony rail.

Overhead, swallows were diving and weaving, snatching insects from the air. For a while, Lambros watched them, until he thought the hour was late enough, when he went inside to pour the first whisky of the day.

Sixteen

At the Hotel Poseidon, the Scandinavians were gone, but Popi was waiting in their place, a bottle of water and a glass on her table, her two cases at her feet. Behind her sunglasses, her eyes were hidden, and as the fat man approached, she seemed not to have seen him; but as he drew close, her solemn expression became a broad smile.

'*Yassou, koukla*,' he said, and held out his hand for her hand, and when she gave it, he kissed the back of it gently, looking into her face. 'Where are you going? Surely you're not leaving us so soon?'

'Ah, Hermes.' She took off her sunglasses and laid them on the table. 'No reason for me to stay. The case is out of my hands, and all I can do now is go back to my office and write up my findings, which, I have to say, contradict in almost every way those of the ignorant, sexist, chauvinist Dr Nick Vatopoulos.'

'I saw the good doctor earlier,' said the fat man. 'He was holding sway at the police station, drinking himself under their tables and looking very pleased with himself. May I join you, by the way? Where is Pericles? Are you really leaving? Won't you join me for lunch before you go?'

'I have plenty of time for lunch, as it happens. They wanted me out of my room to make way for the next guest. So I am condemned to an afternoon as a stateless person. My boat isn't due until this evening.'

'Then I shall wait with you. Where is that man?'

He wandered towards reception, where Pericles was hunched over a desk with a calculator and a pile of invoices.

The fat man called out to him.

'Hey, *patron*! Why are you neglecting your guests?'

'Hey, Hermes!' Pericles put down his paperwork, and removed the wire-framed glasses through which he had been peering at figures. 'What will you have? I'll bring it out immediately.'

'Cold water, and a bottle of chilled wine, a Santorini if you have it. And the lady and I would like lunch. What do you have?'

'Ah, now,' said Pericles, standing up, smiling, 'with you in mind, I managed to find something a little special on my travels around the harbour this morning. Trust me, you won't be disappointed.'

'I do trust you,' said Hermes. 'And where is your lovely wife?'

'She's upstairs, lying down,' said Pericles. 'She has one of her bad heads. She blames it on me, of course, but at least she's out of the way. Go and make yourself comfortable, and I'll go and tell the sous-chef to start cooking. Shall I bring you a little something to start?'

'Of course. Bring us your tastiest and most delectable. The lady is out of sorts, and I want to improve her mood before she leaves.'

'You'll be sorry she's leaving,' said Pericles. 'You and she were getting on very well, I thought.'

'She is both interesting and intelligent, and I appreciate intelligence above all else in a woman.'

Pericles smiled.

'OK,' he said, walking away towards the kitchen. 'If you say so, Hermes. If you say so.'

The fat man returned to the terrace and took a seat opposite Popi. Pericles brought out a bottle of cold water and one of Santorini Nykteri, from which he removed the cork with a flourish.

'You'll like this, I think,' he said. 'I've only a few bottles left and it's impossible to buy more, but I regard you as someone who'll appreciate it.'

He filled their glasses and left them. The fat man raised his glass in a toast.

'To fortunate meetings,' he said. 'And thank you for your company.'

'To fortunate meetings,' echoed Popi, and she tasted the wine. 'It's wonderful, but I'm not in the habit of drinking at lunch time. Still, today I feel the need of something to lift my spirits.'

'Tell me what happened.'

'I intimated to you before that the arrogant but ignorant Dr Nick decided to go running off to the Chief of Police shouting murder before he had possession of all the facts. I mentioned knife wounds on the corpse, he leapt to his erroneous conclusion and of course set everyone running in the wrong direction. So when I spoke to him this morning to correct him – and I must admit, I was very firm in my correction – he couldn't do an about-face without making himself look a fool. Naturally, he took the only route open to him to preserve his stupid male ego, and denounced my professional capabilities to the chief. In short, he derided me, questioned my fitness and qualifications for the job, and persuaded his buddies – without too much difficulty, I should say – that an incompetent drunk with a penis will always know better than any woman.' There were tears in her eyes. 'I'm sorry, Hermes. Sometimes the struggle gets the better of me. So now I have no choice but to go back to the office and enrol the help of a male colleague to back me up and have the file corrected, which makes me look incapable of doing my job without a man to hold my hand.'

Pericles brought out the first of their lunch dishes. Popi replaced her sunglasses to hide the frustration and sadness in her eyes.

'Beetroot dressed with local olive oil, sea salt and crushed garlic,' said Pericles, placing a bowl at the centre of the table. 'I grew the beetroot myself.' Next to it, he put a bowl of grainy hummus sharpened with lemon, crusty fresh bread and a plate of thinly sliced tomatoes and red onion. 'The tomatoes are mine too, picked less than an hour ago. *Kali orexi.*'

'Thank you, my friend,' said the fat man, but he said no more until Pericles was out of earshot. 'To begin with, please, eat something.'

Popi shook her head.

'I'm sorry,' she said, 'I'm really not hungry.'

'Good food always makes the world look kinder, and Pericles will be heartbroken if you don't try his hummus. He never lets anyone else make it. I've been eating his hummus for more years than I care to remember, and I can vouch for its restorative powers.'

He picked up a fork and held it out to her, and with reluctance she took it, dipped the tines into the creamy mixture and tasted it.

She smiled.

'I have to admit, it is good,' she said, and reached for more.

The fat man tried the beetroot.

'I understand completely the misery of your position,' he said. 'But it remains a fact of life that, even in those nations calling themselves enlightened, men still hold the upper hand. Which, in a case like this, could have serious consequences.'

Popi forked a slice of tomato onto her plate, elegantly cut it in half but left it lying there whilst she spoke.

'The knife wounds were, without question, post-mortem,' she said. 'Any first-year pathology student would tell you that. Which still leaves us with the very interesting question of why anyone would stab a corpse, but doesn't help explain the death. Did you come up with anything of interest today?'

'So far, no.' The fat man dipped a piece of bread into the beetroot's oily dressing. 'Who would stab a dead body, in your experience?'

'We do see it, from time to time. Usually someone wants to disguise either the cause of death, or less commonly, the time of death. Very occasionally, they're looking to do both. Sometimes a family is wanting to disguise a suicide and the disgrace that brings, the problems with burial in sacred ground. Quite understandable, but often clumsily done.'

'Would you say it was clumsily done in this case?'

'On the contrary, I'd say it was carefully done. Cautiously, almost. The wounds were quite shallow. If he hadn't been dead already, he might have survived the knife.'

Popi drank more wine, and seemed to be thinking.

'What is very interesting in this case,' she said, 'is that it really isn't obvious from the body how he died. A layman might easily assume water was involved, and that he drowned. In other words, the death might easily have been – unless someone knew better – accidental. And that begs the question, doesn't it, why someone might go to some trouble and some risk to prove otherwise, by tampering with the body to suggest a violent death.'

The fat man frowned.

'That is interesting,' he said. 'What you're suggesting is, the death might easily have been ruled accidental, and yet someone seemed not to want that. Maybe someone wanted you to look more closely than you might otherwise have done.'

Popi raised her eyebrows.

'Are you suggesting I wouldn't have looked closely without a fake stabbing to focus my attention? I am no Dr Nick, Hermes.'

The fat man shook his head vehemently.

'I'm not suggesting that for one moment. But there are plenty of Dr Nicks who would have been all too glad to act exactly as our man has here – a superficial examination, a wrong conclusion and a case either closed, or progressed on the basis of an error.'

Pericles was approaching their table from the kitchen, carrying two pasta bowls.

'*Pedia*,' he said, 'prepare for a feast! A wonderful dish for you – lobster linguine!'

He placed the bowls in front of them, and the aromas of garlicky tomato sauce and lobster rose to their noses.

The fat man was grinning.

'My friend, you have outdone yourself! This looks fantastic!'

'There was lobster at the fish market this morning,' said Pericles. 'I was there early, and beat them all to it. It was a beauty, so I hope you've got good appetites!'

'My appetite is always good,' said the fat man, 'and I hope this will sharpen Popi's too.'

Popi was already twirling strands of hot pasta around her fork.

'My favourite dish ever,' she said. 'You've made my day much brighter.'

'I'll leave the other plates,' said Pericles, walking away. 'Call me if you need anything.'

'This really is superb,' said Popi, taking a second forkful of linguine. 'Thank you, Hermes, for making the day seem not so hopeless.'

'It isn't hopeless at all. Quite the reverse. I think Dr Nick may have played into someone's hands. I'm going to ask you to go along with a plan of mine. You don't have to do anything, in fact you literally have to do nothing, except write your report as you would normally write it, and keep it somewhere safe.'

'What do you mean? I'm legally obliged to file my report as soon as I'm back in the office. The family has a right to know how Tassos actually died, and if I have to sacrifice my pride for that by bringing in a colleague to back me up, so be it. At least the body has been released, so the family can bury him. It's always distressing when there's a delay, and especially when he has been so inadequately looked after in the medical centre. I think they're burying him this evening.'

The fat man poured more wine, and they touched glasses again.

'What would you say is at the heart of your work?' he asked. 'What drew you to this career above any other?'

'The puzzle it sometimes presents. I enjoy the challenge of putting together physical clues to come up with a diagnosis, if you will. I enjoy the knowledge in criminal cases that I've helped put someone behind bars, brought them to justice.'

'Ah, justice. Justice is the guiding principle in all I do, too. But you know, that occasionally brings me into conflict with the law.'

Popi frowned.

'How so? Surely the law is the instrument of justice?'

'More often than you think, the law is an ass, and the guilty go free whilst those who are innocent, in terms of humanity and the heart, are punished. I am afraid we are in danger of seeing such a case here. Tassos's death has some very interesting features, I'm sure you'll agree.'

'It does, and some of them I'm frankly unable to explain. The dual condition of the body, for example, seeming decayed in part, yet with decay that has no smell, and the remainder of the body well preserved. I haven't seen that before, and I shall be consulting with my colleagues when I get back.'

'What if I were to ask you not to have that conversation for the time being?'

'You would have to give me an excellent reason not to.'

'The reason would be justice. Tassos's death is, I think, a case which won't be solved immediately. What I propose is that I speak to the eminent head of your department – who you describe as the stern and scary Professor Maglinis – and get his agreement to hold this case in hiatus. It won't be for long, I'm sure. When the time is right, you will publish your report, which will be a few weeks or months delayed. You remember we spoke about sacrifice, the sacrifice at the bridge of Arta? I am not going to ask you for anything like so big a sacrifice as that poor woman made, but I am going to ask you to temporarily sacrifice your professional reputation, and to leave here allowing Dr Nick and the Chief of Police to believe that Dr Nick's misinterpretation of the facts is correct. You have my word, they will be put right in the end.'

Popi looked doubtful.

'Would you be persuaded if Professor Maglinis spoke to you himself?'

She laughed.

'The great man would never speak to me!'

'I think he will. If you will go along with this plan, you have my absolute assurance you will be persuaded in the end you did the right thing.'

Popi drank more wine.

'It sticks in my throat,' she said, 'to allow that arrogant, opinionated idiot to think he has won. But you seem determined, and if you truly can persuade the great professor, then I will go along with it too.'

'Thank you, Popi. Your sacrifice won't go unnoticed by those in high places. In the meantime, I shall stay on the case, and find out what it was that terrified Tassos so much it stopped his heart.'

Seventeen

The Marie-Crysanthe arrived a little after four, only thirty minutes later than she was scheduled. The fat man stood with Popi on the quayside while the ferry docked, and as the ramp came down and the truck-drivers waiting to board revved their engines, he kissed her on both cheeks.

'Don't worry about anything,' he said. 'I shall get word to you when I've spoken to Professor Maglinis, and you should expect a call from him. After that, I'll let you know when the time is right.'

'Right for what, Hermes?'

'You'll know that too. *Kalo taxidi, koukla mou.* I hope we shall see each other again.'

'I hope so too,' said Popi. 'You know where to find me.'

As the boat's ropes were cast off, she waved to him from the rails of the upper deck, conspicuous in her business clothes amongst the tourists in their sundresses and shorts. The engines rumbled, and the expanse of blue water between the boat's stern and the dock grew wider, until the captain began to turn the vessel, and steer towards open sea.

Popi blew the fat man a kiss. As the *Marie-Crysanthe* sailed away, he walked alone along the harbour-side, back in the direction of the Hotel Poseidon.

Outside a supermarket, Elias was loading cartons of milk into the back of a battered Nissan flatbed.

'Man of Athens!' he called, when he saw the fat man. 'How are you enjoying your stay?'

'I am finding it interesting,' said the fat man, 'and as usual, I am as interested in what people don't say as in what they do. You, for example, omitted a very pertinent piece of information when we were talking about your wanting to buy the Neraida. You never mentioned that your landlady is Tassos's mother.'

'What of it?' asked Elias, throwing another pack of milk onto the truck. 'That's a fact most people here already know. Are you trying to frame me for his murder?'

'Are you calling it murder?'

'What else do you call it, when a man is done to death by a person or persons unknown? But you're barking up the wrong tree with me, my friend. I had nothing to gain by Tassos's death. Quite the reverse, in fact. And if I weren't telling the truth, don't you think Vaios would have already thrown me in his makeshift little prison? If you're going back to your hotel, I can give you a lift part of the way.'

'Thank you, no,' said the fat man. 'I prefer to walk.'

'You have the shoes for it.'

The fat man smiled.

'I call them my winged sandals. And they serve me very well.'

'Don't be a stranger, then,' said Elias.

ထထထ

The fat man slept for an hour, then showered and changed into trousers and a shirt, and slung a cotton sweater round his shoulders. Pericles was already behind the bar, and a few tourists returned from the beach were at the terrace tables.

The fat man ordered Greek coffee, and sipped it looking out across the water, judging the mood of the sea where a brisk breeze was raising whitecaps beyond the harbour's shelter.

Behind the hotel, a funeral bell began to toll, a dour note rung four times followed by a pause. When the bell had rung out twice, it was echoed by a second from a chapel beyond the hill, and quickly picked up by a third.

Pericles came out from behind the bar to clear a table, and as he picked up the empty glasses, the fat man asked, 'The funeral bells – are they for Tassos Hardouvelis?'

'They are,' said Pericles. 'And not before time. The family will be pleased to have him back with them and decently buried. What did your friend find out about that business, by the way? There's a rumour going round that he was murdered.'

'Is that what people are saying?'

'It's what I heard. They're saying there was a knife involved.'

'That sounds like the kind of detail which the police should be keeping close to their chests.'

'Pah! It's not their chests that are the problem. Their mouths leak like sieves. As soon as there's anything interesting going on, they trade information like currency. They sit down in any bar they like and the drinks are on the house, as long as they tell what they know.'

'Hence the warm welcome you provide for the chief of police.'

'It never hurts to cultivate a source, Hermes. You of all people know that.'

'A source of information is not the same as a source of gossip.'

'Ah, but gossip so often hides information! You told me that yourself, last time you were here.'

'Did I? And will the chief gossip-monger be here this evening?'

'If he's on duty, he'll no doubt be here for his beer later on.'

'Then maybe I shall come and hear what he has to say about the progress he is making in Tassos's case, if I am back in time.'

'Are you dining out?'

The fat man shook his head.

'I ate too well at lunchtime. Anyway, I have work to do. I'm thinking of going fishing.'

Pericles glanced out at the water.

'It's not fishing weather now,' he said. 'Look at the sea.'

'It will blow itself out, before long. And anyway, whether it's fishing weather or not depends on what you're fishing for.'

Pericles studied him for a moment. The mournful bells were still tolling, slow and sad.

'And what are you fishing for, Hermes?'

The fat man smiled.

'I cast my net wide,' he said, 'and wait to see what kind of fish swim in.'

ꝏꝏꝏ

As dusk drew close and the fishing boats began to leave the harbour, the fat man stepped aboard Pericles's boat, placed his holdall on one of the benches and started the engine. At first he stayed close to the coast, heading again towards Ammoglossa and the Holy Unmercenaries, but when the fish-farm came into view, he set his course for there instead.

The circular tanks loomed ahead of him in the gloom, their walls rising from the deep waters and appearing to move on the swell, like rafts adrift. At first he gave them a wide berth, passing to the south where he had a clear view of them all and could be sure no-one was there. When he was certain he was alone, he moved in close to find a place he could tie up.

The structures were industrial, a major investment for those who had committed to the enterprise. A vertical ladder with its lower rungs immersed in the water led up to a walkway made of aluminium trellis, the spine of the frame supporting the tanks. The manoeuvre from the boat onto the ladder was tricky; the swell was heavy, and with each passing wave, the boat rose and dropped unpredictably. Choosing his moment, he established a footing on the rungs, and climbed up to the walkway.

The place felt lonely and desolate, a man-made island vulnerable to the whims of the sea. With the light almost gone, the water inside the tanks was dark. In the one to his left, there was a disquieting sense of constant movement, the slithering of too many slippery creatures trapped together and all seeking a way out. To his right, the water was unnaturally still, protected by the tank walls from the waves, empty of the fish which had escaped when the nets were cut.

He made his way along the shifting walkway to its end, where – with no railing or rope to hold on to – a man might easily lose his footing and plunge into the sea. Making his way back to the ladder, he crouched down and found a place to the side of the walkway which he judged to be relatively dry. There was a matchbox in his pocket, and he left it there.

The climb back into the boat was an act of faith and judgement, but he managed it with confidence.

He cast off and pushed away from the tanks, but instead of re-taking his seat at the stern, he settled himself on the bench across the bows and fitted the oars in the rowlocks.

In no hurry he began to row, heading for the twinkle of Liteos's lights, in silence except for the clatter of the oars and the trickle of water running from their tips. The night was fully black and the stars were breathtaking in their magnificence, and he paused from time to time to admire them.

An hour into his slow return, he heard an engine across the water, and before long, the lights of a boat came into view, heading in the direction from where he had come. The fat man shipped his oars, and waited. The boat passed him close without the crew seeing him, but the fat man could make out both of them: Dinos the fisherman and Orestes Stangos's cousin, Vassilis.

The noise of their engine faded in the dark. When he could hear it no more, the fat man moved to the stern, and started up the outboard motor.

∞∞∞

As the fishermen manoeuvred alongside the platform, Dinos switched on the floodlight screwed to the wheelhouse roof. White light flooded the black sea. Vassilis was poised to make the jump from deck to ladder and tie up, but the water around the fish-farm seemed unusually turbulent, and the boat swayed from port to starboard as if unseen hands were rocking them from below. Dinos put the boat into reverse, afraid of catching a blow to the prow, and came at it again, starboard side on. Vassilis had his feet braced on the deck, but he was struggling with his balance as badly as he would in an autumn squall, and almost made a fatal error by moving when the boat suddenly dipped, coming close to a dunking in that perilous spot between hull and mooring.

'Steady, *malaka*! Keep it steady!'

Dinos was busy trying to protect the hull from damage and didn't hear him. A moment came at last when the distance between deck and ladder seemed an easy leap, and Vassilis committed himself; but somehow in that moment the boat rose so the height between the deck and the rung he was aiming for halved, and he landed with too much force. He felt the jolt in his knee, and yelped with pain.

'*Yia moto!*' He struggled up to the walkway, and rubbed his knee. The boat was still being drawn in too close, then drifting too far away.

'Tie her up!' shouted Vassilis. 'Make her secure!'

Dino finally got a rope around a ladder strut, brought the vessel level and tied a second rope at the stern. He cut the engine.

The quiet fell like a blow, leaving the sucking, trickling slurp of the water and the creak of the hull as the boat rocked. The wheelhouse light was a beacon towards Ammoglossa, but it lit almost nothing of the ranks of fish-tanks and their water moving weirdly independently of the sea.

'It's too rough,' said Vassilis, still rubbing his knee. 'I told you we should come tomorrow.'

'Tomorrow, when it's calm and everyone and his brother's out here fishing,' said Dinos. '*Malaka.* Help me up.'

Vassilis offered his hand; in three steps, Dinos was beside him on the walkway.

'This place makes me nauseous,' said Vassilis. 'How can you keep your balance when your body's doing one thing, the sea's doing another and the tanks another?'

'Shhh!' Dinos held up his hand, demanding silence. 'What was that?'

'What?'

'I thought I heard voices. Didn't you hear it?'

'Voices? The only voices you're hearing are in your head.'

'Shhh! Listen! There's someone in the water!'

'I can't hear anything. What do you think it is, mermaids singing?'

Vassilis moved forward between the tanks, where there were splashes and flickers of silver as the teeming fish swam over each other, fighting for space. Dinos peered down through the walkway trellis, convinced someone was there, and as he looked, something caught his eye, almost hidden in the dark. He picked it up: a matchbox, identical to the one in which Sammy kept his pearl. The little box was heavy for its size. He glanced over at Vassilis, and slipped it into his pocket.

'Where shall we look?' asked Vassilis. 'Where would they be?'

'Well, not somewhere obvious, *malaka*,' said Dinos. 'If they were somewhere obvious, people would find them. They must be strung on the outer wall, at the furthest point from here. That's where I'd put them.'

'One of us will have to swim.'

'Swim? I'm not going in there. Not at night.'

'Don't be such a pussy. The water's warm enough. I'll toss you for it.'

'Warm or not, I'm not going in. There might be anything in that water. The thought of it makes me shudder.'

Vassilis had a coin.

'Heads or tails?'

'Heads.'

'Lucky bastard. Heads it is. You can hold my clothes.'

∞∞∞

When the fat man reached the port, he tied up close to the coastguard office and went inside.

A young officer was seated at the front desk reading the sports pages of a two-day-old newspaper, which he folded hurriedly when he saw the fat man and slipped out of sight.

'*Kali spera sas*,' he said. 'Can I help you?'

'I think it is more a case that I can help you,' said the fat man. 'I am aware via my friend Pericles

Kassimis that there have been issues regarding damage and vandalism at the fish-farm, and I'd like to report that I have just seen two men heading in that direction.'

The officer stood up and he reached for his cap.

'When did you see them? Are you sure of where they were going?'

'No doubt whatsoever. As a concerned citizen, I thought it my duty to tell you.'

But the officer wasn't listening. He called to his colleagues, and made for the door.

Outside, the fat man watched the coastguard fire up their launch, cast off and speed away. When they were out of sight, he climbed back into Pericles's boat, and motored at a leisurely pace back to its usual mooring.

∞∞∞

Vassilis began to take off his trousers and shirt, his boots and socks, until he stood in his underpants.

'I'll keep these on,' he said. 'I don't want anything nibbling my *poulaki*. And I need somewhere to hold my knife.' He stuck a hunting knife in the band of his underpants, and his mate handed him a mask and snorkel pipe.

'Your *poulaki*'s not big enough to see in daylight, never mind in the dark. I'll turn that light off before you go in. It's drawing too much attention.'

'Well, bring me a lamp, then. I don't see how I'm to find anything in the dark.'

'By hand, *malaka*. They're strings of shells, so they must be tied to something. If you work your way round, you'll find them.'

Dinos made his way back to the boat, his hand on the matchbox in his pocket. He had a feeling that he didn't need to worry if Vassilis never found the oyster strings, a feeling he'd already got his prize. But getting himself back aboard was tricky, and despite his years at sea, he found himself hesitant to make the jump. In the end he took a risk, and knew he'd been lucky to stay on his feet. At the control panel, he threw the switch to turn off the spotlight. When it went out, the darkness was oppressive. Suddenly, he didn't want to be alone.

'Vassilis!' he shouted.

There was a splash. Briefly, Dinos heard Vassilis moving in the water, and then there was nothing but blackness, the lapping of the waves at the tank-sides, the slithering of the fish and the trickle of water running from the ladder. Clumsily, he climbed back up to the platform and made his way to where Vassilis must have gone in, and looked down on the bituminous sea.

He waited, and waited. Too long, surely? But just as the first flutters of panic were stirring his stomach, Vassilis's head broke the surface, blacker by a few degrees than the starlit sea.

Spluttering and blowing water from his snorkel pipe, Vassilis pushed up his mask and wiped his face.

'Found anything?'

‘Nothing yet. I’m going to start at the far end, at the seaward side.’

Vassilis swam away leaving Dinos alone, swaying with the heaving of the platform, a man who’d been all his life on the water, in fear of the sea. Instinct told him to take a step closer to the centre of the platform, then a few steps closer to the boat. He listened again for Vassilis, and heard in the distance a powerful engine running at full bore.

He waited for the engine noise to fade, but it grew louder. Hurrying back to the end of the platform, he scanned the black water for Vassilis’s head. No damage had been done. If they could get out of here now, they’d be untouchable.

But Vassilis was nowhere to be seen. Dinos watched and waited, listening both for him and the approaching boat, which sounded light and fast, certainly no fishing vessel. A boat like that on the sea at night was either someone up to no good, or someone in pursuit of someone up to no good. Maybe someone in pursuit of them.

He ran back to the ladder, took too big a risk climbing back in the boat and almost fell on his face. If he fired the engines, Vassilis would hear the vibrations and get the message. In the wheelhouse, it was too dark to see the dashboard, but any light would give them away, so he found the magnetos by touch and turned on the ignition. The engine was too loud, but whoever was approaching had loud engines too and that would give them some cover.

Scrambling back up the ladder, he ran again to the end of the walkway. He could pick out the top of Vassilis's head, and willed him to lift his face out of the water. He could see navigation lights now, green and red, and when Vassilis finally raised his head and pushed his mask up to his forehead, he saw the lights too. As the water ran from his ears, he heard the engine.

He pulled the pipe out of his mouth.

'What the hell is that?' he shouted.

'Get out!' Dinos shouted back. 'You have to get out! Swim round, swim round to the boat!'

Vassilis set off in that direction, but the approaching launch switched on its floodlights, and the whole sea was ablaze.

Dinos shielded his eyes against the light, and thought he caught a flash of white on the launch's flank.

The officer at the helm spoke into a microphone, broadcasting his voice through speakers on the roof.

'This is the Hellenic Coastguard. Stay where you are.'

Vassilis threw back his head, and yelled at the sky.

ooooo

The coastguard officers were jubilant, laughing as they towed Vassilis's boat back to port. In the launch's stern, the two fishermen were sullen and silent.

'Got a cigarette?' asked Vassilis.

Dinos put his hand in his pocket. The matchbox was still there. He considered for a moment. Vassilis was going to lose his boat. They might both go to jail.

'It might not be so bad,' he said, and discreetly showed the matchbox to Vassilis. 'I found it on the platform. It's the kind of box Sammy had. I reckon that fellow he was talking to dropped it. We might still be in the money.'

'What's in it?'

'I don't know.'

'Well, open it, *malaka*.'

Careful they weren't observed, the two men leaned together. Dinos slid off the cover, waiting for the glint of luminescence, the soft glow of creamy pearls.

The matchbox was filled with sand.

ꝏꝏꝏ

The fat man wandered up the steps onto the terrace. The hotel was busy, many of its guests returned from dinner and enjoying a night-cap in the evening's coolness.

Pericles was behind the bar, whizzing a pineapple cocktail in a blender. Music was playing over the speakers, a singer currently popular, a handsome young man whose tortured voice persuaded every woman who heard him his love-songs were meant only for her.

The fat man took a seat at the bar, on a free stool next to the chief of police.

'Hermes, *kali spera!*' Pericles shouted over the blender. 'Sit, sit, and I'll be with you in a moment.'

The chief of police was half-way down a large beer. Condensation from his tankard had pooled on the bar-top. He picked up a fistful of salted peanuts from the bowl in front of him, popped several in his mouth, and wished the fat man *kali spera* as he chewed.

Pericles turned off the blender as the singer reached a crescendo of heartbreak. He poured the frothy cocktail into an ice-filled tumbler, dropped in two artificially red cherries, stuck in a straw and balanced a segment of fresh pineapple on the glass's rim.

'What can I get you?' he asked the fat man cheerfully, putting the cocktail on a tray with a can of Fanta and a bottle of Heineken. 'You want to try one of my specials?'

'Not this evening, no,' said the fat man. 'Take care of your customers. I'll decide what to have when you get back.'

Pericles came out from behind the bar and carried the tray over to a table of Germans.

'Very wise,' said the chief of police, chewing peanuts as he spoke. 'Steer clear of his cocktails if you value your liver. Whatever's gathering most dust on the top shelves is what goes in them in the largest quantities.'

'I have been bitten that way too many times to fall for it again,' said the fat man. 'I keep my drinking simple, these days. I'm glad I bumped into you, as a matter of fact. I wanted to ask you whether you've solved your major crime, and whether the bottle I brought you was of any assistance.'

The chief of police took a long drink of his beer.

'I'm afraid not,' he said. 'We can't see any connection between the bottle and Tassos Hardouvelis. He was an ouzo drinker, never known to drink whisky, as far as we know.'

'Interesting,' said the fat man. 'Wouldn't you agree?'

The policeman frowned.

'Why is it interesting?' he asked. 'If there's no connection, there's no connection.'

'Are you sure there's no connection? One hundred percent sure? I still would strongly urge you to check the bottle for fingerprints.'

Pericles returned to the bar, his tray laden with empty glasses, cans and bottles.

'So, Hermes,' he said. 'What can I get you?'

'A Campari and soda, if you please. Chief, may I offer you a drink?'

Vaios considered his almost-empty glass.

'The night is young,' he said. 'Thank you. I'll have another beer.'

Pericles reached up for the bottle of Campari, and Vaios drained his glass.

'You're too set in your ways,' said Pericles, as he made the fat man's drink. 'You're as bad as Vaios here with his beer.'

'I know what I like,' said the chief, reaching for more peanuts. 'Nothing wrong with that.'

Pericles filled a bowl with little fish-shaped snacks and placed it on the bar alongside the fat man's Campari.

'Have you tried these?' he asked. 'They're German, cheese flavoured. Bit of a novelty, don't you think?'

The fat man tried one of the snacks.

'Not bad,' he said. 'But shouldn't fish taste of fish?'

Pericles took a frosted tankard from the freezer and held it under the Amstel tap.

'People don't want fish with their piña coladas,' he said, reaching out to help himself from the fat man's bowl, 'but cheese is always acceptable. I think they're pretty good. Children love them. Vaios, did you go to Tassos's funeral?'

'I did,' said the chief. 'It was a sombre affair, as you'd expect. They kept his mother away. They say she's too far gone. Better for her, I suppose.'

Pericles put the cold beer in front of the policeman and began making up a drinks order for the table he had just cleared, filling glasses with ice and hunting in the fridges for lemonade.

'I heard Papa Alex made a bit of a scene,' he said.

'A scene? Well, yes.' The chief tasted the cold beer. 'He was – I suppose the word is distraught. I didn't see it myself, but they say he fell on the body, begging his brother's forgiveness.'

'Forgiveness?' asked Pericles. 'Why would he need forgiveness?'

'Damned if I know,' said Vaios. 'People get emotional, they say odd things.'

The fat man cleared his throat.

'Maybe I can shed some light on the matter, if you'll permit me. I told you I met Papa Alex this morning at the Holy Unmercenaries. He talked about his brother and about how upset he was. They had fought, apparently, just before Tassos died, a big argument. He was feeling guilty that the last words they spoke together had been in anger.'

Vaios looked at him. The fat man tasted his drink.

'By the way, Pericles,' he said, 'did you know Papa Alex has some talent as an artist? He was working on a carving of a bird, a thrush. I suppose he didn't realise when he started it, but the thrush in some cultures is regarded as a harbinger of death. In others, it is said the thrush appears in times of trouble, as a sign that help is on the way. Which of the two might it be in Papa Alex's case? I was thinking possibly both might apply. His carving really was the most beautiful thing, quite lifelike. He keeps the carving and the knife in the pocket of his cassock, so he can work on it when he has a few minutes to spare. You know, my friend, you really do mix your drinks too strong. Do you think you could spare a little more soda?'

Eighteen

Having missed dinner the previous evening, the fat man felt inclined to do full justice to breakfast. He began with feta and black olives, a few slices of tomato and fresh bread, and moved on to yogurt with a compote of local peaches and a scattering of walnuts. Then he noticed on the buffet some two-bite spinach pies, and tried one of those, and Pericles had fetched almond croissants from the bakery, still warm and syrupy at their marzipan centres, so he ate one of those too. He drank Greek coffee and apple juice, and when he had finished eating, made the rare decision to order a second coffee, which he drank with a cigarette, watching the comings and goings of people and the traffic on the sea.

When Pericles came to take away the fat man's dishes, he looked harassed.

'She's in a terrible temper this morning, Hermes,' he said. 'The laundry hasn't delivered enough clean sheets. Why don't you come and talk to her, exert your charm and calm her down?'

From the direction of the kitchen, the shouts of an angry woman could be heard, alongside the banging of pots and the slamming of doors. The fat man glanced at his watch.

'My friend,' he said, 'you know I would help you if I had time. But I have business to attend to, and having lingered so long over an excellent breakfast, I fear I'm already late.'

'Take me with you,' urged Pericles. 'Tell her you need my help.'

The fat man looked doubtful.

'I think if you go missing in action now, it will be the worse for you in the long run.'

A woman's voice, shrill with annoyance, was calling Pericles's name.

'I wish you good luck.'

'I'll need it,' said Pericles, resignedly.

The fat man made his first stop the *periptero*, where Noula was re-stocking the fridges with chocolate wafer biscuits. When she saw him, she stopped what she was doing, went inside the kiosk and smiled at him from behind the display of chewing gum which spread over the little counter.

'*Kali mera, kyrie*,' she said. 'Are you wanting more cigarettes?'

'No, no thank you. I'm only wanting directions from you this morning, if you don't mind.'

'Not at all. Where are you going?'

'I'm looking for the house of Papa Alex.'

Noula pulled a face, and made three crosses over her chest.

'An unlucky house,' she said. 'You shouldn't go there.'

'I think I shall be immune to the family's misfortune. I have my talismans in my bag.'

'I keep mine here,' said Noula, pointing up to a space above her head not visible to customers. 'I think they're bringing good luck.'

'How so?'

'Stathis has asked me to go fishing with him.'

'I'm very pleased indeed to hear that, for you both. I think you could make a good team. When will you go?'

But Noula wasn't listening; she was looking over the fat man's shoulder.

'Nah!' she said. 'Look at him, strutting around like a cockerel! I spit on him! Nah! Go to the crows!'

The fat man turned to see who she was talking about. Dr Nick was talking to a postman with a heavy letter-bag over his shoulder, apparently asking the postman to search his bag for the doctor's mail.

'You don't like the postman?' he asked.

'Not the postman, the so-called doctor,' said Noula. 'He won't come over here. He knows I won't serve him.'

'Why not?'

'You've seen my brother, *kyrie*. His condition, the way he's shunned and despised for his disability, are the fault of that man. The people say it's a curse from

God, but the truth is it was the curse of his drunkenness. If he'd come to our mother when he was called, Sammy might have been delivered more quickly, and he might have grown up handsome and healthy. But Dr Nick had been drinking, and he wouldn't get out of his bed. I swear when his time finally comes, I'll lead the dance on his grave.'

'Those are strong words.'

'Strong words for strong feelings. Believe me, I'm not alone.'

'So why can't he be removed?'

'That's not so easy while he has connections in the prefecture's medical council. His uncle was chairman for many years. Most people think they have to be nice to him. If you need medical attention, Dr Nick may be the best you'll get.'

'I see,' said the fat man. He looked again at Dr Nick, who was laughing at a joke of his own telling, clutching the postman's arm as he repeated the punch-line. The postman was dutifully smiling, but his smile stopped at the corners of his mouth and went nowhere near his eyes. 'It has been very hard on Sammy, I agree, but life has a way, sometimes, of shining light into the dark. So, you were going to tell me where I can find Papa Alex?'

'To the harbour end, and turn left,' said Noula. 'There's a lane just before the souvlaki shop. The house is up there, a pretty house shaped like a triangle at its end, all pink flowers and a big garden. You can't miss it.'

'Thank you.'

'And thank you for your gift to Sammy. It's a beautiful thing. He says when he gets a better job, he's going to have it made into something for me to wear. A ring or a pendant.' She looked down at her hand as if seeing a ring already there.

'Then we must help him get a better job,' said the fat man. 'You deserve such a ring, and a young man such as your brother deserves the opportunity to provide it.'

∞∞∞

It was too early for the Tasty souvlaki shop to be open. As the fat man passed by, the owner was sitting at one of his own tables with his brother, drinking coffee and smoking cheap Greek cigarettes. Both men were wilting with high-season tiredness, puffy-eyed with lack of sleep and too much alcohol, but they were alert enough to be intrigued by the fat man, looking him up and down as he hesitated at the turning into the lane. When the fat man asked for confirmation this was the right way for the Hardouvelis house, neither of them would do any more than nod.

The fat man followed the upward-winding lane, and soon came to a house as Noula had described, with its triangular form and a gorgeous mass of pink-blossomed bougainvillea on the walls. Despite the day's growing heat, the doors and shutters were closed, the gate to the garden shut. He went by the gate a little further up the lane, and came to a neighbouring house where the gate was open and an elderly man and woman were seated by the front door in the shade of a veranda. The old man was relaxing in an armchair, shirtless and cool in shorts and a baseball cap; his wife was dressed all in black, with a black headscarf covering her hair and pink rubber gloves on her hands. She was peeling prickly pears, with the peeled orange fruit in a bowl on the ground, and the discarded skin and prickles on newspaper by her feet.

'*Kali mera sas!*'

The old man, who had been close to dozing, perked up when the fat man called out.

'*Kali mera*, friend, *kali mera*!'

The fat man made a show of being uncertain of his way, going a little way up the hill, then returning to the gate of the old people's house.

'Where are you going, *kalé*?' asked the old woman, putting down her knife.

The fat man looked around, making it clear it didn't want to be observed or overheard.

'Maybe you can help me,' he said. 'I'm looking for the house of Papa Alex.'

'Directly opposite,' said the old man, pointing with a walking-stick towards the house in question.

'You won't get any answer there,' said the old woman. 'They've fallen on bad times. Where are you from, *kalé*?'

'Athens.'

'Ah, Athens,' said the old woman with a sigh, as if he had spoken of the Gardens of Paradise. 'I went there once. So many people! So many things to buy! We ate meat every night and drank wine from Smyrna – do you remember, husband?'

'I remember it was damned expensive,' said the old man. 'And all that walking was tough on your shoe leather. I have a cousin there, in Psiri. Do you know it?'

'I know it very well.'

'He has a sandwich shop, or at least he did. He's retired now. He did all right for himself, as far as I know.'

He caught sight of a black cat moving stealthily through the stalks of his aubergine plants, and stamped his foot and whacked his cane on the ground.

'Pssst! Damned cats, crapping everywhere.'

'So what brings you to Liteos?' asked the old woman. 'Ah, Athens! We went dancing, and they all threw roses at the singer! Do you remember, husband?'

'My dancing days are over,' said the old man. 'They've had a death in the family, at the priest's house. The priest's brother. The funeral was yesterday.'

'So I heard. In fact it is about Tassos's death I'm calling. I'm trying to get to the bottom of what killed him.'

'Drink,' said the old man. 'That's what they say.'

'Drowning,' said the old woman. 'You drink too much and you go swimming, the two don't go together.'

'I have heard drink might have been a factor,' said the fat man, 'but I have spoken to Papa Alex myself, and he seemed most affected by the fact that he and Tassos had a fight, the night Tassos died.'

'Really?' asked the old woman. 'I hadn't heard that.'

'Then Alex was falling out with everybody,' said the old man. 'We heard him having a big fight with his father that evening.'

'With his father? Are you sure it was his father and not his brother?'

The old man looked at him sternly.

'Listen, friend. I've known Lambros Hardouvelis for over sixty years. We've been neighbours for forty years, and I've seen his boys grow up from tiny babies. I hope I know the difference between his voice and his boys'.

'They were beautiful boys, as children,' said the old woman. 'Two years between them but like peas in a pod. In the face, at least. When he was a boy Tassos had blond hair, white blond, like a foreigner. Alex was always dark. But Lambros's father was blond, do you remember, husband? There was always blond in the family line. Those boys are devoted to their parents, and to each other, Agni was lucky in that. My boys, soon as they had the chance, they were gone. One went to America, and the other's in Germany. I've a grand-daughter I've never seen, and that can't be right. Families need families. It's the natural way.'

'And yet there was an argument. What time was it you heard them fighting?'

'The shouting woke us up,' said the old woman. 'Two, three in the morning it was. They were at it hammer and tongs, shouting and yelling.'

'Could you hear what they were shouting?'

The couple looked at each other.

'Not really,' said the old man. 'All I could hear was them saying whose fault it was.'

'Whose fault what was?'

'That I couldn't tell you.'

'What happened in the end?'

'It all went quiet, and we went back to sleep.'

'But arguments in the house were a rarity?'

'They used to be,' said the old woman. 'Sometimes poor Agni, she gets agitated. Then she shouts, and we hear her weeping, poor soul. She was a good neighbour, before this thing took her. You wouldn't know her, to see her now.'

'But you are sure it was Papa Alex and his father who were shouting that night, not Papa Alex and his brother?'

'Lambros was certainly one half of it. Whether it was Alex or Tassos is more difficult to say. And I can't say for definite Alex didn't fall out with Tassos, but if he did, we certainly didn't hear it.'

'Is there anyone at home now?'

'Oh aye, they're home,' said the old man. 'With her in that state, where else would they be?'

ꝏꝏꝏ

Before he approached the house, the fat man took Papa Alex's copy of *The Fourth Suspect* from his bag. The rusted hinges of the gate squealed as he pushed it open and stepped into the garden which was rich with the scents of high summer, of roses and dry earth, of tomatoes ripe on the vine, and alive with bees and cicadas chirruping. A thrush rustled the branches of a plum-tree, and the cat shooed from the old people's garden crouched watchful under a wheelbarrow.

As he walked towards the house, the fat man saw the door was not closed as he had thought but ajar, and through the gap, he heard the sound of humming – a woman's voice, though the humming carried no melody, seeming to skip from one tune to another. For a few moments, he listened. From time to time a man spoke, not making conversation but giving instructions for the woman to take care, or to desist.

The fat man knocked gently on the door, and the humming stopped.

'Who is it?' demanded the woman's voice, and there was anxiety in the tone. 'Who's there?'

'Don't worry,' said the man. 'There's nothing to worry about.'

Papa Alex opened the door.

'You,' he said. 'What are you doing here?'

'Who is it, *kalé*?' asked the woman's voice. 'Is it Yorgia? Tell her to come in, but the food isn't ready.'

'It isn't Yorgia, mama,' said Papa Alex. 'It's just a visitor.' He turned back to the fat man. 'If you've come on church business, I shall have to ask you to come back another day.'

'Not church business. I've come to return your book.' He held it out.

'That wasn't necessary,' said Papa Alex, taking it. 'As I said to you, you were welcome to leave it at any chapel.'

Agni appeared at his shoulder.

'Is it Yorgia?' she asked. 'Tell them to come in, come in. Don't keep our guests on the doorstep.'

Papa Alex hesitated.

'Come in, then,' he said to the fat man, and stepped out of his way.

The kitchen had been a pride-and-joy but neglect was everywhere, allowing dust to dull the polished copper pans hanging over the fireplace and spatters and splashes to harden in the heat of the stovetop. The air was sweet with vanilla and powdered sugar, and Agni, seeming immediately to forget the fat man was there, went back to the end of the table to stir a bowl of cake mix, beating and beating, muttering to herself and lost in her task, surrounded by a child-like mess of spilled sugar and flour, dribbles of batter, melting butter, empty eggshells and a waiting cake-tin.

'You'll have to excuse my mother,' said Papa Alex, quietly. 'She wants to do nothing but cook. She's preparing for visitors who will never arrive, but I suppose it's harmless enough. The oven is turned off. She'll put her cake in the oven and forget she ever made it, and I shall pour it away.'

'That's very sad.'

'It is,' said Papa Alex. 'She was a good cook. She cooked for us every day and fed us well. We indulge her because it keeps her occupied, for a few minutes at least. We can't make her sleep all the time. And if she sleeps in the day, she's wakeful at night, and that's far worse for all of us.'

'Your care for her is a credit to you.'

'It's no more than she deserves. A son has a duty to his parents, but I hope we act from love, rather than duty. And the blessing of her condition – of her madness, to give it a name – is to spare her the pain of my brother's loss.'

He turned his face away to hide tears. Agni stopped mixing the cake, dipped in a finger and tasted the batter.

'Lemon,' she said. 'It needs lemon.'

'Mama,' said Papa Alex, going to her and touching her arm, 'you said you were going to make a plain cake, do you remember?'

Agni looked at him with eyes that showed no recognition; her face had the blankness of a stranger who passes another on a city street. Not recognising him yet feeling his hand touching her, she looked affronted and angry, and stared down at his hand on her forearm as if trying to make sense of his presumption. Then she noticed the fat man as if for the first time, and shocked to see a stranger in her kitchen, clutched Papa Alex's hand.

'Who's this?' she asked, and then addressed the fat man directly. 'Who are you?'

'A visitor,' he said. 'An acquaintance of your son's.'

She accepted his answer, but looked around now bewildered by the whole situation, as if she had been elsewhere and had just landed in the kitchen, with no memory of cake and baffled by the mess on the table.

'Is Yorgia here?' she asked, and Papa Alex said, 'Not yet, mama.'

At the other end of the table was a basket of bean-pods from the garden, and Agni fixated now on them.

'I'd better get on with shelling those,' she said. 'They'll be here soon.'

'Why don't you sit outside to do them?' asked Papa Alex, and he guided her towards the door, picking up the basket as he went. On the table behind it was a half-bottle of Johnny Walker Black.

The fat man followed Papa Alex outside, where the priest was settling his mother into a chair under the shade of an awning, the basket of beans on the ground beside her. Agni picked up a handful of pods and put them in her lap, then squeezed one to pop it and deftly ran her thumb down its innards to loosen the beans. With the beans in one hand and the empty pod in another, she seemed at a loss.

'Wait a moment, mama,' said Papa Alex. 'I'll fetch a bowl.'

He went back into the kitchen. The fat man watched Agni, who seemed to have forgotten the beans and was gazing round the garden as if she had never seen it before, looking up at the thrush which was still in the tree.

Papa Alex returned with a bowl and put it on his mother's knee with the bean-pods.

'Put the shelled beans in here, mama,' he said, and she gave him another look which suggested she had no idea who he was, but she seemed content, and did as he suggested before going on to empty the next pod.

'I shall leave you, then,' said the fat man. 'By the way, I've heard the police are close to making an arrest in the case of your brother's death.'

Papa Alex looked at him, startled.

'Where did you hear that?' he asked.

'I saw the Chief of Police last night. I think they're putting two and two together. The question is, will they come up with four, or five?'

'What do you mean?'

The fat man didn't immediately answer, but looked out across the garden. Agni was humming as she shelled the beans. The cat under the wheelbarrow was sitting on its haunches, washing its back leg.

'I so admire the way cats do that,' said the fat man. 'It should be an impossible trick to pull off, and yet they manage it so gracefully. A small daily miracle if you will. There are, of course, much larger daily miracles, the love you have for your mother being one. What is her prognosis?'

The priest looked over at Agni.

'A slow deterioration. It'll be hard, but she will be ignorant of it. I look at her and can't believe how time has passed. I see her sitting there and think back to the days Tassos and I were playing round her feet, the days she would tell us stories. She was a wonderful teller of stories, old stories she'd been told as a child herself, and stories she'd just make up on the spot. You wouldn't know it to see her now, but she had such imagination! Wild landscapes and faraway places, places she could never dream of going. We used to beg and beg her to tell us stories, Tassos and I. And yet poor mama, she herself can barely read.'

There were tears in his eyes.

'Yet she gave you a lifelong love of fiction.'

'She did. When I grew too old for her stories, I began to seek out others. But I've never read anything that holds a candle to her inventiveness.'

'Maybe her imagination is serving her now,' said the fat man. 'Who knows how bright and beautiful she paints the world she's living in?'

'I wish I could believe that,' said Papa Alex. 'Whatever world she's in, many of the paths she treads there are dark and fill her with fear, and she falls into rages so terrible she makes us afraid. Us, the men who have always loved her! Before she was ill, she was always bright and cheerful. Now this – disease, this degradation of the brain, whatever it is, has taken that woman away, and left us with a stranger who seems to hate us all. And she drives us to distraction! I'm ashamed to say she's become a burden to us, our cross to bear, but we must shoulder it with good grace, as she would do herself.'

'Alex?'

The voice came from the kitchen, and was followed by the slow slap of slippers on the floor-tiles. Lambros appeared in the doorway in shorts and a vest, his hair dishevelled with sleep, though if he had been sleeping, it had done nothing to remove from his face the impression of a man to whom the restorative of rest was elusive.

'We have a visitor, papa,' said Papa Alex, and the fat man noticed a nuance of warning in his tone.

'Ah.'

Lambros came forward, offering the fat man his hand.

'Lambros Hardouvelis. Welcome.'

'Hermes Diaktoros. Thank you.'

'The gentleman was returning a book of mine,' said Papa Alex.

Lambros shook his head.

'You and your books, son,' he said. 'From a boy, *kyrie*, he's always had his head stuck in a book. Through there, every shelf is full of them. And yet I'm sorry to say, my wife and I can barely read the baker's bill. That's a legacy of the war. There were other things to think about than school, in those days. And how is my princess?'

He looked over at Agni, who seemed oblivious to them all. She was holding a bean pod in one hand, staring at the shelled beans in the bowl and the empty pods on the floor, unable to work out how they were all connected.

Lambros moved close to her, and bent down to place a kiss on the top of her head, and she jerked her head back to look up at him with bewilderment and anger at the liberty he had taken.

Papa Alex crouched down beside her.

'Like this, mama,' he said, and gently took the bean from her hand, popped the pod and ran his thumb down its inside to drop the beans into the bowl.

Her face grew red with rage, and with a shout, she hurled the bowl away, scattering the beans across the terrace. The bowl landed with a clatter. The cat ran for the shelter of the tomato plants; the thrush in the plum tree flew away.

Agni hid her face in her hands and began to wail. Papa Alex tried to comfort her but she pushed him away.

'Leave me!' she shouted. 'Leave me!'

'*Panayia mou*!' Lambros ran his hands over his face. 'I'll get her medicine.'

The fat man put down his holdall, unzipped it and began to hunt in its depths until he found a brown glass vial with a dropper in the top.

'You might try this,' he said to Papa Alex.

'What is it?'

'A herbal remedy I was given by my cousin in Macedonia. Its ingredients are natural, but potent. She distils water-cresses with gentians and other plants to make a sedative which I think your mother would find soothing. Two drops on the tongue is all she'd need. It's less brutal than what you probably have from the pharmacy, and it will go a long way towards calming the demons she's facing inside. Please, take it, try it. I promise it will do her no harm, and it may do her untold good. You may give it as often as you need, but its effects are cumulative, and within two or three days you should find her more peaceful.'

Lambros came from the kitchen with bottle of tablets. Agni was still weeping, pitifully now, like one whose heart was irrevocably broken.

'I'll leave you,' said the fat man.

Lambros was unscrewing the cap from the prescription medicine.

'The gentleman has offered us this as an alternative,' said Papa Alex, holding up the vial. 'Maybe we should give it a try.'

'It's your decision,' said the fat man. 'I shall go.'

'Stay,' said Lambros. 'My wife would think us very rude to rush you away. Let us offer you a drink, a cold beer or coffee, though we don't make very good coffee.'

'Whisky,' said Papa Alex. 'We always keep whisky in the house. You're fond of your whisky, aren't you, papa?'

But the fat man shook his head to decline.

'You are under pressure to cope with this lady,' he said, looking at Agni, who had wrapped herself for comfort in her own arms, and was rocking on her chair, tears running down her cheeks. 'Another time, perhaps.'

As he left, he pulled the gate closed behind him and stepped out into the lane. From there he heard Lambros's voice, asking his son who their visitor was and what he wanted, and Papa Alex's reply.

'He's just a stranger, papa, returning something to me. There's no need to worry yourself about him.'

∞∞∞

As the fat man reached the bottom of the lane, two police cars were pulling up at the kerbside outside the souvlaki shop. The early diners beginning their lunches paused with their forks half-way to their mouths, anticipating being witnesses to a drama. The owner of the shop froze in assembling a *gyros*, the knife in his hand still dipped in the *tzatziki*, and watched in apprehension as four officers climbed from the car, preparing a guarded smile to welcome them.

But the policemen weren't interested in him. Leaving one of the constables waiting by the cars, the other two, led by the chief of police, headed up the lane the fat man had recently descended. The fat man was ready to greet the chief as he passed, but the chief's face was set and grim, and he went by the fat man without acknowledgement, his subordinates hurrying at his heels.

The smell of grilling meat from the souvlaki shop was tempting, and so the fat man went inside, finding himself a table on the terrace with a perfect view of the parked police cars. Using him as an opportunity to interrogate the constable, the shop-owner dropped his knife, left the sandwich he was making on the counter and came running over to the fat man's table with a menu.

'*Yassas*,' he said to the fat man, but as the fat man replied he was ignored. The shopkeeper was already calling out to the constable.

'Hey, Pavlo! *Vre!* What's going on?'

The constable put on a serious face and wagged his finger to indicate he was on confidential official business, but the shopkeeper was determined to know.

'What's happening, *vre*?' he persisted. 'Is this about Tassos? Do they know who did it?'

'I can't comment,' said the officer.

'Are you thirsty?' asked the shopkeeper, and he called out to the boy washing plates in the back to bring the officer a Coca-Cola, which the youngster carried to the policeman solemn-faced.

The policeman popped the cap, drank and nodded his thanks, and though he said no more, signalled to the shopkeeper that he should wait.

With less than half his attention on his customer, the shopkeeper took the fat man's order for a *gyros* with tomato, *tzatziki*, onions but no mustard, and a lemonade. The shopkeeper wrote the order down, but realising he was on the edge of a scoop, was reluctant to return to the kitchen. The policeman finished his Coke, dropped the can in a bin, and settled himself, arms folded, on the bonnet of the car.

The shopkeeper hovered for a minute or two by the fat man's table, but realising there was as yet nothing to see, took the order inside and went back behind the counter, trying as he worked to keep the policeman and the vehicles in view.

Service at the fat man's table was very speedy. In less than five minutes, the shopkeeper was back with his *gyros* and his drink, though the drink was orangeade rather than lemon, and despite the fat man's request there was mustard in the sandwich. The fat man began to eat without complaint. The shopkeeper took a seat at the next table, ensuring he had a clear view of the proceedings.

A pretty girl came down the lane, and stopped to talk to the constable, smilingly trying to extract from him what he was doing there. Though he ate as slowly as he could, the fat man finished his sandwich, folded the paper it had been wrapped in and tucked it under his plate, then poured the remainder of his orangeade into his glass, found his cigarettes and offered them to the shopkeeper, who took one and accepted a light from the fat man's gold lighter.

The girl gave up on the constable and walked away with the constable's eyes on her rear view until she was out of sight. The policeman looked at his watch; the fat man did the same. A bus pulled up on the opposite side of the road, and as passengers were disembarking, the driver signalled to the shopkeeper, asking what was going on. The shopkeeper replied with a shrug, and the bus moved on.

The fat man's cigarette was almost gone when he heard the tramp of men's feet in the lane. The shopkeeper stubbed out the remains of his cigarette and stood up, ignoring the call from one of his customers for their bill.

The chief of police was first into view. The two subordinates followed behind, and between them was Papa Alex, his head low, one of his wrists linked in handcuffs to one of the officers.

'*Panayia mou*!' said the shopkeeper, and crossed himself several times. 'They're taking his brother! How could it be his own brother?'

The fat man rose to his feet, shaking his head.

'Families,' he said, picking up his hold-all. 'They have secrets which run deeper than outsiders can ever know.'

Nineteen

After his siesta, the fat man sat for a long while on the balcony of his room, watching the sea change colour as the sun went down, losing its blues to indigo, its indigo to burgundy until the water was finally burnished with rippling gold.

He went inside to shower, and when he had dried himself, he wrapped a towel around his waist and stood before the bathroom mirror to comb his hair. Unscrewing the top from a jar of English shaving-cream, he lathered his face with a badger-bristle brush, then opened an alligator-skin case and took out an engraved safety-razor. He shaved with great care, and when he was done, splashed on a French cologne scented with bitter-orange neroli, earthy vetiver and the honeyed sweetness of immortelle.

From the wardrobe, he chose a white cotton shirt and camel slacks. Beyond the window, a ferry blew its horn, the melancholy note of countless departures. He stood before the full-length mirror, smoothed his shirt over his ample stomach and ran his hand over his jaw to check his shave; and finding nothing in his appearance to detain him, he left the bedroom and went downstairs.

There was a table free towards the back of the terrace, close to the bar. Discreetly, he surveyed his fellow diners and drinkers. The girl he had seen with Costas was seated with her parents, and a waiter was hanging over her shoulder, his mouth close to her ear as he helped her in her choice of dishes. The girl was smiling, though her father looked annoyed and her middle-aged mother a little crestfallen at her own invisibility. There was music on the loudspeakers – an upbeat tune from a female star of Greek music whose face was on posters plastered on every Athens street – and the fat man was happy to sit back and listen as he waited to be served.

'Eh, Hermes!' Pericles came smiling from the kitchen and clapped the fat man on the shoulder as he carried a refilled ice-bucket to the bar. 'Are you eating with us tonight?'

'I am. My business here is almost done, and I wanted to spend time with you before I go.'

'You're leaving so soon? You've only just arrived! Stay a few more days, relax, go fishing! Why rush away? I've barely seen you, and Tina hasn't seen you at all! She's in a better mood this evening, by the way, which is good news for us all. And she's doing something special with pork. Go and see her, Hermes. Go and say hello. I promise you, this evening there are no flames coming from the dragon's mouth.'

The fat man was dubious.

'You promise?'

'I swear it. Anyway, if she throws anything at you, you're quick on your feet. No, I'm joking, really. Go and talk to her. She's been looking forward to seeing you. I'll have a special aperitif ready when you come back.'

'Nothing too special,' said the fat man, getting to his feet.

He wandered through the hotel dining room and pushed open the swing doors into the kitchen. Two waiters were loading food onto large, round trays; at a huge stainless steel sink, a youth was up to his elbows in hot water, scrubbing out pans. A grey-haired woman in a faded cotton housecoat was making up bowls of Greek salad, distributing sliced cucumber and peppers onto chopped tomatoes; and at a range a chef was stirring a sizzling pan, from which rose the aroma of sautéed garlic.

The chef was slender, with a white apron wrapped tight around her waist and tied in front. There was a little grey in her long hair, which was fastened up in a loose and untidy knot whose tendrils fell enticingly round her face; and though pink from the heat of the kitchen, her face was very attractive. She had heard the doors swing open, and without looking round from the pan, called out, 'Is that you, Pericles? If the Germans want bream, you'll have to clean it. They're on the board over there.'

Without a word, the fat man crossed to the work-surface, where two of Tassos's and Orestes's escaped fish lay clear-eyed and shining on a board, a knife beside them. Seeing him, the old woman making salad was about to speak, but the fat man smiled and put a finger to his lips, and keeping an amused eye on him, she went on with what she was doing, scattering garnishes of black olives and red onion.

'I shall need an apron,' said the fat man.

At the sound of his voice, the chef turned sharply.

'Hermes!' she said in delight, and hurried across the kitchen to greet him.

'*Yassou*, *Kyria* Tina,' he said, embracing her. 'You are yet again more beautiful than the last time I saw you.'

'You rogue,' she said, kissing him on both cheeks. 'Sneaking into my kitchen, pretending to be him. And no, I won't give you an apron. You're our guest, and guests don't work. But you've been here days already, and I haven't seen you. Where have you been?'

'Busy, alas. I have been interesting myself in a little matter here in Liteos, and suddenly it's almost time for me to leave. Of course I couldn't go without seeing you. And you look radiant, radiant! How have you been?'

'Busy, too busy. And oh, that man of mine torments me! He's more work than five children, always full of crazy ideas and never wanting to get on with the job in hand. But I keep him on a short rein, and we do all right.'

'I heard you won a prize for your food.'

She looked bashful, but pleased.

'You heard about that? It was just a regional competition.'

'Just a regional competition? *Kyria* Tina, you are far too modest! I read of it in an Athens newspaper. It is just the thing to bring wealthy Athenians to your door.'

'Wealthy Athenians can be difficult customers,' said Tina, smiling. 'Present company excepted, of course. Are you dining with us this evening?'

'I am. What's on the menu?'

'Come and look,' she said, and taking his hand, led him to the stove, where several pans stood. 'Shall I make my recommendations?'

'Of course. Everything smells wonderful. But I don't want bream.'

She laughed.

'The whole of Liteos is sick of bream. I have something better.' She lifted the lid from a pan, and he leaned across her to look inside. 'To start, maybe a warm salad of fava beans and chick-peas with roasted tomatoes and spinach, served with olive oil croutons.' She replaced that lid, and lifted another. 'And for a main course, I suggest pork – from our neighbour's pig – slow-roasted with marjoram, served on a bed of smoked aubergine. How does that sound?'

'Irresistible.'

'Shall I send you out a bottle of something special from the wine cellar? It's on the house.'

The fat man squeezed her hand.

'You are the brightest star in my firmament, and queen of my heart, always,' he said, and Tina laughed.

'Same old Hermes,' she said.

As he re-took his seat on the terrace, Pericles hurried over with his drink.

'I made you a Martini,' he said. 'An American classic. Have you been flirting with my wife?'

The fat man looked at the Martini. Pericles had put it in an appropriate funnel-shaped glass, and garnished it with a green olive on a stick.

He tasted the drink.

'Very good,' he said. 'A pleasant change. And how could you think I would flirt with your wife? What in heaven's name do you take me for?'

ꝏꝏꝏ

Tina sent out a bottle of red wine from Thessaloniki, a blend of Limnio, Mavroudi and Mavrotragano grapes. Pericles removed the cork and poured a splash into a glass, and waited as the fat man tasted it. The wine was ruby in the glass, rich in blackberry fruit, dry with a hint of spice.

'Excellent,' said the fat man.

He ate his food slowly, savouring the complex flavours Tina had brought to the dishes, the tenderness of the pork and the melting smokiness of aubergines and peppers. He drank a single glass of wine, but when Pericles came to pour him more, he declined.

'I shall wait a while before I have another glass,' he said. 'I'm waiting for news.'

'What news?'

'News of the fratricide. I'm hoping the chief of police will be here before long, and that he'll fill in all the details of the priest's arrest.'

'You have to give him credit for solving the crime so speedily, though, don't you?' asked Pericles. 'How long ago is it since Tassos died? Two, three days, and the guilty party already in custody.'

'It is impressive, yes,' said the fat man, and gave his attention back to the last of his pork.

The chief arrived just after eleven. Though the night was hot, he appeared cool and fresh, still wearing his uniform, though his shirt was unbuttoned well below the neck.

'I haven't had time to go home,' he said, taking his usual seat at the bar. 'Maritsa will forgive me on this one occasion. The phone's been going mad. The press all want the story. I've left Tomas and Panos fending them off. No doubt we'll be seeing TV crews in Liteos tomorrow.'

'All good for business,' said Pericles. 'A beer, I presume?'

'A large one,' said the chief.

The fat man half-filled his wine glass, picked it up and made his way to the bar.

'Do you mind if I join you?' he asked, taking a seat without waiting for an answer. 'I want to congratulate you on your success in this case. Would it be impertinent to ask how you came to identify Papa Alex as the killer?'

Pericles put a saucer of pickled sea-snails in front of the chief, and a stand of cocktail sticks to pick at them with.

'Something special,' he said, 'for a special occasion. So come on, how did you know it was him?'

'He was careless,' said Vaios. 'Simple as that. When I started to focus on him and his movements, it was pretty clear he was guilty. With that in mind, it was a matter of seeking out the proof, and that was relatively easy.'

'How so?' The fat man asked the question, but Pericles was equally interested in the answer.

The chief took a long draft of his beer.

'He seemed to think a double-bluff would save him,' he said. 'Once we'd established that Tassos had died of knife wounds, you find the knife, you've found the killer. Now, the temptation in these cases is to go looking everywhere for the weapon, but our man was clever. He kept the knife on him. See what I mean by a double bluff? How likely were we to go looking in the man's pockets?'

'That's where you found the knife then, as I suggested?' asked the fat man.

The chief gave him a hard stare.

'I don't remember you saying that,' he said. 'But you did bring us the whisky bottle. That's where his whole plan fell apart.'

'How?' asked Pericles, intrigued. 'It's like a detective novel, isn't it?'

'The whisky bottle was what you might call a red herring,' said the chief. 'Alex was getting too clever for his own good. He was trying to throw us off the trail with that one, but we soon figured it out. He was trying to peddle the story that his brother had been drinking and drowned, which was nonsense with the knife wounds, of course. He set the body up with an empty bottle, but when we asked around, Tassos never drank whisky, only ouzo, so there was his first mistake.'

'I suppose Papa Alex couldn't go out and buy ouzo,' said the fat man. 'If he had, that would have registered with someone.'

'His father's a whisky drinker,' said the chief. 'There was an identical bottle to the one we had right there on the kitchen table, when we went to the house. We'd gone to ask about the knife, and when I spotted the bottle, I knew we'd got him before we even found the knife in his cassock pocket. And he'd made a really stupid mistake with that bottle. The cap was screwed on. What drunk screws the cap back on an empty bottle?'

'I see,' said Pericles, admiringly. 'That's right! You wouldn't do that, would you?'

'That's very impressive, Chief,' said the fat man. 'One thing I don't understand. If Papa Alex's father is the whisky drinker, how come he wasn't on your list?'

'An old man like that? He could never have moved the body. Coupled with the fact Papa Alex had been seen – again by you – going backwards and forwards to the scene of the crime ...'

'Where was the scene of the crime?' asked the fat man.

The chief hesitated.

'At the house. They had a fight – over something and nothing – and tempers were lost. Anyway, we put a bit of pressure on him, and he caved in and confessed. Now he's cooling his heels in our cell. He'll be off to the mainland in the morning.'

'How did he get the body onto that beach?'

'He took it to his boat in a wheelbarrow,' said Vaios. 'Simple, eh? Then he tried to disguise the death as an accident, suggesting Tassos had gone swimming drunk from the fish-farm, and died of a heart-attack. I think he thought if the body was wet for a while, it would disguise the knife wounds. Unfortunately for him, we're smarter than that.'

'Indeed,' said the fat man, and took a drink of his wine. 'Well, congratulations, Chief. You've come to exactly the conclusion I might have come to myself. Case closed.'

'Thank you. But with him in custody, Liteos will be looking for a new priest. I'll have another beer, please, Pericles.'

'Certainly,' said Pericles, 'and with the grateful thanks of all our citizens, this one is on the house. It's old Lambros I feel sorry for. He's lost two sons now in just a few days, and he's left with caring for the old girl, in the state she's in. And no-one to pay proper attention to poor Tassos and his grave. It's going to be very hard for him.'

'Someone will help him, surely?' asked the fat man, but Pericles shrugged.

'Who is there? He'll probably find someone to help with the grave. But with Agni, I doubt he'll want to let anyone in the house to take care of her. You know how it is, Hermes. Mental illness is very shaming.'

The fat man was thoughtful.

'You're right,' he said. 'I'm afraid he will struggle.'

'Not much to look forward to in life, has he?' mused Pericles. 'And any day, his son going on trial for murder.'

'Not any day,' said the chief, picking up a cocktail stick and beginning to winkle one of the snails from its black shell. 'The backlog in the courts grows longer every week. He won't see the inside of a courtroom for at least six months.'

'A lot can change in six months,' said the fat man, 'and time has a habit of making things right. If you gentlemen will excuse me, I am feeling rather tired. I shall take my wine upstairs, and drink my nightcap on my balcony. Pericles, Chief, I wish you both goodnight.'

Twenty

On his last morning in Liteos, the fat man was amongst the first for breakfast. As he drank his coffee and ate the last of a piece of almond cake, Pericles brought a bowl of apricots to his table.

'A gift for you, from my mother's garden. Fresh-picked and sweet as any you'll find.'

'The golden apples of mythology,' said the fat man, taking one and examining its rose-tinted skin. 'In the myths, Zeus's wife Hera grew an orchard of them guarded by a hundred-headed dragon.'

'Why did she need a dragon?' asked Pericles. 'They're common enough, surely?'

'Hera's golden apples were the fruit of immortality,' said the fat man. 'If I may, I shall take some with me when I go. I had some from the tree at the Holy Unmercenaries which were delectable. I hope these are half as good as those.'

'Why are you going, Hermes? Why don't you stay?'

'Much as I would wish to, there is business which calls me. I shall be leaving on this morning's ferry.'

'There's another ferry, around five o'clock. Why not at least stay for lunch? Tina is complaining she's barely seen you.'

'Ah, Tina. You remind me I have a gift for you too. Sit down with me a moment.' As Pericles took a seat, the fat man reached down into his hold-all and took out a slender leather case. Inside, lying on taupe velvet, was a necklace of pink-tinted pearls. 'This is for you to give to your wife. I will be honest with you, and tell you it doesn't have huge monetary value. If these stones were from South Sea oysters, they would be worth millions of drachma, but these are pearls I have gathered myself over the years. To my mind, they're as fine as any from Pacific waters. They're from Mediterranean oysters and mussels, and though they're irregular in form and not the pure cream colour jewellers prefer, I think you'll agree they're still things of great beauty.'

'They are,' said Pericles. 'She'll be delighted.'

'She will be more than delighted. There is a gift in this for you too, my friend. Pearls come from the deep places, from Poseidon's world beneath the waves which is always slow and calm. They are the product of inflammation within the mollusc's shell, the result of binding and soothing an irritant and turning it into treasure. I know you love your wife – of course you do, she is a wonderful woman – but she allows life's stresses to impact her too much. In possession of these pearls, you'll find she takes on their influence. They are naturally calming, a balm to the soul. Give them to her, and watch them ease the stresses and worries which are her irritants, and remind her we are here to smell the roses along life's pathway.'

'You mean they'll make her reasonable and relaxed?'

'In time.'

'Then they're worth their weight in gold!'

'Some men do say so, yes.'

Pericles took the fat man's hand between both his own, and shook it heartily.

'Thank you, my friend!' he said. 'If they have the effect you say they will, my life will be transformed!'

'I think you may hope for a little more domestic harmony, at least. But I am sorry not to have spent more time with you both.'

'Then come back,' said Pericles. 'Tina has her birthday in September, and it's one of those significant ones that make women think there's only grey hair and varicose veins on the horizon. Come and join us, and she'll look forward to the date rather than dreading it.'

'I will,' said the fat man. 'You have my word, I shall be here for the occasion. In the meantime, there are things I need to do before the boat departs. Could you get a message to Orestes Stangos, and tell him I need to speak with him? I shall be paying a visit to the Neraida cafe, so perhaps he could join me there.'

∞∞∞

When Stathis arrived at the Turkish quay, he found the fat man waiting at *Panayiotissa*'s mooring, looking down into the water.

'*Kali mera!*' said the fat man. 'I believe I've found an octopus, but it's hiding in the shadow of your hull.' He held out his hand to Circe, who approached him submissively and sniffed at him before licking his thumb. 'May I say, by the way, what an improvement you've made to your boat? She looks all ready to sail.'

'I made a few repairs,' said Stathis. 'I decided you were right, that she deserved a better fate than being left here to rot, or burned. I've found myself a mate, and she and I are going to make a little trip and see how we get along. Come aboard, have a look around.'

He himself climbed over the deck-rail, and laid out the gang-plank for the fat man and Circe, who lay down in the shade of the wheelhouse roof. The boat looked very different to how the fat man had last seen her. She had been washed and sluiced down, her railings were repaired and the *ballones* protecting her hull were inflated and doing their job on new ropes, and the barnacles and deposits below the water-line had been scrubbed away. There were baskets of tuna-fishing lines tied to the engine-housing, and bottled water and fresh bread stored in the wheelhouse.

'All tidy,' he said, and the fat man agreed.

'She's certainly looking sea-worthy,' he said. 'I hope you and your new mate work well together. I realise it goes against common superstition to employ a woman, but I have a feeling you and she might make a lucky team.'

ooooo

At the Neraida café, Elias was at the top of a step-ladder, taking advantage of the quiet early hour to touch up the turquoise paint on the plaster mermaids' tails.

'*Yassou*, man of Athens!' he called down to the fat man. 'Give me a moment, and I'll be there!'

The fat man wished *kali mera* to the only other customer, and sat down at the table under the window. For a few moments he closed his eyes, and listened to the noises of the morning: the chirruping of sparrows and the plash of the calm sea, the bark of a distant dog and the metallic chink of a yacht's rigging. When he opened his eyes again, Elias was climbing down his ladder, and Orestes Stangos was walking through the gate.

Elias greeted Orestes, and headed towards the kitchen. Orestes joined the fat man at his table, and Elias came to stand by them, rubbing his hands.

'Gentlemen,' he said, 'what can I get you? I remember you were a Greek coffee, no sugar. And Orestes, you'll be an extra-sweet.'

'On my bill,' said the fat man. 'And when you've made them, maybe you'll have time to join us for a few minutes. There is a matter I wish to discuss with you both.'

'You want to talk to us together?' Orestes looked baffled.

'I have a proposal to put to you,' said the fat man. 'It is a business matter which will ultimately benefit you, and the people of Liteos. I won't take much of your time. I know you are both busy. But what I have to suggest is important for you all.'

Elias went inside to brew the coffee. Orestes was looking weary, and turned his face away to hide a yawn.

'Did you make any progress with the police?' asked the fat man.

'I needn't have worried,' said Orestes. 'I think they had already figured out that Papa Alex was their man. Hard to believe he would do what he did to his own brother! But then, we never know people like we think we do.'

'You sound as though you speak from experience.'

'Oh, I do! You may not be aware, but there have been other arrests, apart from Papa Alex, in connection, I should be happy to say, with the sabotage of my fish-farm.'

'As a matter of fact, I had heard that,' said the fat man. 'Why does that not make you happy?'

Orestes shook his head.

'*Koproskila*,' he said. '*Yamyiotes*. Two men were arrested, one of them none other than my own cousin Vassilis, the very man who was wanting, so he said, to buy into the business with me. Such a treacherous bastard, as it turns out, he thought it a good plan to ruin me first, so the business's value was low enough for him to be able to afford it. If he hadn't been caught red-handed, I'd have tied myself to that snake-in-the-grass! Now my regret is that I didn't listen more closely to Tassos. At least with him, there was never any doubt that he wanted the business to grow.'

The fat man took out his cigarettes, and offered them to Orestes, but Orestes declined.

'I think you're right,' said the fat man, lighting one for himself. The scent of brewing coffee was reaching them from inside the café. 'It was unfortunate that he never got the chance to turn his plans to reality, but you know it may not be too late.'

Orestes gave a bitter laugh.

'You think not? I'm a man with two halves of a failing business and no-one to share the burden. I'm looking forward to the prospect of double the work and half the profits. I'll need a miracle to survive.'

'Ah, but miracles do appear,' said the fat man, 'and often in the guise of the mundane and every-day.'

Elias brought out a tray of coffee and churros, which he laid out on napkins.

'So,' he said, tucking the tray under his arm. 'You wanted to speak to me?'

'Please, sit with us,' said the fat man, stubbing out his cigarette, and Elias did so. 'I want you to regard me as a kind of broker, a middle-man, if you will, who can bring you mutual benefits. I have a proposal to make, and in doing so I am going to reveal to each of you details of private matters, which I want you to undertake to keep to yourselves.'

Elias shrugged his agreement; Orestes nodded.

'Elias, you wish to acquire this building. That is understandable. Its acquisition would give you scope to develop this business, and thriving businesses bring benefit to the whole island. Orestes, you are looking for investment in the fish-farm, to replenish the stock, improve efficiency and expand your market. Yes?'

'Yes.'

'So here is my proposal. I think I can, in time, persuade the owner of this property to part with it for a fair sum. My suggestion – and it is radical, I know – is that you, Elias, pay part of the value of the building to the owner, and part to Orestes to invest in the fish-farm. My instinct is that the owner will want only a nominal amount from the transaction. That would give you, Orestes, a significant amount to invest.'

Elias was looking puzzled; Orestes looked pleased.

'Why would I do that?' asked Elias. 'I don't know anything about fish.'

'You don't need to. You would give the money as a one-time gift. Which you, Orestes, would receive with certain conditions attached.'

'What conditions?'

'That you designate a certain amount of your resources – two of your tanks – for the replenishment of marine species. In short, you will provide safe havens for creatures which are almost extinct in this region to thrive. I will give you the name of contacts who will supply the spawn and fry, at no cost to you. Like your commercial enterprise, they would grow in captivity, and when they are big enough to be released, you will let them go, and replace them with fresh stock. I am thinking of fish and shellfish, the edible and the inedible, all those creatures which the ocean needs for good health. Thus the sea will be replenished and provide for Liteos's fishermen, and your businesses will prosper at the same time. Elias, for your part, I think the owner would want this building honoured, improved but not demolished. It has a past and a history that deserves to be preserved. Gentlemen, what do you say?'

'But how will you persuade the Neraida's owner to part with it for almost nothing?' asked Orestes. 'It makes no sense.'

'When you are in possession of the facts, it makes perfect sense,' said the fat man.

'If you think they can be persuaded, it's a brilliant idea,' said Elias. 'In fact, I'd go so far as to say it's genius.'

ooooo

On his way back to the hotel, the fat man stopped to buy cigarettes at the *periptero*. The place was undergoing changes: the cards of fish-hooks had made way for island maps and postcards, and the contents of one of the bait freezers had been transferred to its neighbour. Sammy was leaning over it with a sponge, cleaning it with a strong solution of bleach in hot water.

'*Kali mera*,' said the fat man. 'You look very busy.'

Sammy straightened up and, dropping the sponge into the bucket, wiped his hand dry on his shorts.

'*Kali mera!* I am busy! This freezer stinks, and I'm expecting a delivery of ice-cream at lunchtime.'

'Ice-cream in the freezers? What will your sister say?'

'My sister has given me full permission to do what I want with this kiosk, to run it on our family's behalf.'

'And where is she?'

'Noula's going fishing with Stathis. She's first-mate on the *Panayiotissa*.'

'I'm very pleased to hear that,' said the fat man. 'I'm sure she'll love life at sea. And I'm sure you'll do an excellent job of running this place. Let me be one of your first customers. Do you have any of these?'

He showed Sammy his pack of cigarettes with the starlet on the box, and Sammy grinned.

'I have them ready,' he said, going inside the kiosk. 'Noula put them out for you. She thought you'd be coming by here before you left.'

'And matches, too,' said the fat man.

'You use a lot of matches,' said Sammy, placing a box alongside the cigarettes.

'In truth, I don't use many at all,' said the fat man. 'Matchboxes, though, are another matter.' He put money on the counter, and Sammy reached for change. 'May I ask you a question? The people here have not always treated you kindly. Do you think they will behave better, now you're a man of business?'

'I don't care,' said Sammy. 'Those I've placed orders with for stock have been reasonable. Money is money, after all. But there are always foreigners in Liteos, tourists and Greeks. I'll make enough from them to keep us going. I'm going to make this place a tourist-friendly place. I've already started teaching myself English.' He reached under the counter and showed the fat man a book: *English in Twenty Easy Lessons*. 'I don't think the lessons are easy, but I have a brain. There are plenty less intelligent than me who master English. Then I shall learn Italian and German. There'll be plenty of customers for my ice-cream.'

'I think you're right.' The fat man pocketed his cigarettes and matches, and held out his hand, giving Sammy's a firm shake when he took it. 'It's been a pleasure meeting you. I expect our paths will cross again before long.'

'Shall I say goodbye to Noula for you?'

'Please do. Tell her I shall see her next time I am here. And you have my best wishes for this enterprise, Sammy. I see no reason at all why it shouldn't flourish in your care.'

After the fat man had vacated his room, he carried his bag down to the terrace where Pericles was sketching out a sign to advertise his happy hour prices.

'I gave Tina the pearls this morning,' he said. 'She put them on straight away, and I think they're already working their magic. When I told her the laundry's come back short, she hardly batted an eyelid, and just said Raoul is quite capable of serving a few Greek salads for lunch if she takes an hour off to sort it out. What do you think of that?'

'I am glad to be leaving you with life looking rosier,' said the fat man. 'For now, I must say farewell.'

'Let me walk with you to the dock,' said Pericles, putting down his pencil.

'No need, no need,' said the fat man. 'You are busy, and the walk is short. Tell Tina I shall see her again, before the summer is out.'

Pericles stood and embraced the fat man.

'*Kalo taxidi*,' he said. '*Kali epistrofi*. Are you going far?'

'Not too far.'

'To a place free from drama, I hope,' said Pericles. 'I shall be glad to see us return to dull, quiet Liteos.'

'Beneath the surface, no place is ever free from drama, but what has happened here has been especially unfortunate.' The fat man fixed his gaze on the sea. 'Yes, terribly unfortunate. Though I remain confident those involved in that sorry story will live to see better days.'

He walked alone to the dock, where the ferry was almost loaded and preparing to leave. Making his way through the boarding passengers, he climbed the steps to the upper deck and found a space at the rail, looking down on the harbour. As the ramp was raised, the boat began to move, churning the water to white foam at the stern.

From the quayside, a small boy cast his fishing-line. The sun was at its zenith, and the crowded deck was hot. Picking up his holdall, the fat man took a last look at the island, and wandered away amongst the tourists and the travellers, seeking out a comfortable place in the shade.

Summer's End

Twenty One

In a sublime blue sky two eagles soared, spiralling on thermals rising from the valley floor far, far below. The sinuous road which traversed the mountainside showed silver through the dark-green pine-forests; the rocky peaks stretched to the limit of the human eye's seeing, losing their solidity in the smokiness of the horizon's haze.

Delphi's amphitheatre lay on the shelf of an alpine meadow, the ragged tiers of its stone benches concentric like the rings of a felled oak, the curving floor where once musicians had played corrupted from the level by centuries of shifting soil. The fat man climbed to the uppermost seating, and from there looked down at the wandering crowds, laughing Japanese taking photographs of each other, loud Americans wearing money-belts and hats more suited to the tropics, an intense French schoolteacher lecturing a party of flippant teenagers. The sun was hot on his back. In the withered grass growing up between the stones, crickets were singing.

For a while, he watched the eagles, but with the amphitheatre's excellent acoustics, their melancholy cries were lost in the babble reaching him from the tourists below. When a trio of Danes began singing to test for echoes, he gave up his seat, and making his way back down the uneven steps, followed the Sacred Way amongst the fallen stone blocks which had once been the walls of Athena's sanctuary. At the Temple of Apollo, an Italian guide holding up a red umbrella was calling to the stragglers from his group. Someone had left an empty Coke can on the temple steps.

Enrico had found a place in the shade on the far side of the car-park, away from most of the other cars, minibuses and coaches. Waiting at the wheel of a rusting Lada Niva, he was eating roasted peanuts, dropping the empty shells back into the paper bag he had bought them in. When he saw the fat man approaching, he used the rear-view mirror to check his teeth and black goatee for debris, and smoothed his Mephistophelean eyebrows with his finger.

As the fat man opened the Niva's door, the hinges squealed.

'Zeus released two eagles to found Delphi where their flights crossed,' he said, settling into the sagging passenger seat, 'and declared the oracle to be the centre of the world. Now the world and his brother have come to visit, and Delphi has no more significance for any of them than your empty peanut shells.'

'I bought you a fresh peach juice,' said Enrico, reaching down to his feet for a plastic cup balanced on the rubber floor-mat. 'And a sesame *koulouri*.'

The *koulouri* was warm, though the fat man was unsure whether the warmth was from its baking, or from having been lying in Enrico's lap.

'I'm not going to ask how much you paid for them,' he said.

'Five times what they're worth,' said Enrico, cheerfully. 'But don't tell me they didn't rob the visitors to the oracle, back in the old days.'

'I'm sure you're right. You've probably paid no more, relatively speaking, than Xerxes paid for bread and wine when he came visiting two thousand years ago. Even so, the place makes me melancholy, and it's time for us to go. My appointment is fixed at two, and I don't think my hosts will be flexible.'

'Better drink your juice first,' said Enrico, rolling up the top of his bag of peanuts and tossing it onto the back seat. 'If the gears keep jumping, you might spill it.'

The fat man drank down the juice, finding its sweetness improved his mood.

'Let me take that,' said Enrico, holding his hand out to take the empty cup. The fat man gave it to him and bit into the *koulouri*, grateful to discover the dough's warmth seemed to be from the oven rather than Enrico's thighs.

Enrico was a short man and the Niva's driver's seat controls didn't function, so he drove with one cushion at his back, and another under his backside. He turned on the ignition. The engine fired, but ran with a strange knocking noise, loud enough to catch the attention of an American who pointed his camera to take a picture of the dilapidated vehicle.

'I'm not used to travelling in a tourist attraction,' said the fat man, irritably. 'When I accepted the loan of your cousin's car, I think you should have warned me of its condition.'

Enrico patted the steering wheel.

'Reliability, that's what these old troopers have,' he said. 'Go through anything, she will.'

'You over-estimate the perils of the national routes. A saloon car would have done. I only wish to be carried to my appointment and to arrive on time.'

'We have plenty of time.'

Enrico put the Niva into gear, and moving forward slowly, began to turn in a half circle, at the same time winding down his window until he was lined up along-side an over-filled rubbish bin. With relaxed accuracy, he lobbed the fat man's cup onto a heap of ice-cream wrappers and empty water-bottles, and pulling away towards the car park exit, turned the window-winder. There was an odd twang. The window didn't rise.

He looked embarrassed.

'I forgot about that,' he said. 'My cousin told me not to open it.'

The fat man stared fixedly forward.

'We shan't be needing the air-conditioning, then,' he said.

They took the major roads, following the E65 down to the Gulf of Itea, tracking the coast as far as Galaxidi and on to Erateini, where they headed into the mountains, away from the sea. They passed a cemetery filled with silk flowers and white memorials, and a builder's merchants where the yard was stacked with roof-tiles; they drove by a gorge where a number of cement-trucks had been pushed over the edge and dumped. The road now was winding and climbing, stretches of straight carriageway leading to alarming hair-pin bends, and as Enrico went into the turns much faster than was comfortable, the fat man held himself steady with a hand on the roof.

'Corners well, doesn't she?' asked Enrico.

The fat man didn't answer, but looked out over the landscape of rocks, ravines and brush, until Enrico made another turn and there before them again was the azure sea. They passed olive groves and farmsteads, drove through villages and hamlets, until they reached a broad valley stretching between two mountain ranges. Here, unexpectedly, the road improved, becoming newly laid tarmac with crash barriers and fresh markings of white paint, and Enrico took advantage of it to speed up. The road ran wide and straight for several miles through the foothills along the east side of the valley, until it rounded a bend and the view was changed again.

'There it is,' said the fat man.

He pointed to a complex of low, white buildings, anomalies in a rural landscape where there was nothing but dry grassland and rough grazing. As they drew closer, the strangeness of the place became more obvious. What from a distance might have been a factory complex, at closer quarters resembled a modern-day fort, a contemporary version of the Byzantine castles which were visible from time to time at the landscape's highest points.

'Quite a place,' said Enrico.

The new tarmac ran out, and Enrico was forced to slow down to navigate the potholes of the worn road surface. They passed a farmer loading olive-wood onto a truck, who waved as though he knew them, and a roadside shrine with candles lit. Beyond the shrine, a road joined the main carriageway at an angle, and that road led across the valley floor towards the buildings. The road was signposted: Malandrino Prison.

'You hear such terrible things about this place,' said Enrico, making the turn, and he drove slowly, as if reluctant to arrive at their destination. 'Brutality and riots, overcrowding. It's full of Albanians and mafia. Do you want me to come in with you?'

'I don't think they'd allow it,' said the fat man. 'I have my visitor's pass, dated for today, and I think that will get me in, but not you as well. Getting into these places is sometimes harder than getting out.'

The road led in a straight line to the prison, crossing flat, open land with not even a tree for an escapee to hide behind, a natural no-man's-land. Behind a steel fence topped with razor wire, high walls loomed, with watch-towers at all their corners.

They reached a barrier blocking the road, a red-and-white STOP sign and a sentry-house. The two men inside shouldered machine-guns over their blue shirts, and walked in no hurry to Enrico's side of the car, their trousers tucked into their boots, their boots dusty. One of them was chewing gum, which he spat on the ground.

They looked in through Enrico's window, eyes scanning the dash-board, the back seat, the foot-wells.

'*Yassas*,' said Enrico. 'This gentleman has a pass to visit one of your prisoners.'

'Let's see it, then.'

The fat man handed his letter of admission to Enrico, and Enrico passed it to the sentry, who read it and gave it to his colleague. He asked for the fat man's identification, which he checked against the letter, before giving both back to his partner for him to verify.

'OK,' he said. 'You, come with us. You, park over there.'

The fat man climbed from the car. Enrico drove away.

'This way,' said the guard, and he led the fat man into the shadow of the high, white walls.

∞∞∞

'Lambros! Lambros!'

Agni's cries were weak, and Lambros heard his wife's voice as if from some far-away place. The pressures of nursing her made him bone-tired, and he slept whenever he could, at odd times in odd places. This afternoon he had fallen asleep in a balcony chair, his head against the glass of the French doors. When her calling roused him, he hurried to her side.

The room which had been their marital bedroom had become her sick-room, and she was dying in the bed where he had first made love to her, on their wedding night. She was calling him by name, and that might mean she was lucid; there was an irony in her deterioration, that as she grew physically more frail, her clear mind seemed more able to gain control over the disease, and there were still minutes to be spent in the company of the Agni he had all but lost.

Her hair had worked loose from the ribbon he had tied it with. When she was young, she always wore a ribbon, catching her hair with it at the nape of her neck. As grey began to show, she'd begun to cut her hair, and the ribbons were put away.

There had been no hair-cutting since her illness began. Around scissors, she was unpredictable. He had found the ribbons in a drawer of her most personal things, coiled loops of colour amongst the lavender-bags and stockings. He liked the red, and sometimes she allowed him, if he was gentle, to comb her hair and tie it back in that same style she used to wear.

He had spent time filling the bedroom with photographs: family, friends and places, people Agni should know very well, occasions she should remember. There was a picture of a bygone St Sotiris's day, Agni with her sisters, frying fish over an open fire, and a shot of himself turning the spit for a roasting goat, one year when they had spent Easter in the hills. Here was Alex's baptism at age two, him in a white sailor suit, red-faced from crying at the priest's hands, and Tassos at four or maybe five, proudly holding up by its tail the first small bass he ever caught.

Agni was lying on her side, staring at a picture on the bedside table of her younger self, smiling and arms round the shoulders of Alex and Tassos together. How old were the boys there? Alex was probably nine. The picture had been taken by a regular guest at the pension, a Dutchman who'd come every year with his wife.

'Lambros!'

He sat down beside her on the bed and stroked the loose hair back from her eyes.

'I'm here, *koukla*. I'm here.'

From the pillow, she looked up at him. He saw the confusion in her eyes, and his heart broke to see her so troubled.

With a trembling hand, she pointed at the picture.

'Our boys,' she said. 'Where are our boys?'

He turned his face from her to hide the tears that came to his eyes. Blinking them back, he managed – for her sake – a smile.

'They're coming to see you,' he said. 'They send all their love, and they'll be here very soon.'

'I had a dream.' She searched for his hand, and finding it, squeezed it tight. 'There was water. I don't think they're coming back.'

'Just a bad dream, my love,' said Lambros. 'Sleep a while, and when you wake they'll be here. Shall I fix your pillows?'

He made her comfortable, and gave her a few drops of the little remaining remedy the stranger had left them. Dr Nick's prescriptions were shut away in the kitchen, where they were less of a temptation. For her sake, he thought, sometimes, of helping her to sleep and never wake; for his own sake, he was desperate for her to stay.

He held her hand, and she closed her eyes. Out in the garden, a thrush flew into the branches of the plum tree, and began its plaintive song.

∞∞∞

The fat man glanced up at the windows of the watchtowers, where sentinels were watching with no interest, just cold assessments of threat. They watched as his identity card was re-checked, and as the gate in the perimeter fence was opened and he was escorted into the no-man's-land between the fence and the prison's outer wall. Behind them, the outer gate clanged shut.

The short walk between the perimeter fence and the wall seemed long. Oblivious of the barriers, darting swallows called. The men waiting at the gatehouse were hostile, edgy and suspicious, and realising it made him look like a journalist, the fat man regretted his jacket. They patted him down, checking under his lapels and in all his pockets, looking for cameras and recording devices as well as weapons and drugs. He spoke only when spoken to, confirming his name, his official address, and the name of the man he'd come to see.

They kept him waiting for no clear reason, long enough to leave him in doubt he would be admitted at all. The senior officer went inside the guard-house to make a phone-call, and watched the fat man the whole time he was speaking. While he was gone, a guard pointed to the fat man's wrist-watch and the ring on his left hand – a gold band mounted with an old coin depicting a rising sun.

'You're taking a big chance with those,' he said. 'Better leave them with me.'

The fat man looked into the guard's face. Behind his scars, there was callousness and cruelty. Without his uniform, he'd be taken for a man at Malandrino to serve his time.

'I'll take good care of them,' said the fat man, and the guard smiled, showing a cracked tooth going rotten.

'Whatever you want,' he said, and he gave his colleague a wink he thought the fat man wouldn't see.

The officer finished his phone-call.

'OK,' he said, to the guards. 'Take him in, block four. Thirty minutes. Tsavaris, stay with him. And keep him out of trouble.'

When the gate was at last unlocked and thrown open, the fat man was reluctant to pass through. The further a free man went inside the prison, the more it felt he risked his liberty, and the less control he held over his own self. The guards and prison officers seemed less than human; they lacked empathy, compassion, fairness and humour, as if the task of jailing others had robbed them of themselves.

Tsavaris was a big man, broad-backed and threatening, thick-necked and with biceps so hefty he carried his arms wide of his torso. He walked with swagger and attitude, but there was a tension in him which smacked of nervousness, a wariness justified by the knowledge that, in a crisis, he and his colleagues were outnumbered hundreds to one.

He led the fat man beyond the gatehouse, onto a vast acreage of empty tarmac, another no-man's-land where the heat was fierce. The fat man looked back and saw the guards in the watch-towers watching him and Tsavaris as they approached the single-storey buildings which were the prison blocks.

Tsavaris didn't speak, but led him past one block, then another. At the door of block four, Tsavaris pressed a buzzer, and they waited. A minute passed, and Tsavaris buzzed again. They heard boots on tiles, and the panel behind a viewing slot slid back.

'Eh, *malaka*,' said Tsavaris, shortly. 'Open up. I've brought a visitor.'

Keys turned in locks: one, then another, and another. The door opened, and the block guard stood back to allow Tsavaris and the fat man entry. The door slammed shut behind them, and they waited while the three locks were refastened.

The fat man looked around. They were in a kind of airlock with another gate to be unlocked before they were properly inside, but the chaos of the prison was all around: yelling, whistling, jeering, the stink of sweat and unwashed men and their excretions, of bad food and desperation, fear and violence. Along both sides of a broad corridor, ranks of steel doors were enclosed behind bars so a man stepping outside his cell was still caged. There were no windows and no skylights, no openings to the outside world which might let in sunlight or provide a route of escape.

The guard who had admitted them searched the key-ring on his belt for keys to fit the locks of the next gate, and when they were opened, stood back to allow the fat man and Tsavaris inside. The gate was locked behind them – the constant jangle of keys, the rattle of locks, put pressure on the nerves – and with Tsavaris behind him and the guard in front, the fat man was marched like a prisoner along the corridor between the cells. There was whistling as they passed, shouts of derision for the guards, a plea for help and manic laughter, a sudden cry of pain. They came to an unfortified door whose front panel was damaged by a hole the size of a boot-print, and the guard ushered them into a windowless room. He pressed a switch, and a fluorescent strip flickered, faltered, then lit them with cold white light. There was a table, and two chairs.

'Wait here,' said the guard. 'You can sit down.'

He left them. The fat man sat. Outside, the hellish clamour of the cell-block went on.

Tsavaris was restless. He checked the corridor, came back inside the room, checked the corridor again.

'I'm going for coffee,' he said. 'Don't leave this room without me.'

The fat man listened to his heavy footsteps walking away, to more keys fastening and unfastening more locks, to the clang of closing doors. There was nothing for a while but shouting and whooping, a fist banging on an unyielding door.

Then there were more footsteps, and the guard led in a prisoner, a gaunt, wasted man in a t-shirt and stained canvas trousers, with many days' growth of beard on his jaw and neck. His head was clumsily shaved to stubble, and there was a scabbed cut on his scalp. He moved with a stoop and a limp, sliding his feet in sandals which weren't his size. In the weeks since the fat man had last seen him, Papa Alex had aged a dozen years.

The fat man offered his hand.

'No touching!' ordered the guard. 'Sit!'

His instructions were for the prisoner, but the fat man obeyed too.

There was a silence as the two men regarded each other.

'How are you, Alex?' asked the fat man, at last. 'I hope you remember me.'

The priest bowed his head.

'I do, *Kyrie* Diaktoros. When you wrote, I had to rack my brain to call you to mind. But now you're here, I remember you quite well.'

'I am heartily sorry to find you in these – circumstances. This place is everything they say it is, and worse. How are you coping?'

Papa Alex looked at the fat man with tired eyes.

'I endure it,' he said. 'I try to use the opportunity to observe my fellow men, to learn about human nature, but you see how cowardly I am. I have abandoned my role as priest, at least temporarily. They warned me it would make me a special target. But I must be honest and say it would take a better man than I to embrace some of these people as Christian brothers. There are men here who have done terrible, unspeakable things, and who do terrible things still. I cannot lie to you. My life here is hellish. But I have brought it on myself, of course, and must take my punishment.'

The fat man leaned forward across the table, and spoke in a low voice.

'Alex,' he said. 'I know you are innocent.'

There was a shout from the corridor, and the guard went to the door.

'You looking for me?' he asked someone outside. Then he spoke to the fat man. 'Stay here. Don't leave this room. Either of you.' And he was gone.

'Innocent,' said Papa Alex. 'Every last man in here claims he's innocent.'

'But in your case, it's true. How much longer must this charade go on?'

'That's a question for lawyers and the courts.'

'When will your case come to trial?'

'The longest they can keep me on remand is eighteen months.'

'And you are thinking that is long enough.'

'I'm sorry, *Kyrie*, but I don't understand you.'

'Did you ever have ambitions to become a writer, to pen one of those detective novels you enjoy?'

'Me? Hardly. I can't find the time to read all I want, never mind write books. Why have you come to see me, exactly?'

'I ask because the clues you laid were ingenious. They missed the mark by just far enough so that Chief Tsinamis would think himself clever when he worked out they were false. The wheelbarrow you used to transport your brother's body, for example. I don't doubt that part was true, that you did make use of it in that way. But I remember seeing it in the garden myself. What killer wanting to get away with his crime would leave such an obvious piece of the jigsaw under the noses of the police? Yet there it was, on view to anyone who came to the house.'

'Have you never heard of hiding in plain sight?'

'Yes, I have. And I assume you'll say that was your strategy, the same strategy you used with the knife in your cassock. But that would make you stupid, and you are far from being that. The whisky bottle, a double-bluff, of course, a clue which shouted *Clue!* so loud, it could never have been genuine. Not with the bottle's pair displayed on the kitchen table. No doubt the chief thought himself brilliant to spot it. The knife, too – if you had killed your brother with it, of course you would have thrown it in the sea, where it would never have been recovered. Heaven knows you spent enough time on the water, backwards and forwards, making sure as many people as possible – including me – saw you returning to what you were selling as the scene of the crime. Were you surprised they took your bait? You owe thanks to the inebriate doctor for that. If he hadn't been involved, you'd have been eliminated from enquiries early on. The doctor's ignorance was certainly a lucky break for you, but the error of his conclusions will of course come out at your trial and exonerate you. If your trial ever goes ahead.'

'Why shouldn't it?'

The fat man spread his hands.

'Because you're not guilty. The trail of red herrings you laid – the knife-wounds, the whisky bottle, the invented argument between you and your brother, your conspicuousness in revisiting the supposed scene – they all add up to only one thing. You didn't do it. So why don't you take this opportunity to tell me who did?'

The priest looked troubled.

'You're mistaken,' he said. 'Vaios identified me as my brother's killer, and it's only right I should be tried and serve my sentence for the crime.'

'Vaios identified you as the killer because I helped him to follow your false trail. I have a little influence in the right places, Alex. Have you had enough of this place yet? Are you ready to go home?'

The priest covered his face, and his thin shoulders shook with sobs he tried hard to suppress.

'Don't torment me!' he begged. 'Please, don't torment me. If they see I've been crying, they'll make it far worse.'

The fat man reached out and touched the priest's arm.

'Be strong, then,' he said, 'and listen to me.'

Papa Alex rubbed his eyes.

'Let me tell you, first, what I think is going on,' went on the fat man. 'Beyond any doubt, you are covering up for someone. Your plan was clever and I'm sure well-meant, but you raised my suspicions by being too obvious. There are huge holes in your story, and if you end up in a courtroom, they'll come to light immediately, you'll be released and the police will go and look for the real killer. Do you understand me?'

'I don't need much more time,' said Papa Alex. 'A week or two, maybe only days.'

'Imagine a worse scenario,' said the fat man. 'Imagine if not enough attention is paid to your case, and the evidence is swallowed as you presented it. Then you will be spending the next twenty or thirty years here. Imagine that.'

'I would kill myself first. I know that would be a sin, but this place is a living hell!'

'Let us make sure then that it doesn't come to that. Tell me what happened, and I promise you I can help you get the outcome that's best for all concerned. Will you trust me?'

Papa Alex shook his head.

'I still don't understand your interest. What does it have to do with you?'

'I represent the authorities – the highest authorities, who have jurisdiction even over the regular establishments of justice. Your case has come to their attention, and I have been tasked with making sure that justice is served.'

'How can you do that?'

'If you will tell me the truth about your brother's death, I undertake to ensure that the one you are protecting will come to no harm. But I will also make sure that you yourself are taken care of. You have been very brave, Alex, in carrying this burden. If you will share it with me, I promise I can help.'

'Can you get me out of this place?'

'I have information which would free you very quickly, though I realise that may not be what you want. Let me remind you of a story with which I'm sure you are familiar, a story which is very relevant to your situation. I'm referring to the Bridge at Arta. Do you know it?'

'We read it at school,' said Papa Alex, shuddering. 'Such a tragic and terrible tale! As a child, it gave me nightmares to think of that poor woman, sealed up in that cold, dark place.'

'And yet here you are, sealed in your own Bridge of Arta.'

The priest nodded.

'I suppose I am.'

'So why don't you tell me how you came to be here? Tell me your story, and let us decide what's to be done.'

'Why should I trust you?'

'Because you have no choice,' said the fat man. 'And because I am the best, maybe the only hope you have if you want to go home. Who else do you have?'

Papa Alex gave a hollow laugh.

'My lawyer.'

'And have you seen anything of him?'

'He came here, once. I signed some papers and he went away. On the few occasions they let me use a phone, he's out of the office.'

'Yet you are prepared to put your future in his hands? I will get you a good lawyer, one who knows the intricacies of the system. But if I'm to brief him, I'll need to know the pertinent facts.'

Papa Alex sighed, and ran a hand over his face.

'Facts,' he said. 'What are the pertinent facts, as you put it? My mother was a good woman, and a good worker. Is that pertinent? She took the best care of my brother and me, and my father. She ran our house as a pension for many years, catering for foreign tourists. She enjoyed meeting people from different backgrounds. She was proud of Liteos, proud of Greece, and she wanted to make them welcome. The one thing she loved in life was cooking, and she was an excellent cook. She made food for the pension guests, for family and friends, for weddings and baptisms. The kitchen was her province, and she was its queen. We grew up, and I trained for the priesthood. My ambitions lay elsewhere, but I wanted to please her. Tassos followed his own calling, and became a fisherman. He married a girl who was one of our guests, a Swedish girl, but they had too little in common. When she went back to Sweden, Tassos went too, but he couldn't live with the cold and the rain. He left her there, and came home.

'But he came home with ideas. He'd seen how they were doing things in Sweden, making good livings from the sea, not just a hand-to-mouth existence like he'd been used to as a fisherman here. He had a little money saved, and he hooked up with Orestes, and they built the fish-farm. They were doing well. They would have been all right. It was a good idea, and he was committed to it. The first two or three years, they made a little money, and Tassos was thinking it was time to expand.

'But then things began to change at home. My mother became moody, in a way she'd never been before, prone to fits of anger and depression. She didn't want to run the pension any more. That didn't matter. She was getting on in life, and my father was already retired. I was bringing in money, Tassos was making something. We were comfortable financially, but things went from bad to worse.

'My mother became seriously ill in her mind, completely crazy, as you saw her. She couldn't be left alone, but with my obligations in the community and Tassos's work that was difficult. She became aggressive, and too much for my father. She couldn't be reasoned with, and he couldn't cope alone. Then she began to break our hearts by not even knowing us. She treated us like strangers, or what was worse, like enemies who were out to do her harm. She didn't want us near her, but still she wanted to be cooking, cooking, cooking. Well, the kitchen is a dangerous place when the chef is unpredictable. She was the mother who had loved me, but I didn't dare turn my back on her when she had a knife in her hand.'

He stopped.

'Go on,' said the fat man.

'I'm betraying her,' said Papa Alex. 'What kind of son betrays his mother?'

'You are not betraying her. You have my word that anything said here in this room remains between us until you say otherwise. What you are doing is paving the road back to your father, who will need you after your mother is gone more than he ever did. Please, go on.'

'My poor father,' said Papa Alex, shaking his head. 'We did our best for her, but my father especially was proud, and didn't want people to know there was madness in the family. We made excuses for her, and we made too much use of the sedatives Dr Nick prescribed. But we all knew Dr Nick would keep no secrets. He'd blab our business across the whole island when he'd had a drink.'

'I have a feeling Dr Nick will shortly begin to appreciate the advantages of retirement,' said the fat man. 'Have no more worries about him.'

Papa Alex wiped his eyes on the back of his hand.

'I'm sorry,' he said. 'I don't like to remember. With mama so ill, all our lives were impossible. I neglected my churches and cut back on services, so I was beginning to gain a reputation for laziness, and the same was true of Tassos. Orestes accused him of lack of commitment, but he was committed, very committed. He was committed to our mother's care.

'We were happy to make sacrifices out of love, because we remembered how she had always cared for us, and it seemed the least we could do in repayment. And there were still occasions – almost daily – when for short periods of time, maybe only a minute, or five or ten, she was back with us and knew us, but she was bewildered, knowing something was terribly wrong. Then she'd be replaced again by the demon she'd become.'

Papa Alex glanced up at a bloated fly buzzing on the ceiling, knocking itself stupidly on the fluorescent light cover.

'We cared for her as best we could,' he said. 'We kept her clean and fed and safe. Tassos wasn't satisfied that was enough. He wanted to do more. My mother had inherited property – the house where we live was her dowry, but there was another house through a maiden aunt, a large property that's now the Neraida café. The owner wanted to buy it, but my mother wouldn't sell. She had always hoped for a granddaughter, and thought it would be a dowry house for her. But Tassos had heard through his ex-wife of revolutionary treatment in Sweden for mental illness, dementia or insanity, whatever my mother has. There's a sanatorium outside Gothenburg where Tassos wanted her to go. It was expensive, but he thought we should try, and papa and I agreed we should sell the Neraida to pay for it. The one person who wouldn't agree was mama. If it was mentioned to her when she didn't know us, she didn't remember the house either. If we mentioned it in those rare moments of lucidity, she just said no.

'All it needed was her signature on a piece of paper. Tassos had the bill of sale drawn up in agreement with Elias. They fixed a price, enough for mama's treatment with enough left over to invest in the fish-farm. With his declining involvement, he felt he owed Orestes that.'

There were shouts in the corridor, the sounds of fists on a steel door.

'This place,' said Papa Alex. 'I feel I'm losing my mind, too.'

'You must be strong,' said the fat man. 'You're almost at the end. What happened to Tassos?'

Papa Alex bowed his head.

'On the night he died, mama was cooking. It was already after midnight, but it was hot, very hot. My father was sleeping, and Tassos and I were with her in the kitchen. He'd been talking to Elias, and he was showing me the bill of sale. She had it in her mind we were expecting visitors, and she was going to make *pasticcio*. There was a great pan of water she'd put on to boil for the pasta, and when her back was turned, I switched off the gas. She didn't know, or care. She was busy chopping onions. Tassos and I were absorbed in what we were saying, when suddenly she spoke to us, in her normal voice, quite rational. "Tassos," she said, "what am I doing?" He got up and went to her, and put his arm round her, and guided her to a chair, and said, "You're going to write your name, mama, on this piece of paper, and then we shall make some tea." And she seemed happy enough, even when he put the pen in her hand, and she looked down at the paper, and she signed it. And Tassos looked at me and he smiled that smile he had, and I thought, Allelujah!

'But she caught that smile, and the demon was back. She began to shout, calling us thieves, saying we were stealing from her. She was so angry, demented, and Tassos tried to calm her while I went to the cupboard for her sedatives.' He lifted his head, and looked the fat man in the eye. 'I only turned my back for a moment. He didn't even scream. I heard him drop to the floor, and there he was, quite still, his hair soaking, and I couldn't work out what had happened. Then I saw she was holding the pan off the stove, and I knew what she'd done. She'd thrown that pan of water in his face, picked it up and thrown it at him. Which wouldn't have mattered very much, except when I turned off the gas, I didn't do it properly. The water she threw was boiling, and she scalded him to death.'

Papa Alex covered his face.

'Every day, I live it again,' he said. 'Every day, I know my carelessness is to blame.'

'If it's any consolation, he died of shock,' said the fat man. 'I don't think he would have known any pain.'

'The night was so hot, he wasn't wearing a shirt,' said Papa Alex. 'All his face was burned, his chest and shoulders. I didn't know what to do. I shouted my father to take mama away while I helped Tassos, but he was already gone. There was nothing to be done, except protect her. If anyone found out how he'd died, they'd have put her away. My mother, in an asylum! How could we have borne that? So we decided to take him somewhere remote, so his body – my poor brother! – wouldn't quickly be found, and nature could do its work and hide how he had died. We staged a row. We wanted to make the neighbours think Tassos and I had argued, and that he'd left the house in a rage. Then we put him in the wheelbarrow and took him to my boat.

'I took him to the beach where he was found. His skin was peeling from his body where the boiling water had caught him, so the plan was to lay him face-down in the water, as if he'd fallen in. But I couldn't do it! I couldn't do it! So I left him on the beach, and I suppose the crabs did the rest. It was my punishment to see him when they called me to the police station.' Tears ran from his eyes. He wiped them away, and shook his head. 'You cannot imagine, you truly could never imagine the horror of seeing him that way! In that moment, I felt so dreadful at what I had done, I almost told Vaios the truth. But mama was always in my mind, so I kept what I knew in my heart, and disguised my dismay at the part I had played in Tassos ending up that way as shock at his death. Vaios saw what he expected to see, and I got away with it.'

The fat man was silent. Outside, a guard rattled a truncheon between railings and began calling out names. Immersed in the recounting of his story, Papa Alex seemed not to hear.

'His body being found so quickly made everything more complicated. We had to do more, come up with a new plan. I thought of confessing, but I wasn't guilty, and mama in her present state won't be with us very long. I had to get myself arrested, but on flimsy evidence which would never hold up in court, so mama would be out of harm's way for as long as she needed. I never wished her a speedy death, but neither am I such a saint that I want to spend the rest of my life in this place.

'So I started to place the clues and make myself a suspect. When they called me to say the final words over the body, I realised the game had changed, and I stabbed him to make his death look like murder, though I didn't think my efforts were very convincing. I hated hurting him, and I couldn't bring myself to wound him deeply, but thanks to Dr Nick what I did was good enough, as it turned out. As unsubtly as

I could, I kept showing people my knife, hoping someone would run to Vaios, and you did. I thought the police would be talking to Orestes, so I told him Tassos and I had argued to give me a motive, and I placed the whisky bottle as an obvious false clue. So the trap was set, and Vaios fell into it, as he was meant to. The difficulty now is, who will get me out of here?'

Outside, the guard had finished his roll-call. There were tramping boots in the corridor, and Tsavaris appeared in the doorway.

'Time to go,' he said. 'Hardouvelis, stay where you are.'

'A moment longer, please,' said the fat man.

'Time's up,' said Tsavaris. 'Hardouvelis, they're coming for you now.'

The fat man rose from his chair.

'I will get you out,' he said. 'If your mother is failing and it is a matter only of days, we may wait, if you wish, until she has passed. The Examining Magistrate's office has a report which should exonerate you, and while there is the chance the stabbing might bring a charge of defacing a corpse, you have done enough time here to cover a possible sentence for that crime. Of course a scapegoat will be needed for this miscarriage of justice, but I have a deserving candidate in mind. Take heart and be strong, Alex. You will leave this place a hero, a man who sacrificed his liberty to save his mother from shame.'

'I don't want to be a hero. Just please, let me go home.'

'Let's go,' said Tsavaris, holding out his hand to usher the fat man away.

As he reached the door, the fat man stopped.

'One more thing,' he said. 'The deed of sale. What happened to it?'

Papa Alex shook his head.

'A disaster. It got splashed with the boiling water. Papa tried to recover it, but he made it look worse and he threw it away.'

'No matter. I have a proposal for the disposal of the Neraida which will honour Tassos's memory. I think you and your father will agree to it, as her heirs.'

'Thank you. Thank you for taking the time to come and see me.'

'How could I not?' said the fat man. 'My dear man, how could I not? The sacrifice you have made has been extraordinary, and the strength of your love for your mother would make the angels weep.'

∞∞∞

As Enrico drove them away from Malandrino, the fat man was deep in thought.

'We need to find a telephone,' he said.

There was a phone in the next village, on a square with a shady plane tree where old men were gathered on wooden benches, resting their arthritic knees and putting their small world to rights. They were interested in the decrepit Lada, and curious about the fat man, who wished them *kali spera* as he made his way to the phone.

The phone-kiosk was dusty and scribbled with graffiti. The fat man dialled the number he needed, and listened to the ringing tone down the line.

'Examining Magistrate's office.'

'Popi? Is that you? This is Hermes.'

'Hermes! How good to hear from you! Are you well? Where are you?'

'I am some distance from you, *koukla*, or I would have come to you in person. I have been visiting a gentleman in Malandrino prison, whose release is overdue. Do you remember the report you wrote in Liteos, relating to the death of Tassos Hardouvelis?'

'I remember it very well.'

'It's time for that report to reach its audience. I shall be getting in touch with Professor Maglinis, and I shall be asking him to call you. Will you make sure when he does so, you have a copy to hand?'

ꝏꝏꝏ

In Liteos, the start of morning surgery was overdue. Dr Nick had stayed out too late, and overslept by almost an hour. When his office door opened, he was searching through the supply cupboard for aspirin to ease his aching head.

'Wait outside,' he snapped, without turning round. 'I'll call you when I'm ready to see you.'

'I think you'll see me now.' The chief of police was wearing his uniform, and his gun was on his hip.

'Vaios!' Dr Nick closed the supply-cupboard door. '*Kali mera, kali mera!* Sit, please, sit. What can I do for you?'

'I won't sit,' said the Chief of Police. 'This is an official visit.' He held up a piece of paper with a government stamp. 'I'm serving you with a summons, regarding professional evidence you gave in the death of Tassos Hardouvelis.'

Dr Nick frowned.

'What the hell are you talking about? Don't play games with me at this time of the morning, Vaios. My brain isn't up to it.'

'They'll be letting Papa Alex go. He didn't kill his brother. By this evening the press will be here, and they'll be wanting pictures of the party responsible for the wrongful incarceration of a priest. That party is you.'

'Don't be ridiculous,' said Dr Nick. He found a bottle of aspirin in a desk drawer, and tipped three into his hand. 'You arrested him. And why do you say he didn't do it? He stabbed him eleven times.'

'He stabbed a corpse, as that woman tried to say. You shouted her down. I should never have listened to you.'

'It's a storm in a teacup,' said Dr Nick.

'It's the screw-up of a lifetime,' said the chief. 'I acted on your professional opinion, and your opinion was wrong. Shall we go?'

Dr Nick spread his hands in supplication.

'Come on, Vaios! We're friends! There's no need for all this drama!'

'Tell that to the magistrates,' said the chief. 'And just for the record, you and I were never friends.'

∞∞∞

Papa Alex was summoned during breakfast. Tsavaris stood in the cafeteria doorway and shouted his name loud enough to make every man in the room look up from his cold, bitter coffee.

'You're in trouble, *malaka*,' whispered the ugly Cretan to his right, and he grabbed the uneaten bread from Papa Alex's plate.

Papa Alex rose and made his way between the tables. The other prisoners paused in their eating, and watched in expectant silence. When Papa Alex reached the door, Tsavaris said nothing, but indicated with a nod that he should follow.

They took the expected route from the cafeteria, but when they reached block four, Tsavaris kept walking. They passed three, two and one, and were heading for the wall.

Papa Alex looked up at the guards in the watch-towers.

'Where are we going?' he asked. 'Do I have permission to be here?'

Tsavaris didn't answer, but led him to a group of men waiting by the gate, three guards, a senior officer, a man in a suit. When Papa Alex reached them, the suited man stepped forward. He was clean and clean-shaven, smelling sweetly of cologne with the freshness of the outside world on his clothes.

He held out his manicured hand.

'Papa Alex,' he said. 'It's truly a pleasure to meet you. I am Ilias Mentis. You don't know me, but you know a friend of mine, Hermes Diaktoros. I'm a man of the law, and Hermes asked me to look into your case, which I was honoured to do. And you'll be very pleased to know I've brought with me a High Court Order for your release.'

Twenty Two

'I see you are wearing your pearls,' said the fat man.

Pericles had laid a table for lunch with three settings. Pouring shots of ouzo, he added a little water and handed a glass to the fat man.

'I am,' said Tina, touching the string at her neck. 'I wear them every day. I find them – soothing.'

'Since this is such a special birthday, I have brought you something to go with them.'

The fat man placed a small jeweller's box on the table in front of her, and Tina opened it. On a lining of taupe velvet was a pair of pearl earrings, their silver settings moulded as scallop shells.

'Oh Hermes!' she said. 'You shouldn't have!'

'I thought they would suit you.'

'That's very generous of you, Hermes,' said Pericles. 'My gift to my wife is a day of leisure, so I shall be doing most of the cooking here on the barbecue, though Tina is making you one dish she says is something special. Now, drink! *Yammas!* You see I have finally given up on introducing you to new fashions. You're old-fashioned to the marrow of your bones.'

'You're right, my friend,' said the fat man, clinking glasses with his host and hostess. 'I'm too old to change my ways, unless those new ways are demonstrably better than the old. And you have failed to convince me that a concoction of pineapple and tinned coconut is in anyway superior to a good ouzo. *Yammas*!'

Pericles put a match to the barbecue. From the fridge under the bar, he produced two plates and removed their covers.

'I caught these myself this morning,' he said, showing off a small octopus and a few sardines, bright-eyed and glistening with freshness. 'You're not the only one who can catch fish, you know.'

'I'm pleased you caught something other than bream,' said the fat man. 'It appears the sea is beginning to be generous again.'

Smoke rose from the charcoal, and was carried away by the breeze.

'Have you seen the news, Hermes?' asked Tina. 'Pericles, where's the newspaper?'

Pericles handed the fat man that day's copy of *Kathimerini*.

'Look there,' he said.

The fat man unfolded the paper, and studied the photograph covering half of the front page. A tired-looking but smiling Papa Alex was shown walking through the gates of Malandrino prison, his hands raised to wave to the waiting photographers.

The headline read, *Free at Last!*

'A miscarriage of justice, and him a hero, is what they're saying,' said Pericles. 'But you'll see the best of it on page two.'

The fat man turned the page. Under a sub-heading, *Professional misconduct*, a distressed-looking Dr Nikos Vatopoulos was pictured alongside the chief of police.

'So chickens have come home to roost, at last,' said the fat man, folding the paper. 'I expect Dr Nick has been barred from practising medicine, pending his trial?'

'He has indeed. There's a new man at the surgery now. He's recently qualified but keen, and perfectly sober.'

'All is right with the world, then, at least in certain quarters. May I assume it will be a while before the coals are ready for cooking? Would you both excuse me if I take a little walk?'

∞∞∞

He made his way to the Turkish harbour, where Stathis was sluicing down *Panayiotissa*'s decks, looking spry and vigorous and hauling up water with the strength of much younger man. When he saw the fat man, he shook his hand warmly.

'*Kalos tou, kalos tou*,' he said. 'I thought we shouldn't be seeing you again.'

'I'm here only very briefly,' said the fat man. 'May I ask when you're leaving port?'

'Late on this afternoon,' said Stathis, 'if we're ready.'

'I wonder if could ask a favour,' said the fat man. 'I have business not far from here, and a rendezvous to pick me up from the islet of Glaros. Do you know it?'

'I do know it,' said Stathis. 'Why would you go to Glaros? There's nothing there.'

'Could you take me? I'd pay you, of course.'

'I'll take you with pleasure,' said Stathis. 'It's on the way to where we're going, so no charge.'

ꝏꝏꝏ

When the fish were cooked, Pericles hurried inside to fetch Tina, who had changed out of her chef's whites and wore instead a pretty sundress. In one hand she was carrying a dish, which she placed in front of the fat man; in the other was a fan mussel shell, cleaned and shining on its inner surfaces with mother-of-pearl.

'Fan mussel croquettes,' she said, 'in honour of you, our favourite guest. The shell, dear husband, is another for your collection.'

'They look delicious,' said the fat man. 'How do you make them?'

'I chop the mussel meat with onion, and mix it with breadcrumbs, an egg, a little ouzo and some fresh mint. Roll into balls and deep fry. *Voilá*. By the way, I found something in the fan mussel you brought us when you were last here which I think belongs to you.'

She held up between finger and thumb a pink pearl.

The fat man shook his head.

'Not mine,' he said, with a smile. 'It must have fallen from your necklace.'

They ate slowly, enjoying the feast from the sea, picking the flesh from the bones of the sardines with their fingers, dipping bread into the octopus's lemony juices. The mid-day heat was soporific, the inebriant qualities of the ouzo relaxing.

'I expect Papa Alex will be back amongst us any day,' said Tina. 'I wonder if he'll go back to his duties?'

'He may not wish to do so,' said the fat man, helping himself to another croquette. 'An experience such as he has had changes a man.'

'People will welcome him, regardless,' said Pericles. 'He was always well-liked. And I never believed he'd done it in the first place.'

∞∞∞

As afternoon was drawing to its end, the fat man said his goodbyes at the Hotel Poseidon, and made his way back to the Turkish harbour. Noula was out on *Panayiotissa*'s foredeck, preparing hooks with her special bait. In a patch of warm sunshine, Circe was sleeping. Stathis saw him approaching, and called out a greeting.

'You look ready to go fishing,' said the fat man.

Stathis clapped him on the back, and handed him aboard.

'We are,' he said. 'We are most certainly that. We shall take you where you're going, and then we'll be close to good waters for swordfish. We took a fair few over there, in the old days. No reason we shouldn't catch one or two, this trip.'

Stathis steered a course for Ammoglossa, then motored on past the islets of Paximadi and Kromithi, to the deep waters where Mikey had believed the mermaids sang. But for the *Panayiotissa*, the ocean was empty. Noula sat straddling the prow, her bare feet dangling in the spray, watching the day's last light spread gold over the sea. A seagull skimmed the water, so low its wing-tips almost touched the rippling waves, leading the way, it seemed, to Glaros.

The island had a quay covered in goat-droppings, and an ancient chapel of St Michael shaded by an olive-grove. Noula roped the boat to a bollard, and the fat man kissed her on both cheeks.

'Look after him,' he said. 'Learn everything he knows. And good fishing.'

'Your friends aren't here,' said Stathis. 'Let us wait with you until they arrive.'

But the fat man climbed over the deck-rail onto the quay.

'No need to wait,' he said. 'They'll be here.'

'Let us leave you water, at least.'

'There's water in the chapel.'

'Take care then, my friend.' He pulled the fat man to him, and hugged him hard. '*Sto kalo. Sto kalo.*'

When they were a hundred metres out, Stathis turned back from the wheel. The fat man was standing on the beach, and raised his hand.

When they were four hundred metres out, Stathis turned again towards the beach.

No-one was there.

Acknowledgements

To my readers who clamour for more of Hermes, thank you for the incentive to keep writing his adventures.

All credit for the idea for this story goes to the beautiful island of Alonissos, where a chance encounter led to talk of tuna fishing. And thanks to all of Greece and its people for providing such riches of inspiration.

Thanks are always due to my 'professional' supporters, Chris, Emma and Jules at the Christopher Little agency, who guide me with such wisdom and encouragement.

To Lorraine and Philip Andrews, I offer my huge appreciation for your editing skills. The restsina's on me.

And last but by no means least, my most grateful thanks to Andy, who keeps the ship afloat.